AMETHYST
OF
YOUTH

Forbidden Conflicts
~~ Book One ~~

ANN M PRATLEY

BY ANN M PRATLEY

Forbidden Conflicts Series
Amethyst of Youth
Ruby of Law
Diamond of War
Sapphire of Prejudice
Emerald of Wisdom

Power Moore Investigation Tales
Resolution of Happiness
Home by the Sea
Tiger in our House
Catch a Catfish Killer
DJ of Incapacity
Hoonigan

Freedom of Flight Series
Christian
Brandon
Trinity

Painful Deliverance Series
Painful Deliverance
Darkness of Heart
Friendship of Desire

Chisholm Manor Series
Alessandra
Elizabeth

CHAPTER ONE

Charlotte Stonewarden. She kept saying her own name over and over again to herself as she sat at the large dressing table in her bedroom. Sitting on the antique chair, she studied her face as she leaned in close to the good-sized mirror before her. She'd never been a girlie girl. Now, at 18 years of age, she suspected she never would be. The attire she currently wore - jeans and singlet - was her standard dress for the summer months. On slightly colder days, a t-shirt would go over the top of the singlet. On colder days still, a zip-up hoodie would complete her ensemble. No, definitely not a girlie girl. It just wasn't who she was. Perhaps having grown up with only a father and five brothers since she was nine had something to do with that.

She leaned back in her chair and let out an audible sigh. Eighteen. What was she going to do with her life? It was expected that she would contribute to her family business. If that had been something ordinary like a retail shop or a bakery, perhaps it might have inspired her more. Not that she really had a choice. Her father, Mitchell, was a strict ex-military man of stature who had lived through the horrors of wartime. Having seen things he'd never forget, he had always ensured all of his children knew their place. After their mother had died, he had raised them alone.

As far as Charlotte knew, all of her brothers were happy to be in the place their father instructed them to be. For her, though - well, *surely* there was something different for her. Something better. Something *more*.

Leaning in toward the mirror again, she lifted both of her hands and ran them through her hair. She lifted it this way and that, then she laughed. It wasn't able to be tamed. Pale mousy in color, it was neither straight nor curly. It had a life of its own. Yes, she knew. It was good that she wasn't a girlie girl because she sure wouldn't have made a very *good* one, even if she'd tried. Even her name, she found too girlie. In the privacy of her bedroom, she let herself pretend she was Charlotte, but in reality, she made sure that everyone called her Charlie. That was who she was really - 10% Charlotte, 90% Charlie. Or maybe closer to 5% Charlotte and 95% Charlie.

Looking at the dresser, she ran her hand along the length of it. It had always been in her bedroom, even when she was very little. She didn't know how old it was, but she loved it. She loved the solidness of the real timber it was constructed from. She loved knowing that it had been made with love by a quality tradesman and was of the highest quality workmanship. She could appreciate that even more now that she had friends who were starting to leave the sanctuaries of their family homes and venture out by themselves. Almost every one of them had succumbed to the cheapness of flat-pack furniture. Charlie had never thought about furniture at all until she started seeing that flat pack stuff *everywhere*. No, that wasn't for her. She would be happy to stay right where she was, in her bedroom in the house where her mother had lived many years earlier. There she could enjoy the fullness of the high-quality items surrounding her. All through the large home was old furniture and old *everything*, but it was home.

"Charlie!" she heard her older brother Max scream out to her from the lower level of their modest home. It was a run-down old two-story bungalow that was unremarkable from the outside, but it was a home that had been large enough to house the whole family in it when they were younger. Her oldest brothers now lived away from home, of course, but her father seemed to not even regard the idea of the remaining household members moving to a smaller home. Charlie was glad. It was the only place she could almost summon memories of her mother having been. Most days, she forgot about her mother. Other days she wished desperately that she was still alive and that whoever had handed out the terminal cancer card had bypassed her mother and passed it to someone else.

"Come on, or I'm going without you!" she heard Max call out again, extreme impatience very evident in the tone of his voice. Although he was twenty-one and they were three years apart in age, Max was the brother Charlie had always been closest to. Each of her brothers had always shown a strong protectiveness over her, but Max was the one who had always ensured he was fairly close by most of the time. He wasn't the youngest brother she had. Fitz - short for Fitzroy (a name he greatly hated) - was twenty, so one year younger than Max and two years older than her. Even though it could have been expected that the two of them would be close, they were as different as could be. He had never shown as much concern for her, or anyone else, as her other brothers did. There was something different about Fitz. She'd never been able to put her finger on it. Something about him had just always kept her wary about him - and out of his way.

Charlie heard the rattle of car keys as they were being picked up off the side table in the large hallway downstairs. At the sound, she finally started to move.

"I'm coming! Wait!" she yelled out, pounding down the stairs.

At the bottom of the staircase, Max was standing still, calmly waiting with a large grin on his face. Never cottoning on to his same technique to make her panic and get moving when they had to get going somewhere, Charlie tried hard to glare at him but ended up laughing softly instead. She followed that up with a traditional punch on his arm.

"Ouch!" he called out, sounding like a young child as he rubbed the spot she'd punched.

Charlie shook her head at him and grabbed her bag from the coat stand beside the door. No snazzy handbag for her. Nope. A man's duffle bag was far more useful and comfortable to wear. Having slung it diagonally across her body, the two of them finally headed out the door.

"You have the list, right?" Max asked her, teasing her again because he knew that she always forgot the shopping list when it was time for them to go and buy groceries for the house. Because she was so forgetful, he always grabbed the list, as he'd just done. That didn't stop him from teasing her that she should have grabbed it and implying it might still be inside the house even though it was in his pocket.

Charlie glanced at him, startled before she really read the expression on his face.

"Shut up and let's go already," she responded, pretending to be annoyed at him. She wasn't really. As far as brothers and sisters went, they had an easy-going sibling relationship. He teased her a lot, but she knew it was in good jest. She never regarded Max as having any kind of spite or resentment in his nature. If there were another guy out there just like him, she'd probably consider he'd be suited to be her boyfriend.

They climbed into the old Mustang Max had bought a year earlier and had spent countless hours on, doing it up. Why he thought painting it yellow with black stripes running down the length of it, in an effort to make it look like a Transformer, would turn the heads of the young women he constantly pursued, Charlie just didn't get. Really? A woman would turn her head as a car painted like Bumblebee drove past?

But then, what did she know? She was only 18 - almost 19, mind you - but she hadn't had a boyfriend yet. She'd had crushes. All of them had either been completely one-sided, or they'd been completely crushed by the presence of an ex-military father and four of her five brothers showing their muscles and protective side. She did love her family, but overpowering and overprotective? Definitely!

"So, how's things with the pursuit of … umm … what is her name? The blonde one? No, wait. No, the one with black hair?" Charlie teased her brother as they finally began their journey to the supermarket. He didn't have the nickname of Romeo for no reason. Max was a player. He loved women. All through high school, he had loved to chase girls. In that regard, he hadn't changed a bit. They loved him - *all* of them. Charlie chuckled at the thought of how many young women she'd seen just about hanging off him in an attempt to try and become 'the one' - the one that finally turned the head of Max Stonewarden.

Max turned and grinned at her. As far as little sisters went, he did think he'd lucked out. Charlie was okay. She made him laugh. That was something that none of his friends ever said about *their* younger sisters. His friends seemed to avoid their younger siblings like they had the plague, but Charlie was okay. They had both been young when their mother had been sick and then left them completely. Despite having a brother between them in age, it was Charlie who'd looked out for Max, as much as Max had looked out for Charlie.

"I'm not pursuing anyone, Sis, and you know it. They come to me. Why would I have to go out and chase them?" Max teased. Seeing Charlie roll her eyes at him, he laughed.

She knew he was teasing in his words. She also knew that he was making a valid point. They did chase him, so why would he need to keep chasing them?

"Your modesty continues to astound me," she responded and changed the subject. "Did you check the list before you grabbed it? We've got everyone coming over on Sunday, so we need to make sure we have enough to feed everyone in one sitting that day."

"Yeah, don't panic," Max said. "We'll remember. As a matter of fact, we *are* remembering!"

"I meant when we are actually *in* the supermarket. You always forget the most obvious things, and we always need to come back. Not today!"

After Charlie saw him give her a mock salute, they spoke no more for the rest of the fifteen-minute journey. As they pulled into the supermarket carpark, Max saw Charlie's face sharpen and get serious. He turned and followed her view and immediately saw what had captured her attention.

The local thug gang was out in force. That might have been enough in itself, but it was no ordinary gang, and Max and Charlie were no ordinary citizens at that moment. The gang made their money not through drugs like other gangs. No, that stuff this gang didn't touch. Their income came from theft - specifically jewelry theft. They were so discrete and well skilled in their pickpocketing and small theft ventures that members of their gang rarely got caught. Members of the public might not have even known the gang existed, let alone what they did as their 'job'. But the Stonewardens knew because, in some ways, they were their adversaries.

Stonewardens didn't do small jobs. They were highly trained and masters of world-class heists. The local gang couldn't have pulled off a Stonewarden job even if they tried. That fact aside, the reality was that both sides wanted the jewels that were available for the taking in the city. And while the general public knew nothing of either group, both sides certainly knew about each other. Neither was entirely sure who each other was, but they had strong enough suspicions to be slightly nervous when they were in close distance to each other.

Charlie and Max sat still and waited for the black Chrysler Valiant to disappear from view before they exited the car and made their way into the supermarket.

"Join and conquer, or divide and conquer?" Max asked his sister.

Charlie smiled at him in reply, but Max could see she was tense. She hated the world that their family was part of, and he knew it. She had been too young to be brought fully into the business as yet, but they both knew that the day was coming when their father would call her into his office. She would receive the same speech all of her brothers had received when they had each turned nineteen - the great speech about family and honor. Yep, it was coming, and Charlie wanted no part of it.

"You start at that end, and I'll start at this end," Charlie replied. "We'll meet at the meat section in the middle since that's where I know you'll start arguing with me."

Max grinned at her and walked off, shaking his head in fond mock frustration. Charlie turned in the opposite direction, readying herself for the task ahead.

~~~~~

Serving at the checkout counter was Ash Thomson. Twenty years of age, he'd been working in the supermarket for over a year, and he loved it. It paid him enough so that he could afford his own apartment and be free from his family. It wasn't an independence that was needed financially, but he had desperately needed it emotionally. He loved his parents but hated the feeling of suffocation. He also didn't want to live off them. He wanted to live his own life. He wanted to make it a successful life, on his own, without any influence or help from them.

The supermarket wasn't busy. That always made for a long day. In front of him, an elderly woman he saw every week was chatting to him. He didn't mind. In truth, he quite liked it. Every week she seemed to seek him out and make sure she was in his checkout lane. He smiled
~~~~~

at her and patiently listened to the latest sagas with her cats. Ash wasn't sure how many cats she had, but the list of names she gave when she talked about what they'd been doing seemed endless.

As she informed him of the latest little thing that adorable little Toby did (one of her repeat conversations), Ash noticed that girl walk past him. He'd seen her in the supermarket loads of times over the previous year. He wondered how it came to be that *she* never seemed to grace his presence by going through his checkout lane. To her, he was invisible. To him, she definitely was not. He loved her individuality. He loved that she was so natural but still attractive. She didn't have any airs about her. She didn't make herself up so that she looked completely different from who she really was. He was intrigued by her. He didn't know anything about her, and he'd never had the courage to approach her, but one day she would walk through his checkout lane. Then he would get to talk to her. He was sure of it.

Today she was wearing her Mickey Mouse t-shirt. That made Ash smile. She was a tough-looking chick, but every time he saw that Mickey Mouse t-shirt, he thought her toughness took her instead to the brink of cuteness. Yep, she was original, and she had definitely caught his eye. All he had to figure out was how to build up the guts to speak to her.

At twenty, he'd had girlfriends. Women didn't throw themselves at him, but he got along well enough in the dating department. The problem was that he got bored with them so easily. Sometimes it felt like all the women he met looked great but had no skills in conversation whatsoever. It frustrated him. He knew it wasn't outer beauty that would secure his interest in someone. It was intellect and passion - not sexual passion, but a passion for *something*.

"Could you help me carry this to my car today? I am not feeling very steady," his elderly customer asked.

Ash smiled at her, having already anticipated the question. It wasn't common practice to do such a thing, but the checkout supervisor gave Ash the nod and quickly stepped in behind the checkout desk to fill in for the following few minutes.

"Of course, I shall help you. Here we go. I have everything here. Now take my arm and let us be off to find that beautiful car of yours," Ash said, enjoying being able to at least pretend to be a gentleman.

"It is an original, you know. Nothing on it has ever needed to be replaced..." began the regular conversation about her classic car.

From the supermarket to the carpark, Ash said nothing. He let her walk at her pace and made sure she was secure in her car before he returned indoors.

"Thank you for letting me do that each week," he said quietly to his supervisor as they changed places once more.

"Ash, there are few men these days who would *want* to do such a thing, and she is a good regular customer," the supervisor said. "Happy customers talk and spread the word. Keep it up."

Ash settled behind the counter again, but with no more customers in the supermarket that he could see, he let his eyes wander to the girl once more. He could see her moving up and down the aisles. Now and then, she would reach his end of one and then do a u-turn to go down the other side. He could look at her all day, suspecting she would never even notice him doing it.

Toward the other end of the supermarket, Ash could see the guy she always came in with. He had pondered if it might be her boyfriend, but their looks made him think they were more likely brother and sister or cousins - definitely some kind of family. He'd never seen her with anyone else.

Expecting it to be a long, slow, uneventful day, Ash thought he might as well lean on the counter and just indulge in watching her.

So he did.

~~~~~

Charlie wandered up aisle after aisle. Upon reaching the meat section, she waited for Max to appear. As he rounded the corner and saw her, they began a lengthy session of chat and negotiation in deciding what would be cooked and eaten by whom in the coming week. It was a usual discussion. He wanted to eat certain things but hated to cook. Their father was on a strict diet in order to keep himself in prime physical condition, so he needed certain foods also.

Catering to a large family was something they'd all learned skills in after their mother had died. Until that moment, no-one had thought about where the food came from or who was putting time in to prepare it for the crowd in the house. Afterward, they'd all gotten a bit of a shock before everything had finally seemed to slot into place. From that moment, they'd started to work as a team to get everything done that needed to be done.

"Right, are we finished?" Max asked and saw Charlie nod in reply.

"Yeah, let's get out of here."

Making their way to the checkout area, the two of them approached what seemed to be the only counter open for the moment.

Ash felt like he was a lottery winner. She was finally there, right in front of him! Now, if only he could summon some courage to speak to her...

"Ugh, Charlie, we forgot the special high calcium milk that Dad wants. You start putting all this through. I'll run down and get it. I'll be back in a min," Max said to Charlie and turned to begin his walk to the dairy coolers at the back of the store.

Charlie turned to the guy behind the counter and managed only to mumble a short 'hi' to him before something caught her eye. Out the front of the
~~~~~

supermarket - directly in front of her - was the gang car. Not only was it in the supermarket carpark, but it was driving along the front of the building, only a meter or so from the large glass windows.

Charlie was fortunate to have enough time to spot the gun as it was brought up and prepared to take aim.

"Get down!" she yelled as she reached around and pulled the checkout guy down to her side of the counter.

Ash didn't know what was happening, but his instincts were fast enough to immediately follow her lead. He, in turn, pulled her right around the back of the checkout counter, to where a deep freezer for ice cream treats stood. They'd just ducked down to safety when they both heard the sound of gunshots and the explosion of glass. Slivers of it flew over the top of them. Charlie silently thanked him for having moved her that small distance further so that the solid metal freezer protected them so well.

They remained absolutely still. Sure it was the day he was going to die, Ash closed his eyes and tried to let himself find peace in that.

Charlie watched him. She, too, was too terrified to move. She couldn't help but wonder if the bullets could have been intended for her and Max…

Max! Not wanting to move from where she crouched, Charlie strained her ears to listen out for him. Turning her head away from the guy huddling next to her, she tried to look down the aisles that she could see. The milk chillers were further away, she knew. He must have made it safely there and be waiting also.

Outside they could hear angry voices. It sounded for a moment like they were moving closer. Charlie felt tears come to her eyes. She hadn't wanted to move forward and become a part of her family business, but she didn't want to die! She wasn't ready to die. She hadn't even had sex yet.

As if tuned into that very thought, she saw Ash

open his eyes and look right at her. It wasn't a conscious thing done, but he suddenly leaned his head that little bit closer and kissed her. She accepted it. They both accepted they were going to die. One kiss would hardly hurt in their final moments.

The sound of sirens broke into their thoughts, followed by the voices outside seeming to become panicked. They could hear the car start up and screech off loudly from outside the window, with what sounded like at least one police car in pursuit, siren blaring.

Other cars could be heard approaching outside, followed by voices. Charlie was relieved to assess that the voices sounded authoritative. The police had arrived. She hesitated before shifting only far enough to be able to look around the side of the freezer they'd huddled behind. Seeing the blue uniforms, she started to stand up slowly. Ash did the same.

"Kids, are you okay? What happened here?" one of the officers asked as he approached. "Is anyone hurt?"

Charlie thought again about Max and turned to find him. She called out to him again and again as she moved from a walk to a jog and then a run.

"Max!"

Calling his name and getting no response placed Charlie into a panic.

Ash and the officer saw her growing more and more desperate and began to walk in her direction to catch up with her. Just as they did so, all three saw blood pooling in a slow progression across the floor. It was flowing thickly, dark and red, from underneath the tall shelving unit they were beside.

Nausea flowed over Charlie as she slowly walked down to the end of the aisle and around to the other side of the shelving. It was there that she finally found Max. She rushed to him, saying his name over and over, but there was no response.

"We need an ambulance!" the officer called out.

In the distance, Ash could hear someone radioing to arrange one to come immediately.

The officer leaned down and checked for a pulse before placing a hand on Charlie's shoulder. "He's alive. The ambulance is on its way. He will be in good hands very soon."

To Ash, it seemed like only minutes before paramedics were securing the young man before him onto a stretcher and easing him into the back of an ambulance. To Charlie, it seemed like hours.

"I need to ask you two some questions," one of the officers started to say.

"I have to go to the hospital," Charlie started to say, not caring about any stupid questions they wanted to ask.

"I'm sorry but…"

"I said I'm *going* to the *hospital*. That is my brother, and these might be the last minutes of his life. Do whatever you have to do to me later, but I'm going with him *right now!*"

Ash watched as she walked away and pushed herself into the back of the ambulance.

"I will answer your questions, Officer," he said, trying to at least attempt to distract the officer so that the girl could get away in the ambulance without any problems.

"Alright. What happened? What did you see and hear?"

As the questioning began, Ash answered all of the questions as much as he could. His mind wasn't in it. That was centered securely on the girl he'd always wanted to meet, and whatever she was having to deal with at that moment. He had no right to be so focused on her since he expected she didn't even know he existed, but he was worried about her. She had just seen her brother lying in a pool of blood, shot. Did she have someone with her to support her? Did she have friends or any other family? The thought of her being alone and having to deal with whatever was happening with her brother became too much for Ash. He probably wouldn't be welcome, but he had to get to the hospital and make sure she was okay. It didn't matter if she rejected him. It didn't matter if she didn't even remember ever having seen his face. He just had to get there and make sure she was okay.

~~~~~

In the ambulance, Charlie sat quietly and out of the way of the paramedic who was moving around and over Max. She couldn't believe what had just happened. She knew there was an ongoing rivalry between her family and another, but shooting? When did that start? Was it something new, or had it been going on for years as one of those things that her family had shielded from her?

The paramedic turned to her with a sympathetic look on her face.

"He's stable for now. It will only be a few minutes before we reach the hospital. Are you doing okay?" she asked.

Charlie nodded in reply. There were no words that she could find right at that moment. She could hardly think until the paramedic spoke again.

"Is there anyone else who should be called to meet you at the hospital?"

Suddenly all the faces of her family flashed over Charlie's mind. Yes, all her brothers would want to be there, but most importantly, she had to call her father.

As if she'd forgotten it was still slung over her body, she looked down and saw the duffel bag, feeling somewhat surprised that it was still there. Reaching in, she found her mobile phone and pulled it out. Because her hands were shaking, she became frustrated that she kept entering the wrong lock code because her hands were all over the place.
~~~~~

"Let me help you with that," the paramedic said, taking the phone from her. "Tell me your code and I can enter it for you."

If anyone else had said that to her, Charlie might have punched them. The whole point of having a lock code on her phone was to keep every other person out. But it was hardly the time to care about things like that. She said the combination of numbers out loud and was promptly handed the phone back in its unlocked state.

"Thank you," she said quietly and proceeded to scroll through her contacts until she found her father's number. She took a deep breath, began the call, and closed her eyes.

"Charlie, I'm busy right…"

"Dad! Listen to me!" she said in a tone that she never, *ever* used with her father. The tone was enough to silence him and make him listen. "Max…" she started to say and suddenly felt the tears begin to flow heavily. "Max has been shot…"

"No! What happ…"

"Dad! Not now!" Charlie exclaimed. "We're on the way to the hospital. Please meet me there. I don't … I don't want to be there alone."

She heard her father take a deep breath as if to force himself to calm down.

"I'm leaving now," he replied. "I'll find you when I arrive."

All she heard then was the click of the call being disconnected. Despite how well all of her family got on together, she suddenly just felt alone. She couldn't lose Max. He was the best man in her family. He was kind and good, and funny. Only *his* jokes made her laugh.

"We're approaching the hospital now," the paramedic said quietly. "It's important that we move him as quickly as we can, so please stay right where you are when the doors open, alright? I know you'll want to be with him, but the best thing for him right now is for you to let everyone here do their job."

Charlie nodded and remained still and quiet, determined not to interrupt anything that the medical professionals needed to do to save her brother.

~~~~~~

Mitchell Stonewarden stared at his phone for a few minutes before he jolted himself to move. His son had been shot. He wanted details about that, but he couldn't ignore the pleading in his daughter's voice over the phone. His natural reaction was to find out what happened and seek justice somehow. Someone had to pay! At the same time, he had to do what was needed, and right now, his little Charlie needed him. She was his only daughter. Raising her without the help of her mother since she was nine hadn't been easy for him. Not only was he a man, but he had been a military man. When he'd first walked away from the military, he had found it hard to let himself feel, and even harder still to let himself *show* how he felt. It just wasn't the way he'd been brought up.

He'd persevered in determination to be a good father to his children when they'd been left without a mother. It had been a long, hard road, but he couldn't be more proud of any of them. They each had their personality quirks, but they were good kids. Knowing he was a full-time dad to six of them, they could have wrecked so much havoc, but they hadn't. They'd all stuck together and worked out systems and processes that helped each other and made things run as smoothly as they could, given the horrible circumstance they had all found themselves in.

No, he had nothing to be ashamed of with his children. Now his son needed him, and his baby girl needed him.

Without any further thought, he got into his modest car and made his way to the hospital accident and emergency department. He needed to call the other
~~~~~~

boys, but that was a secondary consideration. First, he had to support Max and Charlie. Then he would call their brothers.

~~~~~

Ash rushed into the hospital and to the front desk.

"Please, a friend was shot and brought in by ambulance. Where would they be?" he asked with a level of desperation in his voice.

The receptionist directed him to the right area of the hospital before informing him he shouldn't expect to see the patient in question. Ash ignored that. He didn't need to see the patient. He just wanted to see the patient's sister and make sure she was okay.

He moved quickly while avoiding other people who seemed to be in even more of a hurry than he was. When he reached the department he needed to be in, he saw her. She was sitting on a seat, alone, with her head down. For a moment, he contemplated walking away. Just as he was about to do that, he saw Charlie's head come up, and her eyes focus on him. Immediately she stood and walked right to him. She said nothing as she wrapped her arms around him and leaned her cheek against his chest.

Ash was so overwhelmed that he could say nothing. Instead, he tentatively wrapped his arms gently and loosely around her and just let her be still for as long as she wanted to be. He thought that perhaps she was in so much shock that she thought he was someone else, and would soon scream when she looked at him and realized she didn't know this guy with his arms around her. What actually happened surprised and stunned him.

"You saved my life," she said and then pulled away from him far enough to be able to look into his eyes. "You pulled me behind that freezer, and that saved both of us. Thank you."

Charlie watched his face and could see his uncertainty about how to act. For a moment, he
~~~~~

reminded her of Max. The thought began the flow of tears again. She knew she didn't know the guy she was clinging to, but she couldn't find the strength to move away. She needed someone to lean on, and he was there.

"Charlie!" she suddenly heard.

When she started to turn around, her father was already by her side. He had a curious look on his face as he saw Ash, still with his arms around Charlie.

"Who are you?" Mitchell asked.

Ash felt the power emanating from the older man and instantly pulled away from the young woman in his arms. He wanted to simply introduce himself, using the good manners he always had. Something about the presence of the man scared him immensely.

"Dad, he saved me," Charlie spoke up. "He pulled me to safety. He saved my life. Please don't harass him. He's done nothing to deserve it."

Mitchell looked upon the young man who'd had his arms around his daughter. No man would ever be good enough for his little girl. That was his natural thinking. He knew it was also illogical thinking.

"Perhaps you should introduce us then," he said to his daughter and wasn't at all surprised by her being stunned into silence. "Unless, of course, you haven't yet asked him his name."

The situation they were in wasn't funny. Her brother and his son was in surgery with no certain outcome. But just for a sliver of a moment, both laughed softly and then turned to Ash.

"I'm sorry, my dad is right. I don't know your name," she said and held out her hand for him to shake. "I'm Charlotte Stonewarden, but everyone calls me Charlie."

Ash looked at the hand presented to him. He felt full of surprise for so many reasons. He'd seen her at the supermarket so many times, and she'd never even looked at him.

He shook himself out of any thoughts and gladly took her hand in his.

"I'm Ash."

"Well, Ash," he heard Charlie's father say deeply and quietly. "I guess I owe you thanks for saving my little girl."

As Mitchell held out his hand, Ash shook it, extremely intimidated by the man standing before him, exuding an intense depth of power.

"Stonewarden Family!" a voice called out loudly, making all three turn around.

"Yes! Max is my son," Mitchell spoke up, abruptly reminded of the horrible circumstances that had brought him to the hospital.

"Mr Stonewarden, your son has come through surgery but is still in critical condition. The bullet has done serious damage."

"Can we see him?"

"He's in recovery for now, but a nurse will come and get you when you can go in to see him."

"Thank you."

That was all that Mitchell could say. What more was there to say? He was sure they'd done all they could for Max. Now it was a matter of waiting to see if he recovered. As he took in a deep breath and sat down, Mitchell placed his head in his hands. The smell of the hospital reminded him of when his wife Caroline had been ill and later died. The memory felt raw even though it had happened so many years earlier. For a moment, he forgot Charlie was there and let himself go as he wept for his lost wife and his hurt child. No longer a child at all, of course, but still. That was all he had from his wife - their home and their children. He would hold onto all of those as long as he was able.

"Dad?" Charlie asked him tentatively as she sat beside him. "Dad, we need to tell the boys."

Mitchell raised his head and looked at her,

seeming to come back to her from a place of deep thought and reflection. She saw him nod at her.

"Yes, of course we do," he said as he put his arm around her and kissed her forehead. "Just give me a minute, Charlie. Then I'll ring each of them."

Ash watched on, wondering what he should do. He wasn't needed, but he also didn't want to interrupt their conversation. He thought the only option was to remove himself quietly and leave them to it.

When Charlie saw him turn away and start to leave, she quietly and softly extracted herself from her father's hold. After following Ash until they were a distance away from her father, she called out to him.

When he heard her, Ash stopped and turned around. It wasn't the right time to think it, but when he turned and saw her walking toward him as she was, he thought she looked stunning. She had enraptured him months earlier. She just didn't know it.

"Ash, thank you for coming here," Charlie said as she placed her hand on his arm. The movement was nothing to her. With five brothers, it was natural for her to touch a man's arm - albeit usually to punch them in the case of her brothers. To Ash, it felt like *something*.

"It's … you're … I'm … no problem, Charlie. I hope your brother is okay," he stammered out and was about to turn away again to walk out when he felt her approach and put her arms around him once more.

"Sorry, I know you don't know me, but you feel really nice to hug," she said.

Ash smiled even though she couldn't see it with her face buried into his chest.

"Well, then, you can hug me anytime you like," Ash replied and heard her quietly laugh. "Think of me as the hug fairy," he continued and then saw her pull away as she laughed louder.

"I need to get back to my dad," Charlie said and saw him nod with a sad look on his face. "But would …

could … I'd like to see you again. I don't know where or when, with all that is happening…"

Ash took her hand in his, raised it to his mouth, and kissed it.

"I'm going to give you my number. Just call or text me whenever you want to," he said.

She watched as he held out his hand to prompt her to give him her phone. As she watched him enter his number into it, she smiled on the outside and the inside. Once she had the phone back in her hands, she reached up, kissed his cheek, smiled at him, and then turned and walked back to where her father still sat and waited.

Although it had been a horrible day, Ash felt like maybe it was an okay day after all. He made his way out of the hospital, not knowing what to do or where to go. He walked as far as he could to be able to see the supermarket from a safe distance. It was obvious he wasn't going to be going to work for a while. The entire frontage of windows was missing. It looked as if a bomb had gone off, leaving only destruction behind. Police officers surrounded the area within the bounds of the tape designed to keep people out.

Seeing it from that angle shocked him. It was pure luck that he and Charlie had escaped unharmed. If she hadn't been at the counter right at that moment and seen what was going to happen, he would have been oblivious to that car driving close to the frontage. His back had been to it. He would never have seen it.

He didn't know that if Charlie and Max hadn't been in the supermarket, the shootout possibly wouldn't have happened. He had no idea whatsoever that perhaps it was Charlie and Max that the bullets had actually been intended for.

~~~~~

Charlie sat next to her father. He once again had his arm wrapped around her shoulder and was letting her cuddle into his chest. She'd always been a cuddly kid. He
~~~~~

wasn't surprised that even at 18 - almost 19 - she still sought comfort in cuddling into him like she was. If he was completely honest with himself, it felt good to him too. He hadn't gotten involved with anyone after his Caroline had passed away. It wasn't a logical decision to remain single. He just hadn't met anyone who could replace her. Maybe one day he'd be in that place where he could move on, but not yet. Now was for his kids. No matter how old they were, they were always his priority.

He'd made the phone calls to his other four sons, each of whom would be passing through the hospital in the approaching hours. He wanted to ask Charlie more about what happened, but he was scared of what she would tell him. If he heard what he suspected he would - that their adversaries were responsible for shooting his son - he might be driven to do something extreme. He didn't want that. Not now. Now was the time to just sit, wait, and be there for Max when he woke up.

~~~~~

"Dad!" Charlie heard through the haze of her sleep. She woke with surprise at how easy and comfortable it had felt to drift off as she leaned against her father. He was a strict, solid man, but even though he could portray himself as someone no-one would want to be on the wrong side of, Charlie had to admit that he had always been loving toward her and her brothers. He was tough, but he wasn't afraid to show affection and never had been.

When Charlie looked up, she saw her brother James standing before them. As she pulled herself away from her father, she saw he'd also unintentionally fallen asleep.

"James. You made it," Mitchell said as he sat upright and stretched.

"What's happening?" James asked. "How's Max?"

"I don't know. They were going to come and tell us when we could see him," their father said as he stood
~~~~~

up. "Wait here. I'll go and find someone who can give us answers."

As Mitchell stood up and walked away, James sat down in the seat his father had vacated.

"How are you doing?" he asked Charlie as he reached out to hug her briefly.

The two of them got on well, although they weren't as close as she was to Max. The age gap between them meant that James was much more protective of her and fairly often introduced her as his 'baby sister'. She had to keep reminding him that as she was his only sister, then 'sister' was a fine enough way to introduce her to people. But no, always with him it had to be 'baby sister'. She didn't really mind. She was glad to have a big brother who still wanted to spend time with her now and then.

"I'm okay," she started to say.

As her thoughts returned to the moment she'd first seen Max on the floor, with all the blood, tears began to flow. When she felt James tighten his hold around her, she found herself, for the first time since their mother had died, openly and loudly sobbing.

James sat quietly and let her cry. There were many moments when it was good fun to tease his little sister, but that wasn't one of them. He held her close and let her make the decision about when she would want the hold to break.

Charlie felt her sobs calm, and the tears slow down until the flow stopped. She pulled away and wiped her eyes. The expression of concern on James's face touched her, knowing he had a tough streak in him just like their father did.

"Charlie, what happened? Was this some freak instance of being in the wrong place at the wrong time?" he asked.

As she looked closely at him, she felt uncertain whether to tell him her assessment of what had happened. If she spoke her fears, he most certainly might act and do something that would end up very, very bad for him, and possibly for all of them. Could she risk that? She didn't want to be sitting in the hospital with *another* of her brothers having been shot - or worse. It was bad enough that Max was there without having done anything to deserve it.

Before she could answer, they saw their father walking back toward them with a grave look on his face. Charlie felt as if her heart dropped in her chest. Dead? No, Max couldn't be dead. She started to panic. What would her life be like without him to tease her? To tell her jokes that actually made her laugh?

In the short time it took for Mitchell to walk along the passageway and reach them, Charlie had worked herself up into a panic attack, hyperventilating. James saw it and put his arms around her, rubbing her back to try and soothe her. According to their father, Charlie had never had panic attacks before their mother had died. She'd rarely had them since, but when her stress levels rose, it sometimes hit her hard. All of her brothers had seen it at different times and knew what worked for her. By the time their father had reached them, she had calmed slightly and was concentrating heavily on maintaining her breathing steadily.

"Dad, what did they say?" James quietly asked as he continued to hug his sister, still moving his hands soothingly over her back as he spoke.

Charlie turned and looked at her father. Usually a man who emanated strength and power, all of a sudden, he looked worn down and timid. When she saw her father shake his head, Charlie thought the worse. Then he spoke, and she was able to breathe once again.

"He hasn't woken up. They said he's in a coma, so there's no telling when - *if* - he'll wake up."

The siblings heard the words come from their father's mouth and then watched as he seemed to crumple. It was the first time that to Charlie, her father had actually seemed old. James guided his father to a seat and comforted him.

For a long time, Charlie watched the two men hold each other and lean on one another. She looked at the clock on the wall. It was getting late. She could see the dark enclosing them outside the windows. As if sensing her movement, her father looked up at her.

"Go home, Charlie," Mitchell said. "I don't think there is anything more you can do here tonight."

"Dad, you need to come home, too," she said quietly. She didn't often speak back to her father, but tonight she would. And tonight he would accept it, rather than giving her the powerful glare that he'd given her a few times when talking back before she finally learned not to do it. "Please."

"Dad, one of us can stay here, and one of us can go with Charlie and stay at home overnight," James suggested. "We can swap tomorrow. But you choose. Do you want to stay here tonight, and me go home with her? Or do you want to go home and come back in the morning? I don't mind…"

"James, you go and take Charlie back to the house," Mitchell replied, nodding. "Both of you keep yourselves safe. If anything happens here, I'll call you. Keep your phones on charge right beside your beds, please. Hopefully, it will be an uneventful night, but I can't leave him. Not yet."

James nodded and hugged his father before he stood up and let Charlie do the same.

"We'll see you in the morning, Dad," she said quietly.

Mitchell kissed her forehead in affection. Sometimes when he looked at her, she reminded him so much of her mother that it hurt, but he loved her as much as any father could love their child. They were all special, but she was his little girl. He had to keep her safe.

Charlie and James left quietly, both in their own thoughts, wondering if they would get to see their brother again. They also hoped that Max wouldn't slip away in the night without any opportunity to say goodbye.

~~~~~~

"I don't get what happened, Charlie. You need to tell me how you and Max ended up in a shootout at the supermarket!" James asked as he drove to their family home. It was no longer where he lived, having set himself up in a small apartment just outside the city. He did, though, still regard it as his true home. Their father had changed nothing since he and Victor had moved out. It was a run-down old place, but each of them had the same rooms they'd had their whole lives. It made James feel nostalgic every time he entered.

"James, please. I can't talk to you about this right now. I need to turn my mind off for a while…" she said and saw him start to object. Immediately she cut off his words. "*Please*! I will talk to you about it tomorrow if you want, but tonight I just want to get home, go to my room and be alone."

James looked at her as he briefly turned his head from the road. With an eight-year age gap between them, they'd never really had any crossover in their life as far as friends or interests went. When their mother had died, Charlie had been a little kid while James had already become a 17-year-old teenager who wanted to do adult things and get on with life.

He resolved not to ask her anything more. She'd had a panic attack earlier. Knowing that was a strong indicator of her stress level, he backed off. When he really thought about it, it wasn't surprising she would be stressed or exhausted. She'd left home that morning just to go grocery shopping with their brother. Then she'd been shot at and found Max lying still in a large pool of
~~~~~~

blood.

No, no questions for her tonight, he resolved. But he knew he would hardly sleep, knowing that *someone* had tried to shoot her and Max, and they might try again if they knew they had missed her as a target. Silently he put himself on watch duty for the night - just in case.

~~~~~

Once inside the house, Charlie immediately walked up to her room. Knowing James was in the house was a reassurance and a comfort, but she didn't want to talk to him. All she wanted to do was lie on her bed and pretend like the day hadn't yet started. Perhaps she could pretend it was a Groundhog Day scenario, and tomorrow she would wake up and then hear Max calling out to her to hurry up.

No, it was no use pretending. The day *had* happened, and Max was lying in hospital in a coma. How the day could go from just going to buy food to where everything now stood was beyond belief.

Entering her room, Charlie gladly lay down on top of the covers, not bothering even to take off her shoes. Trying to sleep was pointless yet. Her mind was too active. Her thoughts jumped around from here to there and round in circles.

As the day passed through her mind like a movie running, she briefly remembered the guy she'd met - Ash. Somewhere in the mix of the craziness, they'd kissed. It was an odd thing to have happened, but she could remember at that moment thinking that they might be about to die. Now that she was away from the situation, she took a moment to think about how he'd gone to the hospital to see her. It seemed like something that not everyone would do - check that a stranger was okay. She appreciated that he had. He'd even let her entice him into a hug or two at the hospital.

Yes, it was a pity she'd never see him again. He might have been a genuinely nice guy if she'd had any
~~~~~

opportunity to get to know him.

~~~~~~

Across town in his one-bedroom apartment, Ash also lay on his bed, thinking about the events of the day. He'd gotten up as usual and just gone to work. The series of events that had flowed on from that was almost unbelievable. If Charlie hadn't been in the supermarket and right at the checkout counter when the bullets were about to fly, Ash wouldn't have seen anything and would most surely have been shot. That knowledge scared him.

As soon as he'd returned home to his apartment after visiting the hospital, he'd called the supermarket manager. Highly shaken up, the manager had actually seemed worried about Ash and happy he was alright. What Ash was most concerned about was his income. He'd branched out on his own with the determination to not live off his parents' wealth. The wages had covered him being able to rent the apartment, pay bills, and buy food. It wasn't a happy thought that perhaps he might not have any earnings anymore.

The manager had put his mind at rest. Insurance would cover the physical damage to the store, but it would also cover staff wages until everything was back to normal, however long that would take. The news helped Ash to breathe easy again. He would never have been in a dire situation. He knew his parents would welcome him back under their wings at any moment that he wished to return home, but he just didn't want that. He didn't want the easy way out of things. He wanted to do things right and for himself.

After he'd readied himself for bed and climbed under the covers, he took a moment to think about Charlie and her family. He had watched her come into the supermarket for months, and she'd never noticed him. Today, under horrible circumstances, she finally had. They'd kissed in the moment they were both uncertain what was going to happen. But more than that,
~~~~~~

she'd remembered him when she saw him in the hospital and had freely and openly put her arms around him.

Despite the horror of the day, Ash let himself smile at that thought. He would see how he felt about the idea in the morning but considered that he might want to go to the hospital again.

CHAPTER TWO

Charlie stirred to her name being called out from the other side of her bedroom door. As the haze cleared and she fully woke, she realized that it wasn't James who was calling out to her, but Victor, her oldest brother. Although he worked in the family business, she hardly ever saw him. It was a surprise to hear his voice.

"I'm awake!" she called back and waited for him to enter.

"Can I come in?" Charlie heard him ask.

His question made her smile while rolling her eyes to herself. No-one ever asked before bounding into her room. It was another reminder of how little she knew her 30-year-old brother.

After she acknowledged, the door opened, and she saw him walk in with hesitation in his step. He walked over and sat on the edge of her bed, looking at her with a look of sorrow on his face. The look made Charlie want to panic in suspense of what news she thought he was about to deliver to her.

"No, Max is fine. Don't get worked up," Victor said in his calming voice as if sensing her turmoil coming on. "As far as I know, he's still in a coma, and nothing has changed. I've been at the hospital with Dad. He'll come home soon to sleep. He doesn't want to, but he has to. He has to look after himself."

Charlie listened but said nothing. She was very aware of her heartbeat relaxing back into a steady rhythm again after the anticipation of news that would shock.

"I'm going to give James a ride to the hospital," Victor said. "I don't think he should drive since he's had no sleep. Do you want to come with us?"

Charlie nodded. Nothing more was said as Victor ruffled her hair a little and then stood and walked toward the door.

"We'll wait for you downstairs," he said before walking out.

Alone again, Charlie took a moment to lie back and stare at the ceiling, the events of the day before entering her mind again. Less than 24 hours earlier, she'd been sitting in her room, looking in the mirror and asking what she should do with her life. Now she was glad to *have* her life. It was infinitely easier to see today how lucky she was, than how she had perceived it the day before.

~~~~~

The three siblings made their way to the ward in the hospital where Max had been moved for recovery.

Upon seeing her father, Charlie ran into his arms and was lovingly received before she turned and walked to the bed. Seeing Max lying so still and expressionless almost took her breath away. He was always so full of life, smiling and teasing.

"The doctor came through just before and said we could talk to him. He said that sometimes that helps," she heard her father say as his voice began to cave in like it was crumbling. As she heard him desperately try and hold back a sob, she moved to him and put her arms around him.

James and Victor watched on in silence, at a loss for anything to say. James moved to the far side of the bed and looked down at his brother. Five years apart in age, they got on pretty well even though they lived separate lives. Their paths crossed in the business but nowhere else unless a family gathering came up. James liked Max. He was a good kid that everyone liked. He certainly didn't deserve what had happened to him.

"Where are Regan and Fitz? Are they coming to see him?" Victor asked and saw his father look forlorn.
~~~~~

"Regan will be here soon," Mitchell replied. "Fitz … I have no idea where he is. He always sings his own tune except for when we've got a job on. You know that. I left a message on his voicemail, but who knows if or when he'll get it."

Charlie looked around all the faces in the room. There with her were her father and three of her brothers, one of whom was in the deepest slumber she could imagine.

"Dad, you need to rest. Come on, let me take you home. Charlie and James will stay with Max, right?" Victor asked and saw James nod.

Victor walked to his father and reached out to help him out of the chair. Normally an example of prime fitness and health for his age, Charlie thought that at that moment, he looked like an old man. She watched silently as he let his oldest son lead him out of the room and away to go home.

"I can't believe this," James started to say, his voice sounding more like he was talking to himself rather than her. "Max is usually so full of life. I can't believe he's here … like this. Whoever did this needs to pay!"

To that, Charlie had no reply.

They sat silently on either side of the bed, each holding a hand and hoping Max would wake up. Charlie rested her head in her hands. They weren't a religious family, but internally she was praying. Nothing to lose there, she considered. It was well worth a try.

"Hey," she heard from the doorway, prompting her to look up and see her 24-year-old brother Regan entering quietly. The third oldest of all of the siblings, he was the oldest living at home, although now that he was involved with a new girlfriend, he more often stayed overnight at her place.

He approached Charlie's side of the bed and ruffled her hair in his annoying fashion, as he had done all her life. Usually, she gave him a friendly punch on the arm in reply. Somehow, it didn't seem like much of a punch-in-the-arm kind of day.

"How's he doing?" Regan asked.

"He's alive. That's something," James replied.

"Man, you look like hell," said Regan. "Why don't you go back home and get some sleep? I'll stay here with Max."

"No, I'm good," replied James. "I was at home last night. Charlie and I only came in a short while ago."

"You might have been at home, but you look like you haven't slept."

As the two of them kept talking, back and forth, Charlie tuned out to them. Instead, she turned her head as a figure just outside the door caught her eye. Despite the situation before her, Charlie felt a sliver of happiness as she saw Ash. She didn't hesitate to excuse herself from the company of her brothers.

"Ash," she said simply as she walked up to him. She was glad when he slipped his arms around her as if it were the most natural thing in the world, and they'd done that together hundreds of times before. "What are you doing here?" she asked him quietly as she pulled away only far enough so that she could look at his face.

"I just wanted to see how you and Max are doing," Ash answered in almost a whisper.

Inside the room where Max lay, he could see two men conversing together in a way that told him they were also related. "Are they your brothers too?"

Charlie followed his line of sight and then smiled at him with a sad look on her face.

"I have five brothers in all," she said. "Three are in there. The other two might come and go when they're ready. My oldest brother, Vic, brought me here today, but he's taken Dad home to try and get him to grab some sleep."

Ash looked into her eyes as she talked, but made

no move to pull away from her. As long as she wanted to be standing that close to him, with their arms around each other, he was absolutely fine with that.

"Who's this?" he heard a deep voice say from closer than he'd realized anyone was to them.

"Ash, this is my brother Regan. Regan, this is Ash," Charlie said but made no move to pull away from Ash.

"Boyfriend?" the simple question came.

Ash and Charlie both stuttered out a shy 'no' at the same time in response. It could have been a slightly humorous moment, but Regan wasn't smiling.

"Hurt my sister, and I'll kill you," he said.

Charlie saw Ash visibly gulp heavily. She cringed inside, desiring very much to punch her brother in the face for saying such a stupid thing. She then thanked him silently when he smiled and put out his hand. "Just kidding. I'm Regan."

Ash looked at the hand presented to him and reluctantly removed his own from where it had been around Charlie to accept the handshake. He was unnerved by the guy speaking to him. His words had been one thing. Following them up with a 'just kidding' didn't quite put to rest the fear Ash suddenly had.

"Ash," he said simply and then waited for his hand to be let go.

"Regan, you can go now," Charlie said, breaking the tense moment.

Ash saw the brother look at each of them one more time before he turned and went back into the room.

"Sorry. They are a protective lot, my brothers," Charlie explained.

She looked at his face and wondered if he'd just been scared off, but found reassurance when the lost hand seemed to naturally circle her waist once more.

"How are you doing?" Ash asked quietly.

"I'm alright. I don't know how much sleep I got

last night, so I'm tired, but other than that, I'm good." She paused, looked back at the bed once more, and then resumed her attention on Ash. "Do you want to come outside with me? I think I need to get some fresh air."

Ash nodded and finally pulled away. He watched as she leaned into the room briefly.

"I'm going to get some air outside for a while. Back soon," she said.

Ash saw her brothers nod - the ones that were awake anyway. As he and Charlie began to walk down the long corridor and then through the swinging doors at the end, both were quiet. Down the stairs they walked and finally ventured out through the large automatic opening doors at the main entrance of the hospital building.

Ash followed her as she led him around the side of the building and found a spot on the grass that was bathed in sunshine. Gladly, he sank down to the ground, all the time watching her for signs of where she felt comfortable with him being. Not too close. Not too far away. He'd wanted to meet her for so long that he was afraid of doing anything that might freak her out and result in her wanting to walk away from him.

Charlie sat down and then rolled onto her side so that she was facing him. His tenseness was obvious, and she understood. Her brothers could be intimidating. They could also be charming and funny, but to anyone who didn't know them, intimidation was definitely the strength that they all emanated outwards in large waves.

"Did my brother frighten you? Don't take him seriously. He wouldn't touch anyone who he knows is my friend," she said naturally as if they always talked and always had.

Ash moved a little closer and lay down to mirror her position, on his side and facing her, with his head resting on his raised hand. He was happy with her use of the word 'friend' but discretely didn't mention that.

"No, it's fine," he replied. "I can see that your family care about you and don't want you to be hurt in any way. It's only natural, I guess."

He saw Charlie smile. It was a good thing to see. She was gorgeous when she was in her dark and brooding mood that he'd seen her in fairly often when she'd been grocery shopping, but with that smile on her face, she was stunning. He thought she might not consider herself that way, given that once again, she was wearing the usual attire that he'd seen her in, of old t-shirt and ripped jeans. From his present position, he could look at her face closely for as long as she wanted to lie there with him. Ash opted to take full advantage of that and studied her close up.

Charlie watched his eyes as they moved over her face and then seemed to take in the state of her hair. Then his sight moved to her lips, where she saw his attention sit for a few minutes before his eyes came up to meet hers again. She wouldn't normally appreciate any guy looking at her like that. In fact, she might even go so far as to punch or slap a guy looking at her like that, but she was okay with him doing it. In truth, it was kind of nice.

"I think you will remember the placement of each of my freckles if you study me for any longer," she said, teasing him. In response, she saw him smile and blush, making him look endearing to her as she laughed softly with him.

"Sorry. I … hmm…" Ash began to reply. "To be honest, Charlie, before yesterday, I had seen you in the supermarket heaps of times and had wanted to meet you for a really long time."

He watched her facial expression as he spoke, to try and monitor how she would react to that news. He'd contemplated never telling her that, in case she thought him creepy. But it had come naturally to tell her. What would she do with that knowledge?

"Me?" Charlie asked, confused.

"Yes. You."

"I ... I ... what ... *why*?" she asked, sounding as flustered as he was.

The realization that he wasn't the only one who was blushing made Ash relax.

"Because you're you," he said in a whisper.

Charlie heard the words but felt like she couldn't understand them. What was he saying to her? Her logic and skills in comprehension seemed to have left her.

"I don't ... I don't know what you mean," she said.

Ash laughed softly at her. She'd always seemed so strong and staunch. It was refreshing to see another side to her that he hadn't observed before.

"I can't answer *why* because I don't really know, but you captured my attention ages ago," Ash explained.

Charlie was speechless. She had no more questions. She couldn't comprehend anything he was saying, so decided to just be quiet. Instead, she just looked at him and found that she rather enjoyed him looking at her.

"We kissed yesterday," he said all of a sudden and saw her nod. "I know this isn't the right time, but sometime in the future, I'd like to kiss you again..." he started to say but was cut off. His words were cut short by her moving forward and immediately placing her lips on his. He was so surprised that it took him a moment to relax and then start to kiss her back.

Once he did, Charlie let herself indulge in the feeling of her lips against his. The kiss the day before had been quick and desperate in an attempt to fit a kiss in before expected pain, suffering, and maybe even death. There was no longer any need to rush. As she moved her lips over his, it felt like the first grown-up kiss she'd ever had. His lips parting hers slightly, and his tongue moving softly and tentatively to find hers, felt like something new that she'd never experienced before.

She reveled in it. Tasting him. Caressing him. Their bodies remained apart while their lips began the blissful journey of initiation and familiarization. Charlie wanted to move closer to him, but she held back. It was enough for the moment, just enjoying the kiss.

Ash reluctantly pulled back from her. His lips could have stayed with hers forever, he knew, but he desired to look into her eyes. He needed to *see* her.

As Charlie felt and then saw him pulling away, she felt a depth of need inside of her. Who was this guy, where had he come from, and why did she feel so naturally at ease with him when she was *never* like that with guys?

"What's happening with your job?" she asked out of the blue, momentarily surprising and stunning him. "We drove past the supermarket on the way here and it's cordoned off by police. Do you still *have* a job?"

"Yeah, I talked to my manager yesterday," Ash replied. "He said I'll still receive pay while the mess is being cleaned up and the supermarket's being prepared to open again. I'll go in and help set everything back up once the police have finished doing whatever they are doing there, and there are windows in the place again."

"What are you going to do each day in the meantime though?" Charlie asked. "Sorry, I … I don't know anything about you."

"I hope we can rectify that over time if you'd like to," Ash replied as he grinned at her.

His words were replied to with yet another kiss from her. While he was enjoying that, he couldn't help but consider that fate sometimes went to the strangest degrees to simply get two people to meet.

"I'll be here each day for as long as it takes for Max to wake up," she said in almost a whisper, straining to hold back tears. "I don't know what I'll do without him, Ash. I have five great brothers and a great dad, but Max is the one I've always been closest to. He can't die."

Her words faded out and were replaced by peaceful sobbing. Ash stood up, then leaned down and guided her to stand up so he could put his arms around her properly.

As Charlie eased into his hold, she felt safe and at peace.

"I'd better get back inside," she mumbled against his chest. "Regan and James might send out a search party for me if they think I'm gone too long."

Ash nodded and kissed her forehead before they turned to begin their return journey to the hospital room. Neither consciously thought about how natural their hands had reached out toward each other to hold onto one another as they walked.

~~~~~

Approaching the room, both of them saw uniformed police officers outside the doorway, talking to James.

"Here she is now," he was saying to one of the officers.

"Miss Stonewarden?" the officer asked as she and Ash reached them. "I understand you were at the shooting yesterday? At the supermarket?"

"Yes," she stuttered out, wondering why it had taken a whole day before anyone came to question her. "We both were," she then said, indicating her and Ash both with her hand movements.

The second officer stepped up to Ash.

"And you are?"

"Ash Thomson, Sir. I was working at checkout when it happened. I talked to the officer there yesterday just afterward."

Ash saw the officer glance down at his notebook and nod. He didn't seem to have any further questions for him. Not needed anymore, Ash stood off to the side quietly as he watched them question Charlie. Now and then, he saw her glance at him. It made him nervous, like
~~~~~

she was saying something that she didn't particularly want him to hear. Finally, Ash pointed to the waiting area, saw her nod in recognition, and then he walked to take a seat down the hallway.

Charlie was relieved when she saw him leave. So far, he still thought the shooting had been random, and perhaps it had been. Charlie knew there was also a chance that it was intended. She'd heard that a local gang family saw her family as rivals in the gem market. They weren't the same - they were nowhere near the same caliber of thieves that her father, brothers, and all relations before them were. No, the gang worked more along the lines of thugs. They were the ones who would mug someone to steal their watch and jewelry. Then it would likely end up in a pawnshop somewhere.

Charlie didn't know the full story of their operation. She'd purposely tried to not listen to anything about her own family's 'business' for as long as she could remember. All she did know for certain was that on her 18th birthday - as had been done for every member of the family on their 18th birthday - she'd been told that on her 19th birthday she would begin work with the family.

From the day Charlie had turned 18, she had that one year to do what she wanted before she would commit and make their business her life. If she wanted to see the world, fine - but it had to be done before she turned 19. If she wanted to study at college, that was fine too - but get it out of the way before she turned 19. When her father had sat her down and given her 'the talk', she'd initially thought he must have been kidding. Not that her father was the kidding type, but the idea seemed so extreme and regimented. There appeared to be no scope for anyone to go off their chosen path and do something else with their life.

She could still remember that conversation vividly. She'd objected quietly before she'd upped her objections to the level of a teenage tantrum. She didn't want to be a part of that life. She didn't even want her *family* to be a part of that life. She wanted answers about how they'd even gotten there. Her father had been in the military and overseas, so he obviously had gotten a break somewhere. Why hadn't he stayed out of the so-called business? How could a man who had fought for his country turn around and come home to become a full-time jewel thief with expertise in designing, planning, and performing world-class heists?

Her father had refused to give her any answers that day. He'd told her how it was going to be once she turned 19, and he would say no more. Since then, she'd gone out of her way to never hide her klutzy side from him. Always when growing up, she'd been terrified when she'd knocked the hallway table and whatever vase was on it had fallen and broken. Things like that she did all the time. How could he possibly expect her to gracefully enter a room filled with laser alarms and glass cases? The whole idea was preposterous to her.

They hadn't talked about it again over the two months since her 18th birthday. As far as Charlie was concerned, she was *never* going to go out and be a thief - even a high class one. As far as Mitchell Stonewarden was concerned, she absolutely was.

~~~~~~

After the officer had asked her all the questions he seemed determined to, Charlie was finally free to go and find Ash again. For a fleeting moment when she reached the visitors' lounge, she thought he'd left. The thought saddened her. Then she turned and saw him walking back from a nearby vending machine with sufficient junk food in hand.

"I didn't know what you like, so I got a bit of everything," Ash said, making her laugh softly in relief that he hadn't turned away from her at all.

It had never been easy for Charlie to make friends, let alone keep them. For whatever reason, she
~~~~~~

wanted to keep this one if it were at all in her power.

Ash saw stress release from her face after he spoke, and she seemed to relax again. He didn't know what had made her so tense, and he wouldn't ask. As he watched her move closer and put her arms around him, he wondered if he would ever get tired of that. The sad thought in the back of his mind was that she was clinging to him because her brother was in a coma. Would she still want to know him when that changed and her life returned to normal?

Charlie pulled away and grabbed a bar of chocolate from his hands.

"Thank you," she said. "You didn't need to buy all of this, but it means a lot. I'm going to go back to Max's room though…"

"Okay. I'll head off and leave you and your family in peace," he said and started to turn away.

Charlie watched him for a moment and let him move a few meters away before she called out to him.

"Maybe you'd like to sit in there with me for a while."

Ash stopped walking and slowly turned around to face her.

"I don't want to be in anyone's way."

Charlie walked up to him and kissed him on the cheek.

"You won't be," she said. "I'd really like you to stay a little longer. I want to keep talking to you. I just want to also be there with Max."

He nodded his head, and they started their walk down the corridor to the room once more. As they began to enter, Charlie heard Regan talking to James, asking questions.

"Where's his car? It wasn't at home," he asked and James looked thoughtful for a moment before they both turned to her. "Charlie, where's Max's car?"

She had to think, and her thoughts led her to also

be confused.

"It should be still in the supermarket carpark. That's where he left it, but when we went past there before, it wasn't there, was it?" she asked James and saw him shake his head in reply.

"I don't remember seeing it there, and the police said nothing about it," he replied, exchanging a look with Regan before both stood up. "Charlie, we have to go. Will you stay here with Max?"

"Yeah, of course. I'm not going anywhere. But James, you need to sleep…"

"I'm *fine*," he snapped back at her, a good indicator that he wasn't.

"Please don't let him drive," she said to Regan and saw him nod in agreement before they both left the room.

Ash had watched the family interaction and found himself letting out a deep breath when the two brothers left the room. Yes, they were more than a little intimidating, even when they weren't trying to be.

After Charlie had positioned herself in one chair, Ash pulled up another beside her.

"I'd like to hear about your family," he said quietly. The sound that came from her indicated that she didn't want to talk about them.

"I think, for now, it is enough that you've met the few that you have. I have one more brother - Fitz. You might get to meet him, or he could avoid the hospital altogether. He's different from everyone else. I don't know why. He just always has been. When - if - he wants to turn up, he will. If not, he won't."

As she let the last sentence flow from her lips, Ash saw her reach over and take his hand in hers. No more was said, each of them sitting in silence while knowing that silence was quite okay.

~~~~~

Mitchell made his way to the hospital. He'd gotten
~~~~~

a few hours of sleep, which he had to acknowledge he had definitely needed. Now he had to get back to his son. The house had been empty when he'd woken, even though he'd expected Victor to still be there. Keeping tabs on his kids was something he'd given up on a long while ago. As long as they were where he expected them to be, when he expected them to be there, it was okay. They had to live their own lives to a certain extent - except for when it came to business. Then they had to commit to doing what they were told. No arguments. No negotiation. What he said was what would go. It was that simple, and they all knew it.

For the most part, introducing each of them into the family business had been easy. They'd each wanted to play their part and were primed and ready to jump into it when they had turned nineteen. Except Charlie. Getting her to work in the business was going to prove a challenge for him. He'd been in life-threatening situations where he'd had to be forceful to get his soldiers to do what they had to, to get to safety. Sometimes it was tough, but he'd generally always gotten them home. Getting Charlie to accept her role in the family business was going to be much tougher than that, even for him. In his car, he sighed. If he was honest with himself, he didn't look forward to her reaching that age and the fights that were going to happen then.

He dismissed the thoughts. Today he had to focus on Max. There were months ahead to get his daughter in line. Who knew how long Max would be with them.

~~~~~

When Mitchell walked into the hospital room where his son lay lifeless, he first saw Ash, sitting still and doing or saying nothing. As Mitchell moved toward him, he could see beyond Ash, Charlie in the next chair, asleep.

"I ... I didn't want to leave while she slept," Mitchell heard the young man say quietly as if he were
~~~~~

scared to death at that moment.

'This kid's got it bad', Mitchell thought to himself briefly as he smiled inwardly. He would probably never entirely trust any boy with his little girl, but this one might be okay. He at least deserved the benefit of the doubt, having been there for Charlie two days in a row.

"Thank you, Ash," Mitchell replied. "If you want to stay, you're welcome to. If you need to go, I can tell her to call you when she wakes up."

Ash felt some tenseness flow from him. He didn't know what he'd expected Charlie's dad to do to him, but his reaction to seeing him there was much more relaxed, regardless. After inward debate, he stood up.

"Yes, I think I should go. Please, Sir, I would appreciate it if you did ask her to call me … if she wants to."

Mitchell couldn't help it. He smiled. The kid was likable. He could not deny it.

"I'll do that," he said. "Thank you for being here for my little girl."

Ash nodded and walked out as if he couldn't get out of there fast enough. There was no rush to talk to Charlie all day every day. Perhaps it would be better if they spoke only now and then, letting each other reveal themselves a small amount at a time. After all, he'd been watching her for months on her supermarket shopping duties. He could wait more to get to know her better.

~~~~~

James and Regan drove to the supermarket carpark to check if they had just missed Max's car because of tiredness or lack of attention when they'd each passed by earlier. When they got there, their memories proved to be right. His car was nowhere to be seen.

"What the … where the hell is it? What could have happened to it?" James asked, his voice verging on yelling. "Well, at least it's recognizable. We'll ask
~~~~~

around. If a car painted like Bumblebee has been driving around, someone would have noticed it!"

"Alright," Regan spoke up, acknowledging his brother's logic seemed sound. "But first let me call the cop who gave me his card. They might have impounded it as part of the shooting or something."

James watched as Regan pulled out his phone and made the call. It was a brief call, but James suspected he knew the response Regan had gotten from the cop.

"Well, they don't have it," Regan finally said. "He said one of the officers remembered seeing it in the carpark after the shooting, but they have no idea where it is now. So, I guess we start walking the streets, asking. First, though, you need to get home and sleep..."

"I'm fine!" James said with force.

"Nope, I'm not buying it," Regan replied. "If you want to help find Max's car, you need to be much more alert than you are now. I'm taking you home. When you've had at least a few hours, we'll head out." He saw James begin to object, so cut him off before he could. "It isn't going to make any difference to Max, if we find his car or not, so stop acting like finding it is a life or death thing. The fact that you are so focused on this tells me just how exhausted you are."

James knew when to shut up and just do what he was told. He was older than Regan but had always recognized Regan's strength of character. He'd always seemed far more mature than his years and could get James and Vic to bow down to him with enough of his persuasion.

They drove back to the house in silence. Once there, they expected to see their father or Vic. Neither were in the house.

"To bed with you," Regan demanded.

James rolled his eyes at his brother but did as he was instructed. After removing his clothes, he reluctantly climbed into the bed he'd slept in most of his life to date.

He didn't need to sleep, he kept telling himself as he silently cursed his brother for being so bossy.

Immediately following that thought, he fell into a deep slumber.

~~~~~

"Where are your brothers?" Mitchell asked when Charlie woke up. He watched her gather herself and then become fully awake.

"They were going to go look for Max's car," she said, shaking her head as if trying to shake the sleep residue away. "I said I was okay being here with Max."

Suddenly she remembered Ash had been there with her. She looked around, confused.

"He went home," Mitchell said. "I told him you'd call him when you woke up if you wanted to talk to him."

Charlie nodded. She hadn't meant to fall asleep, but something about sitting so close to Ash had made her feel so secure and safe that it had just happened.

Mitchell moved to sit beside his son, taking his hand and holding it firmly.

"Have you heard from Fitz?" he asked her but only saw Charlie shake her head in response. Deep down, he knew Fitz wouldn't call her. The question spoke volumes of the concern Mitchell had for all of his children. "I wish I knew where he was. I wish I knew he was safe."

"He'll turn up. He's always late to everything," she said, making a half-joke, and was glad to see at least an attempt at a smile grace her father's face.

"That's true. Always in his own time."

~~~~~

Ash returned to his apartment. With it still being quite early in the day, he found himself at a loss to decide what to do. Sitting down on his sofa, he found his thoughts focused on the Stonewarden family as a whole - as much of the whole as he'd met, anyway. They looked out for one another. They cared for one another. Thinking about them made him think about his own family.

Nothing bad had ever happened between him and his parents, but they were wealthy beyond how much even he could comprehend. Instead of loving that, he'd hated that while growing up. He didn't want to be a rich kid. He didn't want to live in a luxury penthouse in a rich part of the city. What he wanted was to be a normal kid - one of thousands, not the one rich kid or the one well-off kid or the one wealthy kid. No, he'd just wanted to be one of the many normal kids. Maybe that was why he'd veered toward a low paid job such as he'd gotten in the supermarket. He wanted to live as most people lived, not the select few.

But he did love his parents, and with all that had happened in the preceding day or so, he felt a strong need to see them. Without ringing them or arranging anything with them, he began to make his way home.

~~~~~

"Mum? Dad?" he called out as he entered the large penthouse apartment on top of a high rise in the very center of the bustling city.

He heard movement coming toward him, but the person that came into view was neither of his parents.

"Maria!" he exclaimed as the housekeeper came toward him, full of smiles. For as long as he could remember, she had been in his home. To some, she would be the hired help. To him, she was a lifelong friend who he loved dearly. "You are a sight for sore eyes."

Maria laughed as he threw his arms around her.

"Saucy boy, Ash," she laughed with distinct fondness in her voice. "What brings you home? Your mother and father did not tell me they were expecting you."

Ash pulled away from her and moved back to a
~~~~~

respectful distance before he replied.

"No, don't worry. They aren't expecting me," Ash replied. "I just felt a strong need to come home, that's all. Where are they?"

"Your father is at the head office today. He should be home around 6 o'clock, in time for dinner. Your mother, I believe she said, had to go to a meeting for one of her charities. She shouldn't be long."

Ash nodded and found himself quite eager to see either of his parents, or both. They hadn't all been in the same room together for almost six months. Of course it would be a surprise to them to see him in their home again.

"But you are not feeding yourself well enough. I can see it, you know. You are too skinny," Maria said and saw Ash burst out laughing.

"Now who is being saucy," Ash said, teasing her.

She laughed with him before leading him to the kitchen.

"Sit. I will make you something to eat now," she said. "Dinner is a long way off. Now, what about … pasta carbonara? Hmm? That was always your favorite."

Ash felt his mouth water at the mention of it. There was nothing like Maria's cooking in his own apartment. He nodded and smiled at her.

"That would be lovely. Thank you." He watched her start to prepare and then had a better thought. "Actually, could you teach me how to make it, Maria?"

"What? Teach you? To cook? Now?"

"Yes," Ash replied, nodding enthusiastically. "You have everything there to make it. Instead of you doing the work, tell me what to do and I'll do it. Let *me* cook something nice for *you*."

Maria looked at him. With that request, she knew that he had indeed grown into a fine young man.

~~~~~

"Ash!" his mother exclaimed when the door later
~~~~~

opened and her eyes laid on him. As was always her way, she rushed to him and kissed his cheeks. "What are you doing here? Oh, my, you are so grown up."

"Mum, I've only been gone a few months!" he said, laughing at her.

"I know, I know, but it seems like years to me. Come and sit down and tell me all about what has been happening with you."

Ash talked about the mundane things but purposely didn't mention the shooting. If he did, she would have insisted he move home to where he would be safe, and then things would get uncomfortable as he turned the instruction down. No, better to keep that little tidbit of information to himself.

When his father came home, the three of them had dinner together for the first time in what seemed like forever. Ash admitted to himself that it wasn't so bad being home. Did he wish he still lived in the luxury apartment with them? No. He knew now that he really was over the money and the lifestyle they had to have, but he would make a point of visiting more often. Life could be so short, and anything could happen at any time. Being almost shot had made that point seem so much more clearer.

"Why don't you stay? Just tonight. Your room is as it always has been. It's already dark out there. Stay and then head home in the morning," his mother said with a slight sound of desperation in her voice. It was if she were afraid that if he left, she wouldn't see him again.

Ash smiled at her and kissed her cheek.

"Thank you, I think I will stay tonight."

Later on, he lay in his childhood bed and looked around the room. There were things on the walls from different stages of his life. When he'd reached teenage years, he'd put new things on the walls around the old things. The result was an odd blend of little kids' stuff and then older kids' stuff. He chuckled at some of the things that caught his eye that he'd been into at different times growing up, but liked the feeling it gave him to be in the middle of it. It was like a security blanket wrapping around him, making him feel safe and secure. He didn't want that all the time, but it was nice. For one night, it was nice.

When he finally insisted his mind rest so he could get some sleep, his mind disobeyed and brought Charlie to the forefront of his thoughts. It both frustrated him when he wanted to get some sleep, and made him smile.

As if she could hear his thoughts, Charlie's name appeared on his mobile phone by the bed as the screen lit up. Opening her text, he smiled at her having contacted him, no matter what she had to say, but there was no need for concern.

'Thank you for being there with me today. I'm heading home with my dad now and will be back with Max tomorrow after 10am. Will I see you tomorrow?'

The smile on Ash's face grew as his heart pounded just that little bit faster and heavier.

'If you want to. Do you want me to come to the hospital, or would you like to meet somewhere else?'

'I don't know what time anyone will be there so could we meet at the hospital? If my brothers are there, we could go get lunch or something?'

Hmm, now something was sounding more like a date. His heart grew heavy with the desire to see her again.

'Okay, see you after 10.'
'Goodnight.'
'Goodnight, Charlie.'

CHAPTER THREE

The next morning, Charlie arrived at the hospital with her father to find Vic and James by Max's bed.

"Regan has to be at work today, so I told him I'd stay here as long as I have to," Vic said, reminding everyone that in addition to their family 'business', they did have their own lives and regular income from regular work.

"It's okay," Mitchell said, nodding. "I can be here all day. Did anything change overnight?" he asked, the sound of hope evident in his voice.

"No, nothing," replied Vic. "The doctor came in just before, but said that it was possible Max could be like this for weeks, or even months."

Charlie saw a serious look cross over her father's face.

"Well, we have a job to do together. We've had it planned for months, and we need to get it done. Tonight, at home, I want you two and Regan to be there with me. And Fitz. We all need to call him and do whatever we have to, to get him home tonight. He's going to be a part of this, whether he likes it or not."

The brothers exchanged looks of uncertainty before James spoke.

"But, Dad, we planned everything with Max as part of it. We can't pull that off with just us…"

"We will!" Mitchell exclaimed. "I know you don't want to consider it, but Max might not be able to help us with this again … ever. We'll keep visiting him, but we also need to get on with our lives."

Charlie was shocked by the words coming out of her father's mouth but said nothing. It wasn't her place. As yet, she was lucky she wasn't being forced to do whatever it was that they had planned. It was definitely better not to interrupt and disturb the hornet's nest.

"Charlie," Mitchell said, turning to her. Just him saying her name made her nervous. She was relieved by the words that followed. "From five till eleven tonight, I want you here with Max. I want you to stay here and not leave. One of us will come in at or after eleven, okay? I'd rather you weren't alone, so if that boyfriend of yours…"

"He's not my boyfriend."

"If that *friend* of yours can be here to keep you company, I'd be grateful to him. I don't want you out alone."

"Dad, I'll be in a hospital full of staff, including security…"

"Don't *argue* with me! If Ash can't be here, tell me and I'll find someone else to come in."

"Alright," Charlie agreed. "He's coming here today. I'll ask him then if he can stay with me all day."

Just then, she spotted Ash approaching the doorway, so jumped up to greet him. Mitchell saw the move, and while he was still protective of her, he knew Ash had won him over at least a little bit. He was dedicated, no doubt about that, to be coming to a morbid and quiet hospital room of someone he didn't even know, day after day.

"Are you staying here for a while, Dad?" Charlie asked. "Can I go out with Ash for a while?"

"Yes! Go!" Mitchell exclaimed. "Get out and do something to relax your mind from all of this, Charlie. Just be back by five."

Ash heard the instruction and was pleased inwardly. Looking at his watch, he saw it was only eleven. They would have all day together. It seemed funny to him that he was hearing instructions that sounded like a curfew. Charlie was 18 years old, but he respected that her father must be protective of her - particularly with what had happened. He would be sure she'd be back before her assigned time to show up.

The two of them turned and started to walk out. No words were said until they got right outside the main hospital doors.

"Do you want to go and see a movie?" she asked.

Ash smiled at her, embracing her enthusiasm.

"Okay. What do you want to see?"

He watched as she moved closer to him, put her arms around him, looked closely up into his eyes, and then placing her lips over his. Ash restrained himself from letting go, indulging in the simplicity of the lips-only caress.

"I don't care," she said as she pulled away. "Let's just go and see the first movie that's on."

He nodded at her as they instinctively both began walking in the direction of the mall.

"Did you sleep okay?" she asked him, surprising him but also pleasing him with her question. He nodded in response.

"I did," Ash replied. "I actually went and saw my parents yesterday, and ended up staying at their place. I hadn't been home for a while, so it was nice."

"Oh! Where do they live?"

It was a natural question to ask, but it was one that Ash had always hated. As always, he gave a broad answer that didn't define the exact part of town his parents lived in - the rich part of town.

"In the city. Nowhere special, but it's home," he said. "I don't mind going there now and then, but I prefer to be in my own space."

"Well, where do *you* live then?"

Ash looked at her. It was odd to have gone through so much together but yet not having had a normal conversation like they were having. He felt like they knew each other, but they didn't actually know anything *about* each other.

"I have a small apartment not far from here," Ash

replied. "It's tiny, but I like it. For me, it's perfect, and within easy walk distance to the supermarket, so I don't need a car, which is good."

"You live alone?"

"Yep. For the past year or so, I've been living in my own space. Like I say, it's not much, but it is all mine."

Charlie said nothing more, considering what that meant to her - if anything. Did it make any difference to her that he lived in his own apartment, alone?

They entered the cinema and saw the next movie to show was a historical romance. Both laughed.

"Not my usual cup of tea, but I'm keen if you are," Ash said, laughing softly.

Charlie looked at his face and had to acknowledge that she did love the way he looked and sounded when he laughed. He was a guy that could easily be overlooked if she passed him on the street, but the more time she spent with him, the more she thought he was actually really hot!

Ash saw her looking at him and then saw her blush as she saw he was seeing her look at him.

"Oh! Um … right. Yes, no, it doesn't matter what's on. Let's go," she stuttered out, her voice revealing her embarrassment at that moment.

They stocked up on snacks and entered the theatre, glad to see no-one else was there at that particular session.

"Must be a real crowd-pleaser, this one," Ash said.

Charlie laughed out loud. Inside, she was pretty pleased they were going to be alone.

Once settled into their seats, Ash turned to her.

"Are you happy living with your family?"

Charlie considered the question but nodded.

"I am. They all drive me crazy sometimes, but I like the security of being at home. I don't think I'm ready to be out on my own yet. I'm still trying to figure my life out."

"And what do you want to do with your life?" he asked.

It was a natural question, but it made Charlie cringe inside.

"I don't know. I'm taking a few months to figure that one out," she replied. "I guess I'm lucky that I *can* live at home while I try and make decisions about my future. I know not everyone my age is so fortunate."

The room dimmed, making Ash look at her one more time as the light faded away. As if she'd sensed him looking at her, Charlie turned to look back at him. Without any need for thought, Ash pushed their food aside, pulled her into his arms, and kissed her - passionately. It wasn't his intention to kiss for the duration of the movie, but he hoped the short duration of it spoke volumes to her about how much he'd wanted to kiss her.

Charlie was stunned. It was no lip-only kiss. She felt his tongue seek hers out and caress it with excitement, before he moved away again and sat back in his seat, leaving her breathless.

~~~~~

"Did you find his car?" Mitchell asked James in the hospital room.

"We asked around, but no-one has seen it," James replied, shaking his head. "Which is weird. I mean, the thing is bright yellow. It stands out. Whoever took it must have done it quickly and really late at night. How it wasn't seen by the security guards guarding the place is beyond me. That thing doesn't have the ability to move quietly. It's grunty…"

"Unless they didn't start it," Mitchell suggested.

"You think they somehow moved it without driving it?" asked James. "Pushed it?"

"Or somehow got it onto a truck? Maybe a tow
~~~~~

truck took it?"

They discussed options. It wasn't as important an issue as Max lying in the bed, silent and motionless, but it was his car, and he'd loved it.

"Man, I hope it turns up," James said. "He put so many hours into that thing."

Mitchell nodded in response. He'd harassed Max quite a bit about spending so many hours doing up a car that was hardly worth anything, but there was also a sliver of pride in him for the dedication Max had shown. Even without having had any mechanical training or knowledge, Max had pulled the thing apart, piece by piece, studied each piece, and then put it all back together. It had been painstaking to watch, so must have been painstaking for him to do, but he'd done it. He'd also managed to get it purring like a tiger. It was his pride and joy, no matter how much his brothers teased him about it.

"It *will* show up," Mitchell said. "It has to. But don't stress about it, you two. When it crosses our path, we'll make sure we get it back. For now, let it lie."

~~~~~

As the movie ended, Charlie found herself relaxed and happy.

"That wasn't bad … really," Ash said, making her laugh out loud. "Well, Miss Charlie, what would you like to do now? We still have a few hours before you need to be back at the hospital, or would you like to go back now? I can walk you there."

"Actually, I have to be there from five till eleven tonight. Will you stay with me there, then? My dad thinks I need…"

Ash cut her words short as he leaned in and kissed her.

"Gladly."

"Movie's over, kids," they heard a voice say in suggestion that they needed to leave.
~~~~~

"Come on, let's go," Ash said and held out his hand for her to take as they walked out.

"Oh geez," she exclaimed as they reached the outside of the building and the sun glared into their eyes. "That is something I always forget when I see a movie during the day - the shock of seeing sunlight after being in the dark for a couple of hours … ugh!"

Ash laughed at her. Slowly she was revealing more and more of who she really was. He hadn't really thought about how he'd perceived her to be when he'd seen her in the supermarket all those times. She dressed like a rocker chick or someone who was tough and took no crap from anyone. Each day that he spent some time with her, he could see more and more of her soft self. Her outer image didn't quite portray who she was on the inside.

"Where to?" he asked again as she moved closer to him, almost pushing herself into his arms.

As he wrapped his arms around her and kissed her softly, Ash tried desperately to not think about being so close to her. When his body reacted, he pulled away from her, determined to not scare her off.

"You could show me your apartment," she said.

Ash groaned inwardly. Being alone with her in a private space like that was exactly what he needed to *not* think about. He took a moment to think and consider. Finally, he spoke.

"Alright, but before I do that, I need to tell you something. Let's go sit on that bench over there," he said as he held out his hand to her once more.

Intrigued by what he was going to say, Charlie let him lead her to the seat on the edge of the park. There, they sat down, facing one another.

"What is it?" she asked him, curious.

"Charlie, I need you to know … I need you to know that I'm not a religious person, but even though I'm not, I have always wanted to wait until I'm married …

before..."

"You're a virgin?" she asked, her surprise evident in her voice. "But you said you're twenty, right?"

As Ash nodded, Charlie saw him blush.

"Yes, I'm twenty. And I can't say why I've always felt strongly about this, but I do."

"Why are you telling me this?" Charlie asked.

"Because I don't want you to come to my apartment and have any expectations..."

"Ash, I'm a virgin too," she replied, instantly seeing his head raise as he looked into her eyes.

"What?" Ash asked.

"I am too."

"But I've seen you with guys."

"Oh yeah, I've *dated*! But I've never let anyone touch me like that," Charlie said. "No way. My body isn't for just anyone's use."

Both remained silent as they each processed the news.

"Did you think I'd be worried? That I wouldn't want to see you anymore?" she asked and saw him nod, still looking a little confused.

"Not everyone takes that news well. I've dated girls who..." Ash began to say.

"Okay, stop there. I don't want to hear about the girls you've dated. They're your past, right?" she asked and saw him nod. "Ash, I'm enjoying this time with you. I want you and I to get to know each other better. If anything has become apparent to me with what's happened over the last few days, it's that I need to get on and do what I enjoy. Anything can happen at any time to rip our lives away from us. I enjoy being with you. I want to *keep* being with you."

Listening to her statement, Ash felt his heart pound heavily as he looked at her. It was a passionate statement to make, and she'd done it without any hesitation at all. He couldn't help himself. He passionately pulled her close to him and kissed her deeply until he heard her moan as her arms wrapped tightly around him.

"If we go to my apartment, we can't do much of that," he said quietly.

Charlie understood what he was saying.

"Deal," she agreed as they embarked on a walk to Ash's apartment in silence.

When they entered the small apartment, Charlie was so surprised that she was initially speechless. She lived in a massive house. Her home was run down and old, but it was huge compared to where Ash lived.

"Whoa. I see what you mean about it being tiny."

Right at the doorway, she was already standing in the living room with its one couch, tiny coffee table, and a small desk and chair against a wall. Directly across from that was a galley kitchen. She could see a bench, two-burner cooktop, and a wall covered in cabinetry that encased a small microwave and a small oven. That was the extent of the kitchen, with one end of it opened up and revealing a washing machine. Beyond that were two doors. Charlie assumed one led to a bathroom, and one led to his bedroom.

"I know," Ash said, laughing at her response. He wasn't embarrassed, although he suspected others might be by a living area so small. "It's my home, though, and I love it. Have a seat."

Charlie walked into the middle of the living area - which, in reality, was about three steps - and sat on the couch.

"What can I get you to drink? I have coffee, green tea, juice, water..." Ash asked.

"Um, green tea would be great. It sounds very healthy."

Seeing her still looking a little stunned made Ash smile. He found himself enjoying her response to his little 'bachelor pad'. After passing her green tea to her, he sat beside her, and they both drank, quietly facing one another.

"Sitting in an apartment alone with a guy is kind of new to me," Charlie said, half with humor and half with seriousness.

"Well, I'm a hands-off guy, so you're kind of safe with me," replied Ash.

Charlie looked at him and smiled. Any guy could say what he'd just said. Any guy could say that they were a virgin and that they wouldn't want to have sex. The difference was that when the guy in front of her said those things, she did truly believe it.

~~~~~

After an afternoon of trying to get to know one another more, while trying to not say too much about their individual family situations, they made their way back to the hospital.

"Okay, we're here," Charlie announced as she and Ash entered Max's room. All three men in the room looked at the two of them as if startled. "What? Why do you all look so morbid? What's happened?"

Her father stood up and came to her, noticing she was rapidly moving into a panic attack.

"Nothing," Mitchell said. "Nothing's happened. Everything's the same as when you left. If you guys are here to stay now, we'll take off and head home. I'll be back about eleven to give you a ride home. I'll be able to give you a ride too, Ash, wherever you need to go then."

"Thank you, Sir," Ash said timidly, completely unknowing that every time he said 'Sir' he was becoming more and more of a favorite in Mitchell's eyes.

After the three older men made their way out of the room, Ash and Charlie sat in the same two chairs they had done the day before. Once relaxed, they continued their chat. After a while, Charlie recognized that slowly even she was beginning to forget about her brother. He was right there in the room with them, but
~~~~~

with his motionlessness, she was starting to sometimes forget that he was even there. The thought brought about a degree of sadness in her.

"I miss him," she said quietly. Although she didn't seem to say it to anyone in particular, Ash knew who she was talking about.

"Tell me about him," he said and saw her smile at him before she began talking. The amount of great and funny things she had to say about Max adequately filled in all the hours left for them to spend together on that evening. Ash watched her smile, laugh, and, at times, cry, but he just let her talk and was happy to do so.

~~~~~

"How can we do this without Max?" Vic was asking his father in their family home.

All of the Stonewarden boys were there except for the one lying silent in the hospital. Even Fitz had finally made an appearance. He liked to go off and do his own thing, but he wasn't so stupid as to miss a meeting when his father called for it for the business. Fitz was one of the ones who loved the work. It thrilled him and excited him. In that part of his life, he was a perfectionist. Nothing would ever go wrong when he was in control of anything. He had the most advanced know-how about technology. That flowed on to the importance of being able to research, understand, and deal with high tech security systems.

"It's only a penthouse apartment, Vic. We've got the blueprints here, and I've already hacked into the security firm's system. This is a straightforward job."

"If it's so straightforward, why don't these people have better security?" Victor queried. "Are you sure the gems you reckon are there, *are* there? You couldn't have been misinformed?"

"Trust me," replied Fitz. "Have I ever had bad intel on things like this? Come on, they are rich as sin, and I bet they never even wear the stuff. It will be sitting
~~~~~

in the safe along with other things that they never use. Hell, they probably don't even look at the things. It isn't right that they should be holding value like that when so many people are living on the streets. You know I'm right. I trust my intel. We can do this. The owners are away this weekend. That only leaves the housekeeper, and we can deal with her."

"*Don't* talk like that, Fitz!" Mitchell exclaimed. "We need a plan as far as the housekeeper goes. No-one gets hurt. No-one *ever* gets hurt! Suggestions from each of you about what we do to get in there and out again without her seeing us?"

Mitchell listened as each of his sons spoke up, offering a way to get what they wanted from the apartment Fitz had put them onto without any possibility of the housekeeper getting involved in any way. For five solid hours, they talked it all through, referring to the building blueprints in front of them when they needed to. He didn't worry about these sons. They always acted with utter professionalism when doing a job with him. None of them had been in the military, but they each acted with military precision. It would be different without Max there as part of the crew, but Mitchell conceded that Fitz was right. For this particular job, being only inside a private residence, they could handle it well enough.

"Tomorrow night then," he finally said. "We meet here at six to prepare before we move in. As always, not a word about the details of this job to anyone, even your sister. We need to coordinate so she can stay with Max at the hospital from five-thirty tomorrow night, so we all need to work together and ensure these schedules are maintained."

One by one, the brothers said goodnight. James and Vic left to go to their own homes. Mitchell left to go and pick up his daughter and drop Regan and Fitz off at the hospital.

"Why do we have to sit with him every hour of every day?" Fitz asked. "It isn't as if he would know we're even there. It's such a waste…"

"Enough!" Mitchell yelled at his youngest son. "You get far too much freedom as it is. Don't push me."

With those few words from his father, Fitz immediately shut up. He hated being part of the family. He really did. The problem was that he equally loved the family business, so he put up with them when he had to. At different times, he'd toyed with the idea of doing a business like that alone, or finding his own crew, but the plan wasn't feasible. He might be a brain behind the technology, but his father had a unique military-precision style of thinking that Fitz didn't have. Mitchell could see problems that others couldn't. In their line of work, that was essential to the planning of jobs, especially the higher caliber heists. They'd been in situations with multilayer security levels and had only made it through by Mitchell seeing things and asking questions, which they'd had to work out solutions to before going anywhere near the location of the job.

No, Fitz knew that starting over on his own wasn't a great idea. It was a wish but not an idea for reality. He'd do as he'd been doing - keep away from them most of the time and return to the roost when summoned for the jobs. That, he could live with.

~~~~~~

"Come on, you two," Mitchell said to Ash and Charlie when he arrived with her two brothers. Ash immediately identified the brother who had previously been missing. They didn't all quite look alike, but there was enough similarity in something - their nose shape or their mouth shape? He wasn't sure, but it was enough for him to confidently identify who was her family. "Oh, Ash, this is Fitz, my youngest son. Fitz, this is Charlie's … friend … Ash."

Charlie looked at her father and saw a small look
~~~~~~

of amusement on his face. Usually, it would annoy her, and she would throw in a good comeback, but seeing her father smile was something she could only appreciate. She wouldn't tease him back.

Fitz was slightly alarmed at meeting Ash. His face seemed familiar, although he couldn't place where he'd seen him. He shook the guy's hand and greeted him civilly but kept his mind open to pondering where their paths could have crossed. After trying to pull the memory forward, he shrugged it off, assuming it couldn't have been anything or anywhere important.

Mitchell was silent as he drove to directions provided by Ash. When they pulled up outside the apartment, Ash showed his manners once more before climbing out of the back seat.

"Thank you for the ride," he said before climbing out of the car.

He was about to turn and walk inside when he saw the front passenger door open and Charlie get out. He couldn't help but smile as she moved close to him, leaned her chest against his, and reached up to kiss him. The kiss was soft but very, very sweet.

"When can I see you again?" she asked.

"Text me tomorrow," Ash replied. "I have no plans until my job starts back. I'm yours whenever you want until then."

After kissing her softly, he watched as she climbed back into the car, and the car drove off.

"Just a friend, huh?" Mitchell teased Charlie, but again she remained quiet. Just seeing him smile and be happy was enough. She'd make up for all this no-smart-reply time later on, she was sure.

CHAPTER FOUR

Charlie woke the next morning to the sun trying to shine through the curtains. She took a few minutes to just lie still and consider how every morning it seemed less and less important to get to the hospital. Knowing she felt that way left her feeling incredibly sad. Max was becoming invisible, and that just wasn't how he was supposed to be. He was vibrant and full of life. He'd never been a guy who would sit in the corner and be quiet. It just wasn't right that he was lifeless and silent.

At least he was alive, and that counted for a lot. It had to. She needed him. She needed him to wake up and be her fun-loving brother again.

"Charlie," she heard a voice say outside her door.

"Yeah, I'm awake. Come in."

She saw her oldest brother Vic walk in, just as she was adjusting herself and sitting up in the bed.

"What's up?" she asked.

"I just wanted to touch base with you and check you're doing okay," Vic said, surprising her.

"I'm okay. I just want him to wake up and be himself again," she said, feeling tears come to her eyes. "I do miss him, Vic."

He wrapped his arms around her.

"I know. I do, too." He was silent for a long while before he spoke. "So today it would be really good if you could be at the hospital to sit with him from five-thirty. Is that okay with you?"

Charlie nodded. She suspected her father and brothers were all doing something they didn't want her to know about, and she was perfectly fine with that. She didn't *want* to know about it. She equally suspected they were placing her somewhere in case something went wrong, and she later needed some kind of alibi. She said nothing more though. She never asked questions, and each of them respected her for that. No-one wanted to lie. They also didn't want to tell the truth - not till she turned nineteen anyway. Once that magical age was reached, Charlie would be inducted into it herself. Then she would know *everything* - everything she wanted to know, and a whole lot more she didn't.

"Yep," she said. "I'll fill in my day, and I'll be in Max's room by five-thirty."

"Thanks," her oldest brother said before kissing her on her forehead and then leaving her room.

As she lay back again, Charlie dismissed the upcoming activities of her brothers and father. That was all beyond her control. Even if she'd ever pleaded with them not to do what they did, they never would have listened to her.

Turning to her side table, she picked up her phone. It was still early - too early to text Ash. Instead, she picked up a book she'd started reading weeks earlier. Sometimes life seemed to be too full to allow for something so relaxing as reading. Other times, everything was perfectly aligned for it. She settled back and let herself float into the land of sexy, rugged pirates, their search for treasure, and the beautiful well-endowed women who kept distracting them.

She became so absorbed in the story that it took her a minute to snap out of her focus on the book and realize that her phone was vibrating.

'Good morning,' Ash's text read, making her smile. Funny how he'd sent her a text right when she'd been reading a sexy scene that was very much heating up in her book.

'And good morning to you,' she replied. Once more, she turned her eyes to the words on the paper pages. *He couldn't help but stare as he saw her stand from the tub, naked and voluptuous, and look directly at him. Her large breasts were his focus...*

Oh!

The phone buzzed again.

'What are you doing?'

Hmm. Should she answer honestly? That she was reading a sexy sex scene? No.

'Just about to get up. What are you doing?' she replied

'I'm showered and dressed. Do you want to meet up?'

For a moment, Charlie considered continuing to indulge in the world of fantasy. Then she shook her head and laughed silently to herself. Reality had to beat the woman with large, bare breasts and whatever she had planned for the sexy captain.

'Okay. What if I pick up some munchies and a few DVDs? A day of movie watching at your place?'

She waited a few minutes before his response came. The time-lapse made her wonder if he hadn't liked the idea at all.

'Perfect. I'll be here all day. Come whenever suits you.'

Charlie looked at the book once more. She needed to read that scene, but she also wanted to see Ash. The book lost. She put her bookmark in and returned it to her side table. Captain Sexy Pants would wait for another day.

~~~~~

Ash heard the knock on his door and smiled when he opened it and saw her wearing shorts and a feminine blouse. He was surprised but liked it enough, although he hoped she didn't feel she needed to change who she was to see him. He'd gotten used to her in singlets and t-shirts with jeans - usually ones with loads of rips in them. He certainly didn't need her to dress differently for her to capture *his* attention.

"Do you like horror?" she asked as she stepped
~~~~~

through the door and immediately into his living area. "I didn't know, so I got a crime thriller, a horror, and some diving drama flick."

Ash couldn't help it. He moved straight to her after he closed the door and kissed her deeply. When he pulled away, he could tell he'd surprised her.

"They all sound good to me," he said, pushing his desire aside. "Do you need to get to the hospital today?"

Charlie placed the DVDs on the coffee table and started to unload what looked, to Ash, like mountains of junk food. Chocolate, popcorn, potato crisps … the items kept coming out of what must have been a bottomless bag.

"Oh, yeah, I need to head over there between five and five-thirty," Charlie replied. "Till then, I have the entire day to hang out with you … if you want to."

Ash moved closer and gently nudged her so that she was sitting on the couch, and then he was kissing her again. As she wrapped her arms around him, he felt one hand moving its fingers through his hair as he indulged in caressing her tongue with his. He couldn't deny how much she turned him on He had dated and kissed women - girls - but it had never felt the same as when he kissed her. If he'd wanted to have sex, he most certainly would have wanted to have it with her.

Charlie felt him pull away abruptly. When she opened her eyes, she saw him smiling bashfully.

"You're a very sexy kisser," he said, his voice low and full of huskiness.

Charlie laughed. The seriousness of the moment was broken. That was good. She'd felt like being carried away too, and neither of them wanted that. Not yet, anyway.

"I'll put the first DVD in," Charlie said, standing up and moving toward the small TV and DVD system underneath it. "Which one?"

"You choose," Ash replied. "Anything to distract

me from your lips is good."

He saw her turn around then and give him the most incredible smile. She was so stunning when she smiled like that! He'd never seen her smile before the day of the shooting. Always when she was in the supermarket, whether alone or with someone else, she'd looked morose and serious. He hadn't minded that at all. It had added to her appeal, but to see her look as happy as she did at that moment, his heart almost melted for her.

He watched as she moved back to the couch, slipped off her shoes, and adjusted herself so that her feet were tucked up beside her. As she moved against him, nudged him till he put his arm around her, and rested her head on his chest, Ash wondered if his life could get any more perfect.

~~~~~

"Oh my god, that was brilliant. I did not see that coming," Charlie exclaimed after they finished the last movie she'd brought. "Did you know that was going to happen? Wow, I … holy schmoly, that got me. I'm going to be thinking about that all night now."

Ash watched as she moved to put on her shoes. Glancing at the clock, he was surprised to see it was already five in the afternoon. He hadn't had such a lazy day in his apartment for months. He'd loved every minute of it, and not just the relaxing, movies, and junk food. Having her nestled against his chest for much of it had definitely made the day even more enjoyable.

"Would you like me to come with you? I can at least walk you to the hospital," he suggested.

Charlie leaned in to him and kissed him softly.

"I'd like that very much."

~~~~~

Entering Max's room, even Ash could sense tenseness in Charlie's brothers. They seemed on edge about something, but he was hardly going to ask them -

or her - about it. He was relieved when they both walked out, leaving him alone with Charlie again. Well, except for Max, that was. He was ashamed to admit that he often forgot that he wasn't alone with Charlie in the hospital room. They had finally moved to a place in their friendship where they talked naturally. Even in Max's room, they talked openly and freely, as if they were alone. They didn't censor their conversation at all.

~~~~~

Max always listened to the conversations going on around him. He could hear them, and inside his head he could respond, but he knew that something was wrong. He couldn't seem to get his thoughts to his mouth or any other part of his body.

Listening to his brothers talk about their upcoming job had upset him slightly, although he couldn't present his dismay in any way to them. In his mind, it needed to stop. No matter that it was some kind of family tradition that went back generations to William the Conqueror or whoever it was that decided that his ancestors would be wardens of the gems. Yes, it was something to have such an amazing family history that was well known and documented over the centuries, but he hated the type of work it was. And it was upsetting rivals in the gem trade. Of course it was.

He hadn't seen the Leadbetters in the supermarket carpark, as Charlie had, so hadn't initially understood what had happened. Since then, he'd heard Charlie talking to police. He knew it was their family who had done what they'd done, and that meant there was a good chance that it wasn't a random shooting. He and Charlie weren't just in the wrong place at the wrong time. No, they had been the *targets*. He could at least be thankful that she had survived unharmed. The conversations he'd heard indicated that whoever that guy was that she kept bringing into this room, had helped her out somehow when the shots had been fired. Now he was hanging out
~~~~~

with her … a *lot*. Max hoped he was a good guy. Otherwise, when he woke up he'd…

God, was he ever going to be able to get his body to move and respond to his wishes again? He wanted to yell at his brothers to not go and do the latest job they'd been talking about doing. He wanted to tell his father to let his stupid pride in family tradition go. It wasn't worth it if they were upsetting people enough for those people to want to *kill* them. And now he had to listen to his little sister being gushy with that guy. Hell, he could even hear the sound of them kissing. Ugh. It just wasn't right. He needed to get his body moving. He needed to scream out at everybody - *anybody*.

~~~~~

The brothers assembled with their father in their family home.

"Are we all good to go?" Mitchell asked after they'd prepared all the equipment and tools they would need to get into the apartment and then break into the safe. "Anyone not want to do this?"

One by one, he looked around his sons. Each, in turn, shook their head but said nothing. When they were like that, Mitchell was reminded of his military days, with the junior soldiers standing before him for inspection. He'd never thought about joining the military himself. It had been his father who had pushed him. It wasn't normal for a Stonewarden to leave the family fold, but his father had reckoned that the training would be good to have - and he'd been right. The knowledge and ability to foresee issues and counteract any potential problems, Mitchell knew came down to his training and experience as a soldier - especially his time at war. During that time, he'd been able to experience and see things he never wanted to see again. It had instilled in him a greater appreciation for life, and for *his* life. He would continue the family tradition, but he'd never hurt anyone, and he'd certainly never take anyone's life.
~~~~~

"Okay, let's do this," he said solemnly.

He never appeared it, but when they went and did a job, Mitchell did get excited. With his adrenaline flowing, he felt like for those few hours, he became a different person - not a father, but a jewel heist professional. Not that their current plan was a heist as such. It was just a residential robbery, although the apartment they were going into was apparently built and secured like a vault. He didn't care. He just wanted the job done so they could move the gems to their next location.

"And remember - no-one gets hurt," he reiterated. "The housekeeper shouldn't be there because it's the night she usually goes to her son's for dinner, but if she *is* there, everyone goes silent. No-one speaks, and we tape her mouth and hands so she can't move or scream. That's it! Everyone make sure they have their masks now."

They did so, and then one by one filed out the front door and into two separate vehicles. Both were big enough to hold all of them, but one would be positioned at the side of the building, and one would be at the back. Just in case. They were standard ho-hum vehicles in the current most common car color. There was nothing noticeable about either of them. For the following couple of hours, they'd both have fake plates on them. Each member of the team had a key for each car. They'd never had to use their back-up escape system, but that didn't stop them from always putting it in place. Just in case.

Walking into the building as three separate groups, they looked average. Their black clothing and masks were in their bags. There was nothing remarkable about the people passing in and out of the apartment building at all. Nobody noticed a thing.

First to enter the apartment, Fitz did a brief assessment of the place and was relieved to see it was exactly as on the plans. He'd seen inside before, but only by hacking into the apartment's security cameras. He'd had to do that tonight as well so that it would look as if no-one was there. Overall he knew that the apartment was stark and lacking in any kind of personality. It may as well have been a museum. There were no photos on the walls and no books in a bookcase. Nothing about it said that people actually lived there. Then he spotted a photo on the mantelpiece - the only photo. When he looked at it, he remembered why Ash seemed so familiar.

"Fuck!" he whispered to himself but immediately turned the photo and lay it down. It was a family photo, and Ash was right in the center of it. The discovery that Charlie's new best friend must live in the apartment momentarily freaked Fitz out. He had to close his eyes for a minute and refocus. It was a rule that none of them spoke on a job, so their voices could not be heard, but when he turned around he could tell by his father's face that there was a question there. Fitz turned away and moved to where he knew the safe was. He couldn't focus on that discovery now. Charlie's friend being a part of the family meant nothing. They were there for a job. It was vital they got on with it and then got out before the family came home.

The team worked together seamlessly, as they always did. The job was a success. As soon as they were home again, Fitz readjusted the apartment's security cameras so they were rolling in real time again, and then it was done. No problems at all. He kept to himself the knowledge he'd gathered while there and resolved that once the night was over, he'd disappear by himself again for a while. He couldn't see that guy day after day and smile at him, knowing what he'd done to his family. They might only be jewels but stealing from someone he knew was past what even Fitz could regard as acceptable.

"Good job, boys," Mitchell said as he looked at

his son's faces. "Big John will be over soon to take these and begin the alteration and distribution process, but your part is done. I need to go to the hospital and bring Charlie home. Who's coming to watch over Max tonight?"

Regan put his hand up as if he were answering a question in a classroom.

"I'll come, Dad," he said. "I have tomorrow off work, so can stay up all night if need be."

"Yeah, I'll come too," Vic chimed in. As always, the biggest brother.

Mitchell turned to Fitz and James.

"Are you two staying here tonight?" he asked and saw both nod. "Alright, I'll be back soon. If you need to talk about anything, talk about it before I bring your sister home. She doesn't need to know anything about this. *Agreed*?"

"Yes!" they all replied. It was always the same routine. Always the same question. Always the same answer.

As his two brothers and his father left the house, Fitz went into a panic. The photo. He was always so meticulous in leaving scenes as they had been when they had arrived. By doing that, it could take months before anyone would open a safe and know something was gone. By then, the gems were just not the same gems anymore.

As he remembered, he knew he'd made a vital mistake tonight.

He'd left the photo turned over.

~~~~~

Mitchell, Regan and Vic entered the hospital room and saw Charlie had fallen asleep. With her head resting on Ash's shoulder, the two of them looked comfortable and cozy. Being approached by three of the men in one go, Ash felt a slight concern fall over him. He sat still and said nothing as he watched Charlie's
~~~~~

father lean over and nudge her on the shoulder.

"Charlie. Hey little girl, it's time to wake up and go home," he said softly. It was a tone that surprised Ash. "Charlie! Wake up!"

Finally, Ash felt Charlie's head lift from his shoulder and saw her look around as she came out of her sleepy daze.

"What?" she asked.

"Come on, sweetheart. It's time to go home so you can sleep in your bed," Charlie heard her father say. She nodded as she slowly stood up. "Do you want me to drop you home, Ash?" her father asked.

Ash nodded in reply, very aware of the brothers watching him.

"Thank you, Sir. Yes, please."

Yep, Mitchell thought to himself again. This one can stay. He might indeed be the one guy she'd met and introduced him to, that met the grade and might indeed be good enough for Mitchell's little girl.

~~~~~

The next morning Ash woke to his phone ringing. First thinking it would be Charlie sending him a text, he smiled as he picked it up sleepily. When he saw his mother's name on the screen, he realized the phone was actually *ringing*.

"Mum?" he asked as he accepted the incoming call.

"It's gone, Ash! I can't believe it. That security company said that no-one - no-one would be able to…"

"Mum, slow down! What's happened?" Ash asked, sitting up abruptly at the terrified tone of his mother's voice.

"They took it, Ash. Our family ring that should be yours to give to your future bride. It's gone."

"Someone broke in and stole a ring?" he asked, thinking that made no sense with all of the high tech entertainment gear that was sitting in this parents'
~~~~~

apartment.

"Oh, not just that, but I don't care about the other jewelry. Yes, it was all gifts from your father, so did mean something, but that ring, Ash. It has been passed down from generation to generation. There isn't another like it. It should have been going to your bride and your children…"

"Okay, where are you?" Ash asked. "Are you at home?"

"Yes, the police are here, dusting for fingerprints … or whatever they're doing."

"Alright, stay right there. I'm on my way and will be there soon."

"Yes. Please hurry," his mother said. "I feel so … *violated*. I don't know if it's safe to be here now."

Ash said goodbye and rushed to have a quick shower and get dressed before he bolted out the door. When he was on his way, his phone vibrated. Looking at the screen, he saw Charlie had sent him a text.

'Want to hang out?' she'd asked.

Ash stopped walking for a moment to consider options. If he said what had happened to his parents, he would probably have to come clean about his family's wealth and tell her that he was a rich kid. He didn't want her to know that - not yet, anyway. He wanted to be liked for who he was, not the value of his parents' bank accounts. He pondered different scenarios of what he could say that wouldn't be a lie but wouldn't quite be the whole truth. He didn't want to ignore her text. He had to say *something*. Once more, he started to walk as he typed his reply.

'My mother is a bit upset. Something's happened at home. Sorry but I need to go to her. Can I chase you up later? I don't know how long I'll be.'

Almost instantly, another text flowed in.

'Sure. I hope your mother's okay. Text me whenever.'

He read that last bit. Did she sound annoyed? He hated text communication. He should have just called her. For the moment, he had to put her aside in his thoughts.

As he caught the long elevator ride to the top floor of the building, he took a deep breath. What was happening to the world with someone he kind of knew (well, okay, didn't know - but had seen!) being shot right in front of him, and now his parents' home being broken into?

As he entered the apartment, he was immediately greeted by an officer in uniform.

"Sorry, Sir, but this is a crime scene."

"No! Stop! That's my son," Ash heard his mother call out.

"What do they mean, a crime scene? Ash asked. "Is Dad…?"

"Oh no, Ash. Your father is fine. He went into work to get out of the way. Couldn't stand to see these people here," she said, observing people doing whatever they were doing. "I just … oh!" she started to say before bursting into tears.

Ash moved to her and put his arms around her.

"It's jewelry, Mum," he said as he held her close. "At least you and Dad are okay. And Maria? Is she alright too?"

He felt his mother nod against his shoulder.

"Yes, she was out last night, thankfully," his mother said. "They must have come in when no-one was here, which was a good coincidence. I know you are right. Life is worth more than jewelry. It's just that ring. At least five generations it has been passed down to, and I was looking forward to giving it to you when you chose a wife…"

Ash gulped at the words but said nothing. No matter how trivial he thought the lost - stolen - items might be, he could see how much the burglary had affected her.

"I don't know if I'm safe here," she started to say. Ash could see her get herself worked up to the point where she no longer appeared to hear him say anything to her at all. Then she seemed to slither down through his arms and fall to the floor.

"Mum!" he shouted to her.

Straightaway, a detective approached and pulled out his phone.

"We need an ambulance!" Ash heard him say before giving the address to the telephone operator at the end of the line.

It wasn't long before Ash was in the back of an ambulance. It felt like an irony after what had happened to Charlie's brother just a few days earlier. He looked at his mother. She seemed to be asleep, but he suspected it must be more than that.

Once at the hospital, he walked alongside the transportation of her until she was transferred to a bed in a small room. A doctor and nurse came in and began their assessment, asking him to step aside as they pulled a curtain around her bed completely. Ash was at a loss. He was in the same hospital as Charlie might be right now, but three floors down. Should he go up and see if she were there? After consideration, he decided he could just run up there quickly and see if she was there. If she wasn't, he would just run back down again.

As he approached Max's room, he could see her inside. Turning and seeing him, she walked out quickly to greet him.

"What's happened?" Charlie asked, sensing something was wrong.

"My mother has been admitted. I don't know what's wrong with her. She had a shock, and I think it's affected her somehow," Ash said as he walked with her a little way down the hallway.

Charlie looked at his face and could see his pain.

She guided him to the visitor area.

"But what happened to shock her?" she asked as they sat down.

"Oh, it's something silly," Ash replied. "Well, to me it seems silly but obviously not to her…"

"Ash! What?"

"Someone broke into my family home last night. They stole all of her jewelry, but she doesn't care about all of it. Among it is a ring that she said has been passed down from generation to generation. Apparently, she intended to give it to me for my future bride and children … oh, hmm, just forget it. Sorry, I know you have enough of your own things to worry about," he said, moving closer to her and gently raising his hand to push a small amount of hair back off her face. "How's Max? Has there been any change?"

"No, but Ash, don't change the subject. Your mother is important!" Charlie exclaimed. "I know, because mine died, remember! You need to get back to her. Do you want me to come with you?"

He looked at her, uncertain about what to expect from her.

"Don't look at me like that. You have been beside me for days now, supporting me when I needed someone to lean on. Don't think that kind of support only goes one way. My father and Regan are in the room with Max. I don't have to be there. Let me come with you and be there for you like you've been there for me."

As she said the last two sentences, she reached out and put her hand on his arm. It felt like a calming reassurance. Ash placed his free hand on hers and raised it to kiss her palm before nodding.

"Yes, please," he said quietly, suddenly feeling emotion flow through him. He didn't want it, but he could feel tears threatening in his eyes. No matter what, his mother was his mother. He couldn't comprehend her being in pain - not *any* kind of pain.

"Okay, wait here," Charlie said. "I'll just be a min."

She raced to Max's room and threw her words at the two men sitting in chairs near him.

"I'll be back soon," she said and turned to leave.

"Where are you going?" her father asked, out of character for him over the previous few days.

"Ash's mother has been brought into the hospital. I'm going downstairs with him. It's the least I can do after all he's done for me."

She saw her father nod and turn away from her, resuming his stare at his son. His son who was lifeless, after having always been so full of life.

~~~~~

As they walked to where Ash's mother lay, he could see that she was awake. A nurse was beside her, talking soothingly to her.

"Ash," he heard his mother say quietly. It seemed to him that within only hours, she had aged considerably.

He saw the nurse turn toward him and usher him outside the room.

"Your mother has had a terrible shock, which affected her badly. She is coming around now though. The doctor gave her a once over and believes she's going to be fine, but she should stay here for the next few hours, just so we can be sure."

"Yes, of course," Ash said, nodding. "Has anyone called my father, do you know?"

"Yes, he is on his way here and should be here shortly. Go in and talk to her but keep her calm. She will be fine but try not to let her get worked up like she must have been before this happened."

Ash nodded more and moved back to the bed. He sat on the edge and took his mother's hand in his.

"The nurse said you'll be fine, but you need to stay relaxed and calm."

He saw his mother nod at him before her sight
~~~~~

turned and she noticed Charlie standing not far away.

"Oh! And who is this lovely young lady?" she asked and saw Charlie move forward, smiling shyly.

"Mum, this is Charlie. Her brother is also in hospital at the moment."

"Oh, dear. I'm sorry to hear that. I'm sure he's a good boy too…" she started to say before she seemed to just drift off to sleep.

Charlie looked from Ash to his mother and back again. There was a slight family resemblance in their looks, but she wondered if he might look more like his father. Just as she was wondering that, a tall man in an exquisitely tailored suit walked in. She watched as Ash stood up and shook the man's hand.

"Have they said anything?" the older man asked and listened as Ash repeated what the nurse had said. "It is a sad affair, Ash. We thought our apartment was secure. The thought that someone could just walk in like they did terrifies me. What if we'd been there? The police say the intruder went straight to the safe, so knew what they were looking for. If we'd been there, what would they have done for the sake of getting to your mother's jewelry? It is unbelievable to me that this has happened. Your mother has taken it hard. She was obsessed with that one ring. She always has been. I should have put it in a safety deposit box at the bank. She told me to many times. I always told her that there was no need - the apartment was secure. It's all my fault…"

"Dad, this is *not* your fault!"

As Charlie listened, she felt a sense of dread flow over her. She knew her father and brothers did *something* last night. What were the chances? Really? Could they be the very people who broke into the apartment of Ash's parents, and subsequently helped his mother to end up in the hospital?

Ash saw Charlie's face full of thought and

remembered to introduce her.

"Dad, this is Charlie. Charlie, this is my father."

"I'm pleased to meet you," she said quietly before turning back to Ash. "Ash, I am going to go back to Max's room," she then said even quieter still.

Ash walked to her, and the two of them left the room. Once outside the door, he turned to her and pulled her into his arms. Both of them held on tight as if in fear they might not see each other again.

"I will see you later?" she asked timidly.

Ash nodded and kissed her before watching her turn and walk away.

Charlie walked back to where her father and brother were sitting. Once in the room, she immediately summoned her father.

"Can I please talk to you for a minute?" she asked.

Mitchell gave her a look of surprise. His daughter *never* asked to talk to him, so he knew it must be important. He remained quiet as she led him to the visitor lounge, and was glad to see no-one there.

"What is it?" he asked her, expecting her to perhaps announce something extreme like an engagement. Instead, he was confronted with the question she could have asked many times before but never had.

"Where were you and the boys last night?"

Charlie saw his face turn to stone in deliberation to not show any emotion.

"Why would you ask that?"

"Actually, I don't want to know the answer. It isn't really a question, but let me just tell you something, and I hope that if you are in any way involved, you will do the right thing … for me. Right now, Ash's mother is downstairs. She was brought in here today after her body shut down from receiving a shock after someone broke into the apartment that she lives in with Ash's father and stole a ring that was a family heirloom. It's a ring that's meant to go to Ash, to pass to his future bride and then his future child. It's an heirloom that's hundreds of years old. It would be horrific if such a thing were cut up and made into other jewelry that no-one really cares about."

Mitchell heard the speech and fought to maintain composure, but inside he was cringing. His daughter often tried to strike a nerve in him but rarely could. Today she was succeeding. He remained still and let her continue.

"Do you understand what I am saying? Ash's mother is in this hospital because of this. I know that you, of all people, will appreciate how important mothers are. It would be best that she does not now live in fear for her life, living in an apartment that has been invaded by someone she doesn't know. It would be kind if she could at least know that her family ring was recovered, safe, and in exactly the same state as it was the last time she saw it."

Charlie saw her father finally open his mouth as if to speak. She held up her hand to stop him.

"I don't want to know if you did this," she said. "I can happily remain in the dark about where you were last night. You know what is happening in Ash's family right now. If you have the power, perhaps you can somehow put it right. And if you didn't have anything to do with it, then there is nothing more for me to say."

Charlie looked at her father. She had delivered the speech with pretend confidence, but inside she was shaking. No-one ever spoke to her father like she'd just done - especially her. Despite her nervousness, she stood her ground and hoped that it *was* her own family who had done this. She wanted it to be them because then there might be some hope to at least get the ring back.

They stood in silence for a few minutes. Seeing that her father would admit nothing, Charlie turned and walked away.

Mitchell watched his little girl walk back toward Max's room. She'd put on a good show, but he knew her too well. She'd made a pretty good attempt to be staunch in talking to him. As he watched her walking down the corridor, he could see she was shaking. He could have been angry at her, but he wasn't. This kid, Ash, had already proven his worth by sitting with her day after day. Maybe they deserved to be robbed, being as rich as they were and holding onto that wealth rather than giving it to causes that truly needed it, but the kid didn't deserve to lose his mother over it. Mitchell had seen his six children work through losing their mother. He would never intentionally do anything to cause health issues or worse to another person.

He let her go a few meters before he slowly started to walk behind her. Before he reached the doorway, he heard Charlie's voice call out.

"Max!"

Immediately Mitchell started running, expecting the worst. Instead, when he arrived in the room, he saw his son's eyes slowly trying to open.

"You lot talk a load of crap," Max said softly as he looked around briefly. He then moved his head back into the pillow once more.

Charlie saw her father leave the room hurriedly and then return with a doctor beside him. She wanted to stay full of hope, but at the same time, she didn't want to hope at all. Perhaps it was just a fleeting one-off thing that happened. Perhaps he was about to fall into an even deeper state of bad health.

All of them sat back and watched the doctor do an assessment. When he stood up, he smiled at all of them.

"He's awake," he said. "Well, by that, I mean he's out of his coma. His eyes are shut, but right now I do believe he is only asleep."

"Yeah, yeah, I can hear you. I'm wide awake," Max's voice said, making everyone laugh quietly.

Slowly as the hour progressed, he woke up completely although he was giddy.

"Did they catch the guy who shot at us?" he asked, still sounding sleepy.

"Max, just relax. Don't think about that now," Mitchell said, softly stroking his son's forehead to soothe him, just as he had done when Max was a toddler.

"I've been relaxing for days, Dad. What do you think I've been doing here in this stupid bed? Listening to you all bleat on about everything? Geez, my brothers talk about crap stuff. And as for Charlie and her boyfriend, kissing all the time…"

Mitchell looked sternly at his daughter but he wasn't going to make any kind of deal about it. Her speech was still at the forefront of his mind. He knew he had to act quickly to do the right thing if he wanted to get that ring back. They had a well-oiled system. Gems were quickly processed in his world.

"Max, I have to go out for a while but I'll be back soon, okay?" he said and saw Max try to nod.

"Yeah, I'm going to stay here. I don't think I'm gonna go anywhere anytime soon," Max replied.

Charlie watched her father walk out silently. He said nothing about where he was going. He didn't even look at her, but she suspected - *hoped* - he was going to do what she wished him to do.

Max seemed to wake up more by the minute.

"Hey kiddo," he called out. In response, he saw Charlie turn toward him and venture closer. "Are you okay?"

Charlie took his hand in hers and kissed the back of it. It was soppy for them, but she couldn't help it. She felt soppy.

"Yeah, I'm all good," she replied.

"He sounds nice, whoever that guy is that has been hanging around here."

"You didn't really hear our conversations, did

you?"

"Oh yeah," said Max. "I've been listening to everyone. I was wide awake. I just couldn't seem to get my body to do anything. Otherwise, I would have told the guy to stop kissing you so much."

Charlie laughed softly. He was Max. He wasn't anywhere near 100%, but he was a whole lot closer to it than he had been hours earlier. That was enough for the moment.

She sat back quietly and said no more as she held his hand. When she felt him drift off again, she let his hand go and relaxed back in the chair.

"What's the deal with that guy anyway, Charlie?" she heard Regan ask quietly.

"What do you mean?"

"Come on," Regan said. "You're kissing him? You said he wasn't your boyfriend, so what's the deal with that?"

"Leave him alone, Regan," Charlie said. "His mum is in here now, having suffered a stress attack after finding out that last night someone broke into her home and took a very special ring that was a family heirloom. A ring that should go to Ash, by the way, and any children he has after that."

She'd said it to get his attention, and she sure got it. Regan said nothing about what she'd said but stood up immediately. Before he could leave, she made sure that he heard her next statement.

"We already lost our mother. I hope the stress that is in Ash's mother right now doesn't make him lose her."

Regan walked out. He couldn't listen to that. Silently he panicked. He didn't know what was right. Well, that wasn't quite true. He knew what was right. He just didn't know if he should do the right thing by Charlie and her boyfriend, or he should do right by his own family. In all the years their family had been doing what they did, he didn't think such a thing had ever happened. They lived in a big city. The chances of inadvertently stealing from someone they knew, even indirectly, was remote. It just didn't happen.

Except that on this occasion, it had.

~~~~~

Mitchell drove quickly to see Big John. He was the next person in their smooth-running operation to handle gems once the Stonewardens did their thing and took them. Mitchell knew that Big John was fast at what he did. Everything had been done for centuries, and systems were in place to move stolen gems incredibly quickly. He appreciated how much work his ancestors had put in to make it all work well, no matter the time in history it was happening in. Today was the first time he actually hoped things hadn't moved quite so fast as normal.

It was a long drive to the large homestead far outside the city. To anyone passing by, the home looked like any other old house on a blank canvas of grass. It should have been a working farm. Now there was just grass all around the house. It was unremarkable to look at, and therefore unnoticeable. That was how it had to look. No-one passing by could have any idea that underneath the house was a basement of high-tech gadgetry that was used for transforming jewelry into completely different pieces from what it had arrived as.

Mitchell drove up the long driveway, accelerating slightly in his anticipation to get there. He felt like he was acting out of character. This kind of thing just wasn't done. They never went to save a piece of jewelry and get it back to its owner, but he liked the guy who was devoting so much time to Charlie. Also playing on Mitchell's mind was knowing Ash's mother was unwell because of the stress of what he and the boys had done.

As a family, the Stonewardens did what they did to help people in need. They were really a modern-day Robin Hood, with the way they would take items from
~~~~~

people so rich that usually they didn't even notice them gone, and then worked and sold gems in a new form before using the resulting funds to help out in small communities. Even in the fairly short time since Mitchell had become head of the family business, schools and hospitals had benefited from their help, as had a brand new accommodation shelter for people who had been living on the streets. Knowing his family did things like that made him feel good, even though at the heart of it, his family were thieves. Usually, he didn't feel like a thief. Today there was an inkling of feeling inside of him that he was.

Once parked by the old homestead, he ran and knocked on the front door, hoping desperately that Big John was there. Usually a patient man, Mitchell was wound up by the time the door opened and the man in question was standing in front of him.

"Mitchell, I wasn't expecting you. Come in."

The two men both went into the house, and Mitchell closed the front door behind him.

"I hope I'm not too late, Big John, but there was a piece in the last lot…"

Big John smiled at him.

"It hasn't been processed yet, Mitchell. Come downstairs, and let's look through what you brought to me."

Mitchell felt extreme relief flow through him as he watched Big John unlock the well-hidden and secure entrance down to the basement area. Whenever he visited the processing room under the house, he was always surprised. The movement from the old traditional feel and look of the main house, to the almost futuristic feel of the basement underneath, was sometimes surreal.

He followed the older man to the specially designed assessment table, where the gems were laid out.

"I was just assessing them when I heard you

knock," Big John said. "What are we looking for?"

"A ring," Mitchell replied. "It is apparently generations old so I am hoping it will stand out from everything else."

"I know the piece you mean," Big John said, nodding. "It caught my eye when I first saw it."

"I *hope* you know which piece it is because I have no idea what it looks like, which doesn't make things easy."

"Sounds like there's a story there somewhere," Big John said, chuckling slightly. He'd been in the business much longer than Mitchell and still remembered Mitchell as a child before he even knew anything *about* the business. In Mitchell's time as family leader, he'd never come to even glance at the jewels after they were delivered to Big John, but it wasn't the first time Big John had seen something retrieved moments before it would have been transformed into something entirely different.

Mitchell glanced over the hoard spread out in front of him. He didn't have any interest in gems or any knowledge about them, so he had always been in awe of Big John for the way he could identify something so tiny by an even more minute detail.

"Wait, there are no rings here," he said when he'd glanced over the entire table.

His words were met by another chuckle from the older man beside him.

"No, the rings have been put aside. I do them after the larger pieces," Big John said, moving to another smaller counter off to the side. "Come and look here."

Mitchell moved over and looked at the surface. Instantly it leaped out at him. He picked up the one he thought must be it.

"This one? Do you think?"

Big John nodded at him.

"I do. That is a rare gem indeed. I would date that

back to the mid-1600s, Italy."

Mitchell's breath caught as he looked at the older man sharply.

"1600s? Surely not!"

"Surely so, Mitchell. If I'm wrong, I am not wrong by much. It would fetch a fair price…"

Mitchell groaned at the words. Sometimes he cursed his family business being what it was. Not very often, but certainly sometimes.

"No, we can't do anything to it," he said. "I need to take it with me."

"You have never retrieved anything before."

"No, and I feel wrong for wanting to do it today."

Big John chuckled and placed a hand on Mitchell's shoulder.

"Do not feel wrong, Mitchell. I have been doing this for your family for as long as I can remember. For you and your father and his family before that. This is not the first time something has been taken back. Your father did it once too."

"He did?" Mitchell asked, his voice full of surprise.

"He did. A piece came through that he had second thoughts about because it ended up being a lost jewel of someone in your mother's family," Big John said, laughing softly. "Oh, your father was beside himself when he realized what had happened. It wasn't anything directly related to your mother, but your father was horrified that something had happened so close to home. I still vividly remember his face when he turned up that day. It was much like your face today."

Mitchell tried to imagine his father acting in such a way and couldn't. His father had been such a staunch, strict man with no appearance of sentimentality at all. Did he really do that for Mitchell's mother?

"Here, place it in this here box," Big John said, holding out a standard ring box. "But hold onto it tightly,

Mitchell. That isn't something you want to put down and forget!"

"I know where it has to get to," Mitchell said. "I just don't know how to get it there without the owner knowing it was me or my family who took it!"

"Ahh, yes, the problem of goods return. Your father had the same problem," said Big John.

"How did he do it? How did he return the item to the family without revealing he'd taken it?"

"Well, he was able to get back into the house and replace it where it had been, but that was done in a time when it was easier to be stealthy. How secure is the place this came from?"

"It's a well-guarded apartment now," Mitchell replied. "The police might still be there, for all I know. But the owner is currently in hospital…"

"Hmm. Perhaps a well-timed visit during the night when no-one is around, to slip the ring on the owner's finger?"

Mitchell considered the idea and gave it merit, although he gave thought to the horror that something could go wrong. The ring might fall off the finger in the night, or someone might see him there and think he was stealing it. Regardless, it would be better than attempting to go anywhere near the apartment again.

"Who is this person?" Big John asked. "She must mean something special to you."

"No, I don't even know her. The owner is the mother of someone who is proving to be quite attached to my daughter."

"Ahh, young Charlotte. How is she doing, after the shooting?"

"She's holding herself together remarkably well, considering she was shot at, and Max was hit," Mitchell said. "But this guy who's hanging around her seems to be a good kid. He's certainly eager to be there for her to lean on, and I'm happy about that."

"It usually means something when a father likes the man who's chasing his daughter," Big John said, laughing out loud. Mitchell chuckled with him.

"Yes, I am thinking that too, but his mother is in hospital after the shock of realizing someone was in their apartment," said Mitchell. "I hate to say it, Big John, but this last job has left me feeling pretty horrible about what we've done."

"Mitchell, it is part of the business. Everyone who has done it has felt the same at some point, I am sure. You have to maintain focus on the fact that you don't take these jewels for your own personal gain or for a thrill. You do good. You help even out the wealth of the rich and the poverty of the poor, even if just a little bit. I won't tell you to not feel as you do. Just remember *why* you do what you do - what your family has done for hundreds of years."

Mitchell nodded and placed the ring box into a secure, zip-up pocket inside his jacket.

"I know. Thank you, Big John. I think I really did need your pep talk today. I think I might be getting too old for this now. Perhaps it's time to pass the business to Vic…"

The older man laughed heartily.

"Oh, Mitchell! You are still young, and definitely not too old. Train Vic, yes. But you retire? No! You couldn't do it, even if you tried."

The two men walked out of the basement. Mitchell watched as the door and doorway cover were secured before they walked to the front door of the house together.

"Charlie doesn't want to be a part of the business," Mitchell said. "I don't know what to do about that."

"You have ensured all of the children are part of it. How did you deal with any of them objecting before?"

"They didn't."

CHAPTER FIVE

When Mitchell arrived back at the hospital, he saw Charlie and Max quietly chatting as he entered the room. Charlie looked at her father, wondering if anything might have changed with the situation of Ash's mother's jewels. She knew she could have been wrong in her belief. Her father and brothers might not have had anything to do with the burglary at all. She didn't want to ask. She didn't really want to know. If she didn't know, then she would never have to lie to Ash.

"Where's Regan?" she heard her father ask as he sat on the other side of Max's bed.

"He had to go. He said he'll visit Max again tomorrow," Charlie said.

Max could sense the tension between his sister and his father but said nothing. He was intelligent enough to know that his body had gone through something it seriously didn't like. There was no way he'd be pushing it to do anything much for the immediate future.

"I'm going to stay here overnight..." Mitchell began to say before Max cut him off.

"Dad, you don't need to. I'm fine," Max started to object.

"Don't think that you're well enough to argue with me yet, Max," Mitchell said, trying to sound a little bit humorous even though his words were obviously meant to be heeded. "Charlie, how about you head home now, while it's still light?"

Charlie looked at her father and knew that moment was certainly not the right one to argue with him. Without making any comment, she stood up, leaned over Max, and kissed his forehead.

"I'll come back in tomorrow," she said softly and saw him smile sadly at her.

Charlie said nothing to her father before she walked out. He was right. It was still early enough to walk home safely in the light of the day, but it was also early enough to go and see Ash. There could be no harm in going to see how his mother was doing.

Making her way down the stairs, her mind wandered to her father. Had he gone to find the ring? Was that something he'd ever done or had ever had to do? For anyone? Or was she right off the mark and her family had nothing to do with the robbery at all?

She quickly put the thoughts out of her mind as she walked along the corridor on the floor of where Ash's mother was staying. Walking tentatively toward the room, she could see Ash sitting inside from where she stood, a short distance outside the doorway. As if sensing her there, he turned and looked at her. She saw him say something to his mother before walking out of the room and moving toward her.

"Hey," he said, wrapping his arms around her and kissing her softly.

"How is she doing?" Charlie asked.

"She's going to be okay. She just had a shock. She needs to stay here tonight but will go home tomorrow. I think she's a bit scared to go home, to be honest. I thought I could offer her my apartment to go to, but it's not quite the standard of living she's used to," Ash said, laughing softly through his last sentence.

"What about your dad?" asked Charlie.

"Oh, he's alright," Ash replied. "At the moment, he has a new security system being installed by a new security company. He can afford the best, so the best he will get!"

It wasn't lost on Charlie that the tone Ash used to talk about his parents wasn't so nice when there was living style or money involved. She didn't ask about it at that moment, but she knew she would eventually.

"My dad is in there now, but he said he's going to head back to their place at eight. I don't think either of them needs me here. What are you doing? How's Max?"

"He's awake!" Charlie said, immediately seeing the level of surprise on Ash's face. "He's awake and talking, Ash!"

"Wow, that's amazing!" Ash exclaimed. "That must be a huge relief for you and your family."

Charlie nodded at him, silently hoping his mother would also be in full recovery soon.

"My father has told me to go and not come back till tomorrow."

"Oh, well, we could … go somewhere? Do you want to?" Ash asked, suddenly feeling insecure and uncertain. Max being in a coma had secured a need in her for him. Would she need him now that Max was healing?

"I do," Charlie said, feeling her face begin to blush. "I do want to … go somewhere …with you."

Ash smiled at her, sensing he wasn't the only one feeling slightly timid in the moment.

"Okay. Wait here. I'll just say goodbye to Mum and Dad. Then we'll go … somewhere," he said, grinning before he kissed her softly again.

Charlie watched him as he walked down to the room, disappeared for a couple of minutes, and then began walking back toward her. Looking at him from the distance, seeing him move closer, she felt her heart pounding. In her head, she heard words loud and clear. Yep, he's definitely *hot*.

"All done. Where to?" Ash asked as he approached, immediately taking her hand in his when he reached her.

"Would you like to come to my house? My brothers might be there. Or they might not be. I dunno."

Looking at her, Ash saw her blushing. Even

though it was a direct contradiction of who he'd expected her to be when he'd seen her but hadn't met her, he liked it.

"Lead the way."

With it being a good 45-minute walk to her home, Charlie had time to start to feel nervous. They'd been alone before at his apartment, so she knew it wasn't that which was making her apprehensive. No, it was him seeing where she lived that worried her, which made no sense since she was the one who had done the inviting.

Ash was very aware of the feelings inside of him as he held her hand while they walked. Something about Max waking up made it feel like things had changed, or were about to change. When Max had been in a coma, the situation had felt like some kind of security blanket and comfort. With him now having woken up, that comfort that was peeling away.

"You seem nervous, Charlie," he said to her once he could feel her tenseness flowing through her hand. "If you'd like to go somewhere else, I don't mind."

Charlie stopped walking and turned to face him.

"No, I want you to come to my home," she said. "I want to share with you something of who I am."

"But something doesn't feel right to you?"

"No, I think I'm just nervous about you seeing my home," Charlie replied. "It's run down and, I dunno, maybe I'm a little embarrassed by it."

Ash pulled her into his arms and kissed her, softly at first but then passionately.

"Don't worry so much," he reassured her. "You accepted my tiny living space, and I don't care where you live. I just want to know *you*."

Charlie nodded shyly and turned so they could begin walking once more.

Soon they were on the pavement outside her home. Ash was unaware of why they'd stopped walking until she looked at him and nodded toward the large house beside them.

"Oh, wow, you live here? It's *huge*!" he said and saw her blush. "Charlie, your house looks amazing. Why would you ever be embarrassed by it?"

"It's falling to pieces," she said quietly and saw him laugh.

"Come on, I want to see inside," Ash said excitedly.

Forcing herself to relax, Charlie gently tugged him along, up onto the verandah, and then through the front door.

Upon entering, the first thing Ash's eyes fell to was the ornate flowing staircase in front of him. From directly in front of the front door, it wound upwards and then split off in two directions at the top. It was carved out of solid timber, and the carving throughout the foyer was intricate, created by a master craftsman. Ash was in awe. Everywhere he looked, it was grand. She'd been right in indicating it was run down and had been neglected for decades, but the house structure itself was grand. In its heyday, it would have been a beautiful home - a mansion to some.

"It's pretty rough, huh," he heard Charlie say beside him.

Ash turned to her with awe on his face.

"Charlie, it's incredible," he said. "I've never been in a home like this."

She looked closely at him and believed in his sincerity. The discovery relaxed her.

"Come on, I want to show you something," she said and took his hand once more.

Ash found himself led up the staircase, feeling like he was in a palace. His family might have had money, but they'd never owned a home like the one he was currently in. With his parents, it was all about glitz and glamour. That wasn't Ash. He'd much more likely be attracted to something like the Stonewarden home -

something with character.

He followed her into what he knew to be her bedroom as soon as they entered. With a father and five brothers, the room definitely could only be hers. Hearing the door close behind them, he stood still, suddenly nervous.

Charlie approached him until her chest touched his. When he looked down into her eyes, he was swept away in desire. It wasn't something he wanted to feel, but he couldn't walk away. She reached up and kissed him, her kisses becoming more and more forceful with every second that they stood like that. Ash couldn't stop himself from enclosing her tightly in his arms as his passion struck, and his tongue moved against hers.

They remained like that for a long time until he felt her nudging him backward, and then he was falling back onto the bed. Backing up so that he was fully on the bed, he watched as she lay beside him.

"Charlie, we're not…"

"No, we're not. Don't worry. We agreed, and we're sticking to that agreement," Charlie replied before kissing him again.

Keeping her assurance in his head, Ash indulged in the taste of her lips and her tongue, while he felt her hands moving over his chest, his back … his bum. He didn't stop her. As long as she steered clear from the area where he definitely couldn't hide his extreme arousal, she could touch him anywhere she wanted, as far as he was concerned.

He kept his hips back from hers. It was uncomfortable enough being as hard as he was inside his jeans. He didn't think he could stand it if she were to rub her hips against him.

Charlie reveled in the feelings awakening in her. She loved kissing him. There was no denying it - she was loving everything about him. He was an ordinary guy living an ordinary life, and he turned her on a *lot*!

The sound of a mobile phone going off interrupted them. Ash reached into his pocket quickly, not particularly wanting to feel his phone vibrating in there right at that moment. On the screen, he could see his manager's name appear. He answered it quickly as he sat up and got off the bed.

Charlie watched him as he talked on the phone. She was glad of the interruption. She liked kissing him a bit too much. It was nice to look at him from behind as he looked out the window and indulged in conversation. He had a nice back and nice shoulders. In the t-shirt he was wearing, it was easy to see how defined his upper arm muscles were even though she hadn't heard him mention being a gym-goer. Taking the time to give him a good thorough look up and down, she thought he had a beautiful physique. She wondered why she'd never even noticed him before.

After a few minutes, Ash hung up and turned around, catching Charlie looking at him as if he were the most delicious dessert she'd ever set eyes on. He smiled at her with amusement and saw her blush when her eyes seemed to focus on his, and she realized he was watching her watching him.

"That was my boss. The glass is installed and the cleaners are at work today. I'll be starting work again on Sunday," he said as he walked back to the bed and sat beside her. "Today and tomorrow are the last days of this freedom for me."

He ran his fingers through her hair and kissed her softly before sitting back from her.

"Did you grow up here? You and all of your brothers?" he asked and watched as Charlie sat up, nodding.

"I think this house has been in our family for a couple of generations, at least," she said. "Everyone keeps living in it because it fits a good-sized family in it, but each generation seems to forget to maintain it. It's taken for granted, year after year, which is a bit sad. Oh, but I wanted to show you something."

Ash watched as she jumped up and retrieved a shoebox from a shelf on the wall. Sitting down on the bed cross-legged, she opened the box.

When Ash peered inside, he saw photos - *lots* of photos. He watched as Charlie pulled out one and handed it to him.

"My mum," she said quietly, thinking to herself that it had been a long while since she'd given any thought to her mother.

Ash accepted the photo and looked closely at it.

"She was beautiful. You look like her," he said and saw Charlie smile sadly in response.

"It's the only photo that I have of her. I asked my father once why there weren't more photos, but he wouldn't say. He let me keep that one, but why aren't there others?"

Ash studied the photo, taking note of the area around Charlie's mother.

"That sign that she's standing under - 'Riccarton Ranch'. I've seen that. It's on the bus route out of town, about 20 minutes out."

"Is it? I always wondered," she said, thoughtful. "Do you think the place meant something to her? I mean, it's the only photo of her, and it was taken there."

Ash nodded.

"It must have been a time when taking photos wasn't as common as it is now, so maybe you're right. Maybe it did mean something special to her."

"No-one ever talks about her. They all think it's best not to speak of her, but I don't agree with that. I'd like to know who she really was."

"But you knew her, right?" Ash asked. "Before she died?"

"Yes, she died when I was nine. And I do kind of remember her, but my memories are those of a child for a mother. I'd like to know who she was as a person. What were her passions? How did she meet Dad? What did she see in him that made her want to marry him and have six kids with him? Did she ever have a job? Did she study anything?" she said and paused before speaking again. "I just wish *someone* would talk about her."

As Ash handed the photo back to her, he was reminded of how lucky he was to still have both of his parents, even though he took them for granted so much.

"Well, what happens when you ask? Your father? Your brothers?"

"To them, the subject is a closed book," Charlie replied. "They shut me down and say there's no point in talking about her. They want to forget her, I think. So you know this place then? You know how to get there?"

"Yeah, the bus goes right past it. It's on the main road out of town."

"What are you doing tomorrow?" she asked, her mind working.

"You want to go there?" Ash asked and saw her nod in reply. "Why?"

"Because I have a photo that says that sometime - at least once - my mother was there. Maybe someone there knew her. And if they did, they could tell me about her. I know it's a long shot, but it's only the cost of a bus ride, right?"

He nodded at her.

"True," he said. "Okay. If you want to go, I can go with you to this place tomorrow."

Instantly, Ash saw Charlie's face light up with a huge grin, which in turn made him smile before he found his lips once again being caressed by hers. As the kisses grew more passionate, Ash edged himself away.

"Enough of that, though," he said, making her giggle slightly. "It's going to get dark soon, so I'm going to head home."

"Stay," Charlie said, making Ash's heart feel like it dropped out of his chest. "Not like that! I mean, just stay here for the night. There's room in my bed for two."

Ash gulped at the thought. Of one consideration was sleeping beside her, which in one way was appealing but another seemed would only lead to trouble - or at the very least, a very sleepless night. The other consideration was her father and five brothers. The latter thought made him stand up sharply. Although he wanted to spend time with her, he wasn't going looking for trouble.

"The idea is tempting, Charlie, but I can't stay here with you."

She came forward and wrapped her arms around him, looking up into his eyes.

"Why?"

Ash smiled at her, deciding to leave brothers and father out of his defense.

"Because your kisses are far too delicious," he replied. "I just don't trust myself to lie near you for a whole night. Maybe in the future, but not yet."

Charlie nodded, inwardly kind of glad that he was such a gentleman. She had her own morals, and even though her body was telling her to ignore them, it was nice to be with a guy who would respect them and keep reminding her of them when needed.

After the two of them left the bedroom and walked downstairs, they found her older brother James sitting, watching TV. When James saw Ash, he jumped up, making Ash gulp.

"Stop! Whatever you are going to say, don't," Ash heard Charlie say to her brother. He was surprised to see James do as she said. Right where James had reached, he'd stopped and stood still. "I'm seeing Ash out. Chill, James."

Ash walked quicker to the door than he would have otherwise. Out on the verandah, he stopped and turned to her. Although nervous to do it with her big brother so close, he slid his arms around her and felt her do the same, before he kissed her softly.

"The bus stop is close to my apartment. Do you want to just come over there in the morning, and go from there?" he asked her.

As she nodded, Ash could see the excitement in her eyes at the prospect of finding out something about her mother. It seemed a long shot. He hoped she wouldn't be disappointed.

Charlie watched him walk down the stairs, down the path, and then down the road. When she couldn't see him anymore, she returned inside and sat down on the couch by James.

"I'm not sure I like the idea of you being upstairs in your room with a guy."

"James, I'm almost 19 years old!" Charlie exclaimed. "You were younger than me when you started bringing home girls…"

"That's not the same thing!" he argued back.

"No, it's not. You were having sex with them. I have no intention of having sex anytime soon, and neither does Ash. He's a good guy, so don't freak him out like you were about to."

"I didn't do any…"

"You charged at him like you were a bulldog," Charlie teased him.

James smiled at her terminology and relaxed back.

"Fine. But you better be telling me the truth about the no-sex thing."

"Oh god, I can't believe I'm even having this conversation with you," Charlie said. "And what are you doing here anyway? The drama with Max is over now that he's awake…"

James sat bolt upright.

"He's awake? Why didn't anyone *tell* me?" he

asked as he jumped up. "I have to go and see him! You wanna come?" he asked and she shook her head.

"No, Dad told me to stay here now, so I will," Charlie replied, shaking her head. "I'm knackered. I think I'm going to just go to bed."

"Alright," her older brother said as he kissed her forehead. "Lock the door properly when I leave and don't answer it!" he called out, making her roll her eyes at him.

"I'm fine. Go!"

Once the door was closed and she was alone in the house, Charlie let out a sigh of relief. She hadn't lied to James. She really did feel like she needed an early night - or at least a night of lying in her nice warm bed, reading about a certain sexy pirate captain and his big-bosomed temptress.

~~~~~

Ash reached his apartment just as the sun was starting to go down. He was glad he hadn't stayed any longer. He'd always hated being out at night anyway, but the shooting had freaked him out even more. Even though it had happened in broad daylight, somehow it made the nighttime seem even more dangerous to him, even though he knew that was illogical.

Inside his small living area, he sat down and closed his eyes. His body had been taken to an extreme level of arousal when he'd been in Charlie's room, and he wanted to calm down. Either that or…

"Ugh," he said as he stood up and shook his head. It was good to have met someone who he liked spending time with so much, but at the same time, there was a frustration to it. He'd never felt such a connection with anyone. He'd dated girls who looked amazing, and he shared a physical attraction with, but they'd never seemed very good at conversation. Charlie was like a whole package. She was so incredibly sexy and aroused him so easily without even really doing anything. In
~~~~~

addition to that, she was intriguing and easy to talk to.

He climbed into bed and tried to relax, but it was useless. His body was too electrified. Even with him not having been near her for half an hour or so, his body was still awake in the wake of her kisses. When trying to sleep wouldn't work, he got out of bed and went to the living area to turn on the TV. Flicking through the channels revealed nothing of value to distract him, so he picked out a movie and put it on, relaxing back along the length of his couch. That was fine for half an hour - until his mind turned to her once more. Then he couldn't do anything else. To the bathroom he went and turned on the shower. He was already aroused. His body had hardly rested from that state since he'd been in her bedroom. There was just nothing else for it. He climbed into the shower, soaped up his hand, and indulged in pleasuring himself. Thinking about her lips and her tongue, plus the feeling of her hands moving over every other part of his body when they'd lay down beside each other on her bed, it didn't take long before Ash finally felt the sweet and well overdue release that he'd so long needed.

~~~~~

Charlie lay in her bed, reading the next scene of her pirate adventure.

He watched her standing there, not moving, inside the bathtub, fully naked. He was glued to the spot where he stood, unable to move past the beauty before him. He tried to keep his eyes on hers, but he couldn't help himself. The voluptuousness of her body, the roundness of her breasts, and the hardness of her nipples made him breathless.

Charlie had been thinking about many things before she'd picked up her book to continue reading it. Now she was lost in it again. She wasn't a girlie girl in many things, but a long time before, she had discovered romance novels. After reading one of those, she did find
~~~~~

herself dreaming of the lives her heroines seemed to have. They were complete fiction, but how would it feel to have a man look at her naked, like her sexy pirate captain was looking at his beauty in the book right now? If Ash saw her naked, would he like what he saw? Would he find it difficult to look away? Would he be breathless in the sight of her? Moreover, would *she* be breathless at the sight of *him* naked?

She shook her head as if to shake the thoughts and questions away, and returned to the page before her.

He moved forward and stood with his hand out to guide her and help her step safely out of the bathwater. She said nothing, but she also did nothing. She made no attempt to hide her luscious nakedness from him, and when she was free of the bath, she stood, waiting. Enraptured by her extreme beauty, he could not think what she might be waiting for. He let his eyes glide down her body from head to toe and back again. The glistening of the wetness he could see, he loved the look of. He could hold back no longer, and abruptly pulled her into his arms and kissed her with deep, lustful passion.

Deep, lustful passion, Charlie thought about. Was that what she felt when she was with Ash? Hmm possibly. She bowed her head down again and continued reading. If nothing else, the story was certainly distracting her from anything serious.

CHAPTER SIX

Ash heard the knock on his apartment door just after ten the following morning. After his release the night before, he'd finally been able to relax and have a decent sleep.

Opening the door, the sight of Charlie left him breathless. She was wearing her usual jeans and t-shirt, but the t-shirt was one he'd never seen before, and it fitted her just that little bit more. He looked up into her eyes to distract himself from wanting to look at the outline of her breasts, that were more visible than usual with the added tightness of the top.

"Are you ready?" she asked.

"Come in first," Ash replied, desperate to kiss her.

As he closed the door, he leaned down and placed his lips on hers. Straight away, he felt Charlie heat as her tongue wrapped around his and her arms encased him. It was almost instantaneous, the change from a simple kiss to one of desire. He guided her against the living room wall.

Charlie felt like she was on fire. The wall rigid behind her only drove her on, wanting more from him, but she knew she mustn't. She pulled him as close to her as she could and felt him hard against her. She'd never seen a guy naked, but she read her books. She knew an erection from how it had been described in many of her much-loved stories. It was the first time she'd felt it. The thought excited her because she understood that it meant he was excited. She reached down, curious, but his hand caught hers as if he knew exactly where it was heading.

"Oh no you don't, Charlie," Ash said. "If you do that, we'll go somewhere we don't want to go."

"What if I do?"

He pulled away from her.

"What?"

"Ash, I like being with you like this," Charlie said. "I want to be closer to you."

He was surprised by the declaration but couldn't think about how to respond. In a timely manner, his mobile phone started to vibrate where it sat on the coffee table.

"Mum?" he asked as he answered it. "What? How can that be?"

Charlie watched him from her spot against the wall. She couldn't move. She was alive, and she loved the feeling. She wanted to have more of it. That was all she could think about - until Ash finished his phone call.

"That was my father," he said. "Apparently, Mum woke up this morning with her family ring ... on her finger..."

Charlie heard those words with definite clarity. She felt confused all of a sudden. She wanted to be happy that her father had made that right, but she was very aware that she couldn't *show* she was happy. She stood still and just looked at him, watching his face and choosing not to say anything.

Ash was happy for his mother but he could see Charlie standing just as she had been. He wanted her - badly. He'd never wanted anyone like that, and he knew it made him rethink his decision to wait until he was married before he had sex.

As a distraction, he looked at his watch.

"We have to go. Come on. The bus leaves in 15 minutes," he said, putting his keys and phone in his pocket and grabbing his wallet.

Charlie was abruptly reminded of what they were supposed to be doing that day for *her*. She nodded and left through the front door, saying nothing. After walking in silence to the bus stop, they sat in peace, each in their own thoughts.

"You haven't told me why you don't want to," she

eventually said, her curiosity piqued. "I know we both feel the same way, but what is *your* reason?"

Ash looked at her, perplexed.

"I just … want … to wait. I want to share that with the one person I love enough to marry. I don't want it to mean nothing." He paused to see if she would say anything in return. When she didn't, he continued, taking her hand in his. "Charlie, my body goes wild when I'm with you, and I love being with you. But we don't need to rush … right?"

Charlie nodded at him.

"I know, and I really don't want to either, but I *yearn* for you."

At hearing her terminology, Ash laughed softly.

"Yearn? Who says yearn? Charlie, are you a hidden romance novel reader?" he teased her and saw her blush then laugh herself.

"Okay, yes, I am. Maybe yearn isn't the right - normal - word. When you kiss me, I feel like I want to be closer to you - like I want *more* of you."

He kissed her softly, vowing silently not to tease her again.

"I know what you mean. I feel exactly the same way," he said with a slight smile before delivering one tiny tease. "I *yearn* for you too."

Once the bus pulled up, Ash and Charlie quickly got on and sat down. No more was said for the journey.

~~~~~

As they drove past the ranch entrance, they alerted the driver to slow and stop at the next bus stop.

"Are you nervous?" Ash asked Charlie as they walked back along the road the few meters they needed to. When the large overhead sign came into view, he saw her pull the photo out and compare it, as if making sure they were in the right place.

"Yes, but like you said, they probably know nothing of my mother," Charlie replied. "She might have
~~~~~

visited one time only."

"Only one way to find out," he said, reaching out and taking her hand in his. When she smiled at him, Ash raised it to his lips and kissed her palm.

The driveway seemed to go on forever. As the two of them walked the length of it, they saw horses in the distance.

Eventually, they arrived in a circular drive area. On the far side of it was a large house. It made even Charlie's large old home seem like a small cottage. It wasn't high so much as it was very, very long. Ash and Charlie stood together and just looked at it, speechless and wondering what to do next.

"Can I help you?" a gruff male voice asked from their left.

When they turned, Charlie and Ash saw an older man walking toward them. They saw him look at them front-on. When he did, he stopped, his eyes clearly focused on Charlie's.

"No! Is that you, little Charlotte Stonewarden?" he exclaimed and saw the look of surprise on both young people's faces. "Is it?"

Charlie nodded at him.

"How do you know me?" she asked meekly, instantly seeing the gruffness on his face replaced by a wide grin.

"I don't," the older man said. "We have never met, but you … you are a spitting image of your mother, and I knew her very well."

"Did you? I have come here because of this…" Charlie said as she walked forward to him and handed him the photo.

"Oh," the man said, laughing. "I remember that day. That was taken before your mother attempted to ride her first horse. She didn't look quite so happy afterward," he said, his laugh loud and booming. "Oh, she was a sweet, sweet lass, she was."

Charlie watched his face and thought she saw a tear begin to form. She found herself excited about the possibility that she might learn something about her mother after all.

"Did you know her well then?" she asked.

"Aye, I did, but let us have some introduction here. I know who you are, but I do not know this young man. I suspect you are not a Stonewarden though."

Ash held out his hand.

"No, Sir. I'm Ash. I'm here just as a friend of Charlie's - sorry, Charlotte's."

"Charlie. Oh, that is a nice name too," the man said. "I can call you Charlie. And I am Tom."

Both young people shook hands with the older man.

"I am very pleased to meet you, Tom," Charlie said, hoping the good start would follow through to provide her with what she wanted.

"But what brings you out here today?"

"I found this photograph and I just wanted to see if anyone remembered my mother," Charlie replied. "I don't remember her very well, and I would like to know more about her. Can you tell me more?"

Tom suddenly looked grave and uncertain. He stood like that for a long while, making Charlie nervous that perhaps they were going to be asked to leave.

"I think that before I say anything more, I best make a phone call. Can you two wait here for a few minutes? I'll be right back," Tom said before walking off briskly.

He went into the nearby stable to talk but seemingly did not realize how loud he was talking. Ash and Charlie were unintentionally able to overhear the entire conversation he began.

"The young lass is here with a friend. Yes! Charlotte! No, she said she wants to know more about her mother. Well, how do you want me to handle it?

Yes. Are you sure? Yes, of course. Very well."

When he returned, Ash and Charlie both pretended not to have heard anything and smiled at him.

"Right, well, here's the thing. I only work here on this ranch. I'm not the owner, and I just spoke to the owner. His instruction was that I can tell *you* everything," he said, pointing at Charlie. "But I can't tell *you* anything," he continued, pointing at Ash. "So! I am happy to show you both around the ranch, but I cannot answer any questions. But Charlotte - Charlie - I hope you will want to come back another day. Perhaps tomorrow? Then we can have a real good chat, and I can answer whatever you like."

Charlie was speechless for a moment and wanted to object until she felt Ash put his hand on her arm.

"Charlie, you have the opportunity to learn what you want to learn," he said. "You should come back tomorrow and talk to Tom, or I can leave now if you prefer. I don't mind. This is important."

She looked at him and smiled before nodding to both of them.

"I will come back tomorrow alone with my questions, if that is alright with you, Tom," Charlie said. "But for now, could you show Ash and I around anyway? I've never been on a ranch before."

"Have you ridden before?" Tom asked and saw Charlie laugh.

"No!"

"Would you like to? I can saddle up a couple of small, slow horses for the two of you," Tom suggested.

Ash laughed out loud. "Me? On a horse?"

The thought made him giggle like a child, and Charlie was enraptured as she saw it. He hadn't laughed like that before.

"Actually Tom, I think that is a very good idea!" she said. She grinned as she saw Ash go pale. "Come on. Let's both try it together. We'll either both have fun, or we'll both be in pain. Either way, we can have some fun trying something neither of us has done before. What do you think?"

Ash looked at her face and couldn't say no. She looked angelic and desirable, all at the same time. Yes, having something else to concentrate on couldn't be a bad thing.

"Alright then! Come along, and I'll introduce you to the horses," Tom said, smiling at them both as if they'd just made his day.

After a lengthy introduction to two horses, including general lessons on how to act around them and how not to act, Ash found himself up and sitting on a horse - a *pony*, he'd been told, but to him, it felt like the biggest horse on the planet. He was nervous and shaky but felt a little more at ease as he saw Charlie trying to get up on to her pony too, and the trouble she was having.

Finally, they were both settled with a guide by each of them, teaching them what to do and what not to do as they began to move. It was slow, but that was perfectly fine with both of them. As they were walked around a small enclosed area, Ash and Charlie both became absorbed in conversation with their guides. It was what Ash needed to keep his mind off more pleasurable aspects of spending time with her.

~~~~~

"Oh, Tom, I don't think I was born to be a horsewoman, I'm afraid," Charlie said when they had finished their ride and safely found themselves on the ground again. "But thank you for taking this time and sharing this with us."

"Oh, rubbish," Tom said. "You do that a few times, and you might be surprised how good a horsewoman you can be, Charlotte Stonewarden! Now, you come back and see me tomorrow, and we'll have a good long chat. And you, young man, it has been a
~~~~~

pleasure meeting you. Another time, you are welcome again, but first, this young lady and I need to talk about a great many things personal to her family."

Ash nodded and shook his hand.

"I understand completely. Thank you for your time, Tom."

Tom watched the two young people begin their walk down the long driveway once more. It certainly hadn't been expected, the youngest Stonewarden showing up, but she'd been a pleasure to spend time with. The poor lass had lost her sweet mother so young. It would have been hard for her, growing up with so many men in the house. As he saw the two of them finally disappear from sight, Tom rushed inside to tell his wife about the newest Stonewarden he'd met.

~~~~~

"How do you feel about that?" Ash asked when they were on the bus home again.

"Oh, that was amazing, wasn't it?!" Charlie exclaimed excitedly. "I didn't really expect to see anyone who would remember my mother but finding Tom is incredible. I *will* go back tomorrow. Hopefully, he'll tell me more about her."

"I think he has more to tell you about your whole family, if I interpreted him correctly," Ash said. "You might learn a secret or two. Do you think you're ready for that?"

She reached over and took his hand in hers, pulling it onto her lap.

"I am. Whatever he can tell me, I'm ready for."

As Ash watched, Charlie seemed to bubble over with energy and enthusiasm that was contagious. He couldn't help but smile at her. When she turned to face him directly, he saw a different look on her face, and that was dangerous.

"Do you need to go to the hospital to see your mother?" she asked, surprising him as he'd have
~~~~~

expected quite a different question with that look on her face.

"Yes, I should head in there and at least check she is alright," Ash replied. "Are you going in to see Max?"

Charlie nodded but kept her eyes firmly focused on his.

"I will, but since the bus stops near your apartment, can we stop there for a few minutes first?"

Ash gulped but nodded. It was only a few minutes. What could happen in that time? And why was he so nervous at the thought? Not long before, they had spent hours alone there, watching movies, and nothing had happened. But something *had* changed. He could feel it. It was like someone had ramped up the electricity voltage between them.

Back at his apartment, he turned the key in the door and let her enter first. As soon as he'd closed the door, he was pushed up against the wall and his mouth was enclosed by hers. It was as if she'd been starving, and he was the first meal she'd seen in ages. Ash indulged in it as their hands wrapped tightly around each other.

Charlie felt his lips move onto her neck, making her moan heavily in the delicious feelings evoked in her from it. Ash felt he should stop, but his body was screaming out silently, 'No! Don't you dare stop!'

Together, they naturally moved to the sofa, where she lay down and welcomed him into her arms as he lay on top of her. Her lips were addictive. He couldn't stop. He just couldn't get enough of her. Her tongue was passionately engaging his, and her hands were moving over his back and butt as if edging him to move even closer to him. As she moved her legs, Ash felt his hips naturally slip between her thighs. Even through the two pairs of jeans, he could feel friction that was delicious and haunting at the same time.

Charlie lay in blissful happiness. No-one had ever

before inspired such feelings in her body or her heart. She wanted him - she really did, and not just his body. She wanted all of him, in her life, all the time. Not that she'd tell him that, of course. He didn't want sex before he found the right woman to marry. He had told her that without any doubt in his voice so she would respect it. For the moment, however, he was with her, no matter who the lucky woman was that would secure his heart for the forever after in the future.

Ash stopped his movements and took a moment to get his breath. Looking into her eyes, he kissed her softly on the lips. No tongue. No passion. He just wanted to kiss her softly, over and over. He needed to slow things down, but he also wanted to pamper her, not rush at her like he felt he was doing.

"I think we were going to the hospital," he said quietly, his voice full of desire.

Charlie laughed softly and nodded.

"We were. We *are*."

Ash felt her hands move up his back and begin stroking him. One settled on his back while the other one moved to his hair, caressing his scalp. He lay his head on her shoulder and relaxed, reveling in the simplistic pleasure that came from her touch.

"I love being with you, Charlie," he said softly.

The words were spoken so quietly that Charlie was left wondering if she'd actually heard them or not.

When Ash didn't hear or feel any response, he lifted his head and again looked at her.

"Does that freak you out?" he asked and saw her instantly smile.

"No."

"My body wants yours, in case you hadn't noticed," he said, with a teasing smile on his face, eager to release tension between them.

Charlie laughed and nodded her head as best she could, lying under him.

"I *had* noticed, actually," she said. "But I'm also pretty aware that my body wants yours, too."

He kissed her again before pulling right away from her and holding out his hand to help her stand up.

"Come on. We do need to get to the hospital. There will be plenty of time for more of this later."

Charlie let him pull her up. Once both were standing, they held each other closely before finally moving toward the door.

~~~~~

"Ash! Oh, look!" his mother exclaimed when he walked into her hospital room.

Ash moved forward under the watchful eye of his father and looked at the ring on her finger. Only then did he realize that he'd never really seen the ring - or if it had ever been shown to him, he'd never taken any notice of it. As he looked at it, he was amazed at the intricacy of it and how *old* it looked.

"I'm so glad, Mum. You look heaps better today. Are you feeling okay?"

"Oh, yes! I know they took a lot more, but this is all that is important to me."

"The doctor has said that your mother can go home, so we are leaving shortly," his father said, joining in the conversation. "Do you want to come home with us?"

"Oh, yes, Ash. Come home and stay. It will make me feel better to know you are there."

Ash looked at his mother. Not wanting to let her down, he nodded.

"I can stay tonight, but I have to start back at work tomorrow when the supermarket opens at nine."

"You know you don't need to work, Ash," his father said sternly.

Ash smiled sadly in response. His father and mother would never understand why he chose to work, have his own apartment, and pay for his own living
~~~~~

expenses. They had both been born into money and had just accepted their lives being that way. He didn't know why he saw things differently from them, but he just did.

"I'll stay tonight, but tomorrow morning I'll leave early to go back to my apartment to get ready for work," he said. "I can't miss a day tomorrow. With the supermarket having been closed for so long, my boss thinks it could be crazy tomorrow with people stocking up on supplies they haven't been able to buy lately."

Both of his parents nodded and said nothing more.

As the three of them were leaving the building, he heard Charlie's voice call out to him. When Ash turned, he saw her running toward him. He stopped and pulled her into his arms when she reached him.

"Are you leaving now?" she asked.

"I'm going home with Mum and Dad and I'm going to stay at their place tonight," Ash replied as he smiled at her.

"Okay. Thanks for coming with me today," she said and leaned up to kiss him softly.

"I hope you have a good day back there tomorrow. I think all your questions will be answered, and more!"

"I hope so. Can … can we catch up tomorrow night, if you finish work early enough?"

He nodded and kissed her forehead.

"Yes, please," he said, reluctant to say goodbye to her all of a sudden. He turned and saw his parents waiting. "I have to go. I'll call you when I finish tomorrow, yeah?" he asked and saw her nod before she turned and walked back into the hospital building.

~~~~~

When Charlie walked back into Max's room, he was sitting up even though he still looked exhausted. To Charlie, he'd said it seemed like his brain had woken up and begun talking to his body again, but his body kept
~~~~~

trying to fall asleep again.

"Did you see lover boy?" he asked her as she approached his bed.

Charlie rolled her eyes at him, making him laugh at her. She looked around the two other faces that were in the room. James and Mitchell both sat in chairs on either side of the bed.

"The doctor came by when you were outside," her father said. "He thinks Max will be okay to go home in a few days."

"Nah," Max said with an already cheeky grin on his face, which Charlie took to mean that he was indeed on his way to recovery. "That blonde nurse wants me gone 'cause I was trying to chat her up."

Everyone laughed at him, happy to see his quirky humor at least trying to return.

Charlie looked at her father. She didn't know if he was the person on the other end of the telephone when Tom had made the call from the ranch, but who else would it be? He was the head of the family now. As far as she knew, there were no other relatives living and older. Of course, it might not have been anything to do with her father or their family. Perhaps it was someone else entirely on the phone, who only had a connection to her mother. She could feel herself getting slightly panicked at the not knowing, and closed her eyes to maintain her breathing.

"Are you okay, Charlie?" she heard her father ask.

When she opened her eyes, she saw that he was directly in front of her, placing a hand on each of her shoulders. She nodded in response.

"Yeah, but I feel tired. I might head home if you don't mind."

Mitchell looked at his baby girl. He wasn't sure she had truly dealt with having been shot at. Max having been in a coma had provided her with some protection from thinking about how she had been in the same danger in those few moments when bullets flew into the supermarket. Now that Max was getting better, Mitchell wondered if a delayed shock might lie ahead for her. He was determined to watch her closely.

"That's fine," he said. "I'll give you a ride. I think Vic is coming in soon anyway."

"I don't need babysitters, Dad!" Max cried out, but Charlie could read the mock exasperation in his voice. He was teasing his father, and she knew Mitchell would see it. Max could sometimes get away with anything by teasing and being funny. He was charming. She'd always loved that about him. So had all the girls who had crossed his path.

Mitchell went up to his bed-bound son and playfully messed up his hair.

"I will see *you* tomorrow," Mitchell said before leaning in and giving his son a soppy kiss on the forehead. The sight made Charlie laugh. "James, what are you doing? Do you need a ride?"

"No, thanks," James replied. "I'll stay here till Vic comes, and then I'm going to head back to my place. I'm tired too, and I need to work early tomorrow morning."

Mitchell nodded at him and guided Charlie from the room.

Nothing was said between them on the way home. Once in the house, Charlie made her way up to her room and closed the door. Her father made no move to follow her. She was an independent soul, even though she was still cuddly and needed someone close to her now and then. He knew that she always asked when she needed help or needed to talk. He never tried to force her to talk. She was in a thoughtful mood. If she wanted to ask him anything, she would come back down and do so.

~~~~~

Charlie lay on her bed and looked at the ceiling. It wasn't late enough yet to sleep, but she wanted a few moments alone. Her emotions had run through a few
~~~~~

different levels throughout the day. There was the excitement of finding someone who had known her mother. Another type of excitement was that which she'd experienced in Ash's apartment. *That* she could ponder for a long time, but what was at the forefront of her mind was the coming day. She was going to go back to the ranch and talk to Tom again. She was going to ask questions, and she believed she was going to get answers. She was going to know more about the woman who gave birth to her.

Reaching into her bag, she pulled the photo out again. After looking at it for a long while, she sat it on her bedside table, leaning it against the lamp. She lay on her side and just looked at it. That was her mother. She vaguely remembered her, but she suspected her childhood memories weren't completely accurate. It was like she'd selected a few good parts of her mother being at home with them and saved them, but discarded the rest. It was the rest that she was desperate to learn about. After all, she was half made by that woman. What traits had she inherited from her side of the family? She knew that she had the look of a Stonewarden. Tom's response earlier in the day had proved that. But what aspects of her belonged to her mother?

Hearing and feeling her tummy grumble, she pulled herself off the bed and went downstairs. She was shy around her father because she didn't want to talk about the ranch. She didn't want to talk about it, and she didn't want to ask about it. Neither did she want him to ask *her* about it.

When she reached the lower level of the house, she saw him on the sofa watching sport. He was engrossed in it. Good. No questions then.

"Dad, I'm going to make something to eat. Do you want something?" she called out, but he was well and truly in the zone. She smiled. If he was in his sports zone, there she would leave him.

She opened the refrigerator and pulled out cold meats and whatever salad vegetables were lurking there. It was fairly bare, she noticed. But then, of course, it would be. That was why she and Max had gone to the supermarket that day. She shuddered at the thought. She didn't want to think about that. All that blood...

Grabbing whatever was handy, she put together two plates and walked through to the lounge. Her father was too engrossed in the large screen to notice, which she was grateful for. She walked to him and held the plate out to him. As expected, he took it with a brief glance and a quiet 'thanks' before returning his attention to the game. Some people would have hated being ignored for something on TV, but she was glad of it. It made it all easier for her if he stayed in that zone until she had found out all she needed to at the ranch the following day.

Leaving him, she headed up the staircase once more, eager to eat her salad and cold meat, but also to return to her book. Yes, reading what happened next to the sexy pirate captain and his big breasted naked woman from the bath was a perfect way to turn off her mind from reality!

CHAPTER SEVEN

"Are you sure you have to go to work today?" Ash's mother asked him as he readied to leave the following morning.

"Mum, it's my job," Ash replied. "Of course I have to go to work."

"But after what happened. Are you sure it's safe there?"

He looked at his mother. They hadn't previously talked about the shooting, and he didn't want to stress her out any more than she already was.

"I'm fine," he said. "If the police had discovered something in their investigation to suggest that it was likely to happen again, I'm sure they wouldn't have given the go-ahead for my boss to open the place today." He walked to her and wrapped her in an embrace. "Stop worrying. Everything is fine. Now I have to go."

"I love you, Ash," his mother said timidly.

Ash felt his heart pinched at the thought of letting her down in any way.

"I love you too."

As he walked out of his parents' apartment building, he experienced overwhelming nervousness inside of him. Although he'd tossed her concern aside and told her not to worry, there *was* a growing anxiety inside about going back into his workplace. The police had said nothing about who they thought the person was who had used the gun that had shot Max. With regard to their 'ongoing investigation', Ash had no idea where it was going *to*.

After a long walk home, he approached his apartment block and was surprised to see Charlie sitting on the steps outside his door.

"Hey," he said, running to her and kissing her. "What are you doing here?"

"I just wanted to see you … to wish you luck for your first day back," Charlie said.

As Ash studied her face, he could see something was off. She wasn't her usual chirpy self.

"What's wrong?" he asked, his voice gentle and coaxing.

He waited for a long while, looking at her, and eventually saw tears begin to well in her eyes.

Charlie tried to compose herself, but it was useless.

"Thinking about you going back there … it just … it *scares* me!" she exclaimed as the tears flowed.

Ash reached out his hands and helped her stand. He was glad when she moved into his arms, allowing him to hold her tightly.

"I know. It scares me a little bit too," Ash said. "But it's my job, Charlie, and there are no indications to suggest it wasn't a one-off freak thing that happened." He looked at his watch and then kissed her. "I don't have long before I have to leave. Come inside while I get ready."

She followed him in, surprised by the level of unease she could feel throughout her body. It didn't seem likely that the shooter would return to the supermarket, and if she were honest with herself, she'd been walking around for days. She could have been taken out at any moment if that had been the intent of the supermarket shooter. She had to have faith that it had been a freak incident, not at all related to her or her family.

"How are you feeling about going to the ranch today?" Ash called out to her from the bathroom, where he was shaving.

"I'm okay," Charlie called back as she moved to the bathroom doorway. He'd left it open, so she assumed he meant it was okay for her to watch.

In the mirror, she caught his eye and saw him watching her in return as he slowly continued to use a razor to slide away the white foam on his face. It was an odd thing to see since all her brothers seemed to use electric shavers. Charlie found herself quite intrigued.

"I hope you get all the answers you're looking for," Ash said. "Did you ask your dad about anything?"

"No. I don't want to talk to him about it. He'd only try and talk me out of going there," Charlie said. "This is something I have to do for me, not for the rest of my family."

She continued to watch Ash until he finally became foamless again, rinsing his face off and then moving the small hand towel to his face to dry off.

"Did you enjoy my show?" Ash asked, smiling and teasing her. In response, he saw her move toward him, reach up, and slowly and gently rubbed one cheek against one of his before repeating the action on the other side. It was such a small gesture, but Ash felt himself instantly grow hard at her simple but intimate touch. "I can't be late, Charlie," he finally said, firmly putting her away from him. "And that means I can't be this close to you right now."

Charlie smiled in recognition.

"Okay," she said, nodding. "I don't want to be distracted either, and you *are* a distraction."

Ash kissed her as he walked past her and went to the bedroom to change into his work uniform. It felt like a lifetime since he'd worn it. His life was usually so peaceful and uneventful. It was almost beyond belief how much had happened since the last morning that he'd left to go to work, just as he was about to do.

Grabbing his keys and wallet, he faced her, nervous but ready to go.

"I'll walk you to the bus stop," he said and saw her nod and walk out.

Once at their destination, he held and kissed her

again.

"Ash, be careful," Charlie said as her arms tightened around him.

"I will," Ash replied. "You too."

~~~~~~

As he approached the supermarket, Ash felt apprehension growing. With the new still-shiny glass installed along the entire frontage, the building almost looked new. His eyes canvassed the carpark and street. Not that that would make any difference since he hadn't seen the car the shooter was in, but it felt wise to check, just in case.

Walking in, he was greeted by the store owner and manager.

"Ash, thank you for coming back today. I am sure it isn't easy for you to do so," the older man in a well-tailored suit said, holding out his hand.

Ash shook it and smiled.

"I am glad to be back at work, Sir."

As the owner and manager moved away, Ash's supervisor approached him.

"Hey, Ash, good to see you. We're opening in an hour, so can you do your usual set up to get ready? Take checkout number two. I think it'll either be dead today or it's going to be crazy."

"Sure," Ash replied and immediately moved into work mode. Despite his heart beating fiercely, he resolved to ignore it and just get on with his day as if it were any other regular day in his place of work.

~~~~~~

Charlie had a moment of uncertainty as she sat on the bus. Was she doing the right thing? For all she knew, she was walking into some kind of torture chamber owned by the same people who had shot at her and Max. She considered that and then shook the thought away. Tom seemed genuine. He was a bit old to be mixed up in anything like that, surely.

She disembarked the bus and walked the long journey until she was finally in front of the long, stretched-out house once more.

"Good morning, Miss Charlotte - oh, sorry, *Charlie*!" she heard Tom call out. "I am very pleased to see you back here again. I'm just giving the horses their morning feed. Will you come into the stable? We can chat as I do what I have to," he said, walking toward the structure she'd heard him talk on the phone in the day before. He turned to her with a humorous look on his face as he continued to speak. "They get all huffy if their breakfast is late, you know. A bit titchy, they can be, I tell you!"

Charlie tentatively moved forward until she was at the open stable doorway. Inside, it was dark. Once again, a fleeting moment of fear passed over her, making her question if she was doing a wise thing being there by herself.

"Your mother was afraid of horses too, the first time she came here. She was a city girl, through and through," Tom said, laughing softly as he readied feed.

"How did you meet her?"

"Ah, well, that is why I wanted to speak to you by yourself. Your mother came here with your father, of course. The first time I met her, they were only dating, mind you. Oh, she was beautiful. I can still remember the first moment I set eyes on her. She was a sight for sore eyes, and I don't mind admitting I was rightly jealous of your father for having secured *her* heart."

As Charlie started to relax, she moved into the stable a bit further.

"But why did my father bring her here?"

Tom stopped what he was doing and looked at her.

"This ranch, Charlie, belongs to your family," he said. "It has for many generations."

"But I've never heard of it."

Tom chuckled.

"Yes, it is one of the Stonewardens' best-kept secrets. When I've finished here, I'll take you inside and show you some of your family history. For now, let's just say that this place is a special place. It has stood for hundreds of years, providing refuge to those who need it."

"I … I don't understand," Charlie said, feeling unable to process what he was saying.

"I know. Everything will make more sense when we can move into the house. For now, though, can you pass me that bucket there by your feet?" Tom asked. "Now, how would you feel about doing some grooming? That young lass there that you rode yesterday - Missy is her name - loves to be brushed down first thing in the morning."

Charlie looked at the pony and was uncertain. Once Tom's persuasion won her over, she began receiving instruction on how to groom Missy 'just the way she likes it'.

"Right," Tom said a long while later after all of his morning chores were complete. "Let's go up to the house."

Charlie followed behind him, looking again at the long structure as they approached it.

"Why is it so large?" she asked.

Hearing her question, Tom laughed heartily.

"Because it was built to house a great many people. Your family was always large, no matter what the generation."

"But we don't live here."

"No," Tom said. "This isn't known to everyone in your family now. Even on paper, it's been hidden behind the documentation of trusts and businesses over the years."

"But *I'm* allowed to know?"

"I don't know if your father intended for you to

know, but he knows you made your way here yesterday, and he knows you're here now."

Through a side door, Charlie and Tom entered a large area that looked like it had been designed specifically as an intermediary area between the muddy outside and the clean inside. Charlie watched as Tom removed his boots and the long overcoat he'd been wearing, then moved to the large sink tub and started to scrub his hands.

"Come and wash your hands, lass," he said. "Horses are clean animals, but it's good practice to have a good wash after handling any animals."

Hands washed and dried, and footwear removed, Charlie was led through a door that led her to a main part of the expansive house. The front of the house had given her the impression that it was a fairly modern structure, built perhaps in the 1950s or 1960s. When she passed through that door, she felt like she was transported back into the pages of the history books she'd had to study at school.

Above her, Charlie saw the solid but irregularly cut and shaped rafters and beams. From them hung large black iron structures that still housed candles, although intertwined through and around them, she could see regular light fittings that had been made to fit seamlessly with the old.

Tom turned and watched her as she entered the room. The expression on her face was nothing new. He'd seen it many times before.

"It's a surprise, isn't it," he said. "This is the original part of the home. The front façade was added this century to make it look like any other house in the area."

"But this looks *really* old," Charlie said and saw him nod.

"It has been in the ownership of Stonewardens for a great many generations, lass. Follow me and let me show you something real special."

Charlie let him lead the way through the initial room they'd entered, and then around a sharp corner through another wider foyer area. Through one more door, they walked. On the other side of that lay one long room with four strong pillars evenly spaced in the middle of it, extending from the floor up to the roof. What caught Charlie's eyes were the portraits lining the walls. The room left her speechless.

"Come this way, Miss Charlotte. The story of your family, as far back as we know, begins here," Tom said, breaking her out of her surprise.

Charlie watched him move to the first portrait to the left of the door.

"Edward Stonewarden," he said as he pointed to the portrait. "The man who declared that he and his family would guard the jewels and keep them safe."

Charlie looked at the date on the portrait.

"1565? No, it can't be."

Tom laughed at her.

"Oh, yes it can."

"But this *painting* isn't that old," Charlie said quietly, the words forming more of a question than a statement.

She saw Tom smile at her in reply, silently telling her that it certainly was. Charlie felt her pulse speed increase at the thought of being a descendent of someone from that period of time. She followed Tom from portrait to portrait as decade after decade of century after century was broken down and explained by who was the head of the family of each time.

When they moved into the 1900s, her excitement and curiosity grew even more.

"This was your great grandfather, Richard Stonewarden," Tom continued. "He changed the way things worked forevermore."

"What do you mean?" asked Charlie, eager to

gain a full understanding of her family.

"Up till that time, the Stonewardens had been carers of gems. It was their role to look after them for the rich. Anyone who wanted their jewels kept safe would put their faith in a Stonewarden to do it. Once Richard Stonewarden took the business over, he saw different opportunities."

"You mean stealing?" she asked quietly, her head hung low.

"No! You mustn't think of it quite like that," Tom said. "What he wanted to do was even out wealth with poverty. He decided that he would change things so that a little bit of the wealth of the rich would be obtained, and then a process would happen that would make that wealth available to the poor."

"Like some kind of Robin Hood thing?"

She saw Tom nod in reply.

"In a way, yes."

They still stood before the large portrait of Richard, her great grandfather. To Charlie, he looked like the most morose and serious man she had ever seen the face of.

"He was the one who ensured places like this were secure from anyone else ever having them," Tom said.

"There are more places like this?"

"Oh, yes. Your family owns property like this around the world now, with travel being so easy nowadays."

"But do you really believe the Robin Hood thing is real?"

Tom seemed to disregard the question as he moved them along to the next portrait.

"Here is your grandfather, Thomas Stonewarden," he said. "He lived through the First and Second World Wars, and that made him hone the business systems even more. He watched as the wealthy and the poor grew more distant still, and he couldn't bear seeing people homeless. He helped set things up right and started using the family business to establish long term events such as donations to different charities. He started many of the donations that are still being made today by your father out of respect for the commitment made by your grandfather. He was a great, great man, your grandfather."

"You knew him then?"

"Oh, yes. I was working right here when your grandfather stepped down and your father came home and stepped up. Your father had been away in the wars, you see. No Stonewarden had been granted permission to leave the family like that previously, but your grandfather, in his plans to better secure the family and the business, felt that specialized military training could do no harm. He was forward-thinking for the time, your grandfather. Everything that was invented, he would jump in and buy or have set up. He'd then take the time to find the absolute best way to utilize it to the advantage of the business."

They moved to the last portrait in the line that ran around the walls.

"And now your father reigns the legacy of all these other Stonewardens. He was nervous about taking over the reins, but he is a fine Stonewarden indeed - as are all of you."

"Not me," Charlie said with conviction that made Tom smile. "I don't want to be part of it, Tom - not stealing. I know it's made out to be some kind of glamour, robbing from the rich and giving to the poor, but all I can see is stealing. It isn't right - not for me, anyway."

Tom nodded.

"Aye, I believe a few Stonewardens have felt that way, but all have done their duty when the time is right."

She looked at him, one very significant question

on her mind now.

"But where do *you* fit in, Tom?"

He looked at her and laughed softly.

"I am the last remaining Stonewarden from your grandfather's generation, Charlotte. I am your great uncle - your father's uncle."

"But Dad never talked about having any other living relatives."

"It is our family way," Tom said. "We keep quiet about everything. Each generation, a small crew silently works together to keep doing what the family has always done, but everything is kept quiet. Even this place is kept quiet. Your brothers may or may not know about this ranch, for example. I don't know if your father has chosen to tell them about it or not. Certainly, I've never seen any of them visit."

"But *why*?" Charlie asked, confused. "Why own such a place and never use or even visit it? That makes no sense!"

Tom led her slowly through another doorway and into a small room with only a wooden table and chairs that looked ancient to Charlie's young eyes. As they sat down, Tom saw her run her hands over the tabletop, as if lovingly caressing it.

"You appreciate fine furniture, don't you?" he asked, instantly seeing surprise on her face. "I see that you do. That is your heritage, Charlie. There have been many fine craftsmen in our family, and still are today."

"But who?"

"Well, me for one. Furniture making is a craft of mine. I receive a portion of earnings each month to purchase raw materials - mostly fine timber. I make quality furniture which we donate to schools, churches, and the like."

Charlie looked at him. Her mind was working overtime as if doing calculations in her head.

"So, you are part of my family," she said and saw

him nod. "And yet, *you* don't have to go out on the heists."

"It is true," Tom replied.

"So when my father told me that I had to join the business, he wasn't quite telling the truth."

"No, Charlie, he was telling you the absolute truth," Tom said. "He just didn't explain to you all of the *options* for working in the family business."

Seeing his face full of amusement, Charlie had to let his words play through her mind to make sense of them.

"I told my father I didn't want to steal," she said. "Are you saying that there might be another option available to me to still commit to the family business, but not work on the heists with my father and brothers?"

Tom smiled at her and nodded.

"It is up to your father, of course," he said. "Although I am much older than him, I have no right to tell him how things are to be done. He *is* the family head now. If he says you are to join him and your brothers in their work, I am afraid not much could be done about that."

"But I have no skills in furniture making. I have no skills in *anything*!"

Tom laughed softly.

"Everyone can learn a skill, Charlie," he reassured her. "Yes, even you."

At that moment, the door opened and a woman came through it, smiling at both of them.

"Now Charlotte, please allow me to introduce my wife - your great aunt," said Tom. "Molly, this is Charlotte. Charlotte, this is Molly."

The older woman came forward and reached out to take Charlie's hand in both of hers.

"Charlotte, it is a great pleasure to meet you. Tom was excited last night when he told me you'd turned up here without any knowledge of how special this place was to your family. It was a sign, I told him - a sign that you are meant to be here."

At those words, a light bulb went off in Charlie's head. Tom could almost see it happen. He smiled at her but said nothing.

"Thank you, but please call me Charlie," she replied. "I do prefer it. I'm not really much of a Charlotte."

"Alright, Charlie," Molly said, nodding. "Tom also told me there was a young man with you when you arrived yesterday. Perhaps you would like some girl to girl talk?"

Charlie laughed, instantly liking her great aunt.

"He - Ash - is someone I met a while ago. I do like him … a lot."

"Well, perhaps you might like to bring him out here again sometime. I trust you will be coming back to visit us, now that you know we are here?"

Charlie smiled and nodded.

"I would really like that, but I don't want to put you out…"

"No, not at all," said Molly. "This is a large house. You are welcome to come and visit. Perhaps sometimes you might like to come and stay. Maybe your young man would like to as well."

"Pardon me?" Tom jumped into the conversation, sounding shocked at the idea, and making Charlie laugh at the two of them.

"Oh, I meant to stay in a different bedroom, of course," Molly said before leaning in closer to Charlie. "He's so old fashioned! I remember one time when he was courting me…"

"Molly!" Tom jumped in again, making Charlie giggle loudly. Yes, she definitely would enjoy spending time with *those* two relations.

When her laughter subsided, Charlie remembered the reason she had come to the ranch in the first place.

"I would like to know more about my mother," she said. "I remember her, but I want to learn more about what kind of person she was. What she liked. What she didn't like. Can you tell me?"

Tom replied, his voice full of emotion.

"Aye, your mother was very welcome here," he said. "She was a lovely lady. It wasn't hard to see why your father fell for her as hard as he did. I never would've imagined him to fall for anyone, he was such an independent soul, but he did - and hard! Even your grandfather was surprised, and a little resistant at first. It isn't easy letting people into our family with what we do. You have to know you can truly trust them, Charlie. Make sure that young man of yours earns your trust completely. It's easy to get caught up in the freshness and excitement of … well, I'm sure you know, being the age you are. But you have to look beyond that and see the real person who is there - not through rose-colored glasses. No, you have to take the time and use your determination to really *see* them. Only when you are absolutely sure, let them ease into your family."

Charlie watched as Molly moved closer to Tom and took his hand in hers.

"Yes, it can be difficult for an outsider," she said. "It took a long while for me to get to know Tom because he was so closed off about everything. He had to be, of course, but it made getting to know one another difficult at times. But we persevered - well, *he* persevered - in chasing me. And here we are, having now been married for almost fifty years. Even knowing the things that they do, well, I wouldn't trade my life with Tom for anything."

Charlie felt emotional - so much so that she could feel a tear threatening. She rubbed her eye to stop the tear before it could become visible. How would it feel to experience such love in one's lifetime? *For* one's lifetime? How could she determine how she truly felt about Ash or anyone else she might become involved with?

"You'll just know," Molly said as if she'd heard Charlie's thoughts spoken out loud.

~~~~

After talking and enjoying lunch with her newfound relatives, Charlie withdrew and began her journey home. She had a lot to think about. Before she'd left, Tom had reminded her that her brothers might not know about the ranch. If they didn't, it was because her father deemed it necessary to keep it from them. It was not up to her to take things into her own hands and tell them such a thing. She had nodded and promised she would keep it to herself. She'd also promised that she would return the following week. Now that she'd found Tom and Molly, she wanted to keep getting to know them.

Walking into her home, she wondered if her father would say anything to her when he saw her. She was relieved to see he wasn't at home. She had so much to process in her thoughts. It would be easier to do that alone.

Before she headed up the staircase to her bedroom, she took a moment to sit down in the lounge and close her eyes. So much seemed to have happened in such a short amount of time. Max being in a coma and then waking up. Meeting Ash and starting to realize how much pleasure he could provide her in his company. And now, meeting relations she'd never heard of, who had also known her mother.

Her peaceful meditation was interrupted by footsteps bounding down the stairs. She was surprised to see Fitz appear before her. Even though he officially lived in the house, generally no-one ever knew where he was.

"Hi! Bye!" he threw at her as he sauntered past and out the front door.
~~~~

Charlie moved to the window, curious about where her brother went and what he did with his time. Seeing him simply start to walk down the road didn't help tame that curiosity at all. One day, when everything was completely back to normal, she'd like to follow him. One day.

Next, she heard a car pull into the driveway, followed by the opening of the front door. In walked her father, surprising her while at the same time making her apprehensive about how things would pan out between them. Would he be angry that she'd found the ranch and asked as many questions as she had? Had Tom reported in and told her father everything about the conversations they'd shared?

"Hey," Mitchell said to her when he noticed her sitting in silence in their living area. "Are you alright?"

She nodded but said nothing.

"I need to have a word with Fitz…"

"You just missed him - literally, minutes ago," she said. "I'm surprised you didn't drive past him."

"Ugh! That kid. He *knew* I needed to talk to him!" Mitchell said with determination in his voice.

Charlie watched as he moved into the kitchen, situated across the foyer from the living area. She could hear him opening and closing the refrigerator, then the cupboards, one by one. Shortly afterward, he returned to her side of the house and stood in front of her.

"I'm going to buy groceries," Mitchell said. "Do you want to come?"

Charlie felt herself freeze at the suggestion. It was unreasonable to act in such a way, but she couldn't help it.

As Mitchell watched her face, his previous frustration at his youngest son instantly evaporated. He sat down beside her on the couch, facing her straight on.

"Charlie, do you want to talk to someone about the shooting?" he asked.

"What do you mean?"

"Someone … like a counselor."

Charlie shook her head, slightly annoyed that he would suggest such a thing.

"No! I'm fine," she said. "I'll come with you. Once I've been back there the first time, I won't give the last time another thought."

Mitchell wondered if that were true, but nodded at her.

"Alright, let's go."

~~~~~

As the two of them walked from the car toward the main doors of the supermarket, Charlie felt her anxiety heighten. She slowed her breath and tried to focus on something else. Looking through the new panes of glass, she let her eyes wander until they found Ash chatting and smiling at a customer at checkout. That focus she held, looking at him and forcing her mind to think of more pleasurable things as she walked through the large sliding doors with her father beside her.

Once inside, she did a quick scan of the checkout area and saw that for that moment, things were quiet.

"I'll find you in a minute, Dad," she said and immediately walked away.

Mitchell followed her line of direction and saw Ash on checkout. He smiled to himself. If there was something that could take her mind off the horror of what she'd been through and what she'd seen that day, love could probably be it. He wasn't ready to let himself believe that his daughter would find love so easily or so young, but if for the moment it took her mind off things that affected her, he could accept it.

"Hey," Charlie said to Ash as she approached him when the last customer in his queue had moved away. Instantly she saw his face light up in a large grin.

"Hey. How was your ranch visit?" he asked, trying to keep his mind off the subject of pleasure as he
~~~~~

took in the sight of her lips that he'd very much enjoyed kissing.

Ash watched as she bent forward against the checkout counter, leaning toward him. He didn't think she'd done it intentionally, but the way her v-neck t-shirt gaped as she leaned over made him heated at the view. His thoughts on waiting until marriage before having sex with anyone were always going to be in question when he was around her. She was alluring, and the fact that she didn't know she was alluring made her even *more* alluring.

Abruptly he raised his eyes to hers, to focus on what she was saying.

"I enjoyed it," Charlie said. "I learned a lot today. Some details I will keep to myself, but Tom did extend an invitation for you and I both to go back and visit another time if you'd like to."

He nodded and smiled at her.

"Does that mean we get to attempt riding horses again?"

Charlie laughed at the memory. She could still feel that ride in her butt muscles.

"We could if you want to give it another go. You did look hot on that pony."

Ash laughed out loud at her, knowing he must have looked as uncomfortable as he'd felt on his first attempt at riding a horse.

"Well, if I look hot on a pony, then we should definitely do it again," he said and winked at her, making her laugh softly in reply.

As Charlie saw a customer heading toward the checkout, she pulled away.

"I'm going to go and find Dad. He's in here somewhere."

Ash watched her discreetly while he greeted the customer who approached. While beginning to scan the items on the conveyor belt in front of him, he watched as

Charlie walked away. Front view or back, he wondered if he would ever tire of looking at her.

~~~~~

Back in the hospital, Max was starting to feel like himself again. His family still huddled close by, but he knew he had to appreciate that rather than object to it.

"What do you know about this guy who's hanging around Charlie?" James asked him.

Max prepared himself for some uneasiness for his sister. He agreed that they all should be protective over her to a degree, but she was growing up, and she was strong. He had no doubts about that whatsoever.

"James, he's a good guy," he said. "Don't go making trouble for him. He was here every day for Charlie, when there was nothing in it for him to be. Give him a chance. Give *them* a chance."

"You're getting soft already, little brother," James said partially in jest.

"Yeah, well, it's about time that you found some chick to hook up with, don't you think?"

James smiled at him in his macho pride way.

"I get my share of chicks," he said. "Don't you worry about that!"

Max rolled his eyes as his older brother. With five years between them, they had a brotherly relationship where sometimes they got on and hung out. At other times they had completely separate lives - more so since James had moved out of the family home.

"Well, if Ash keeps being as good a guy as he has been so far, I am happy for Charlie. She needs someone to lean on…"

"She has *us*!" James exclaimed.

"We aren't always there for her," Max replied. "With everyone's jobs and the family business, she's on her own most of the time. You know she's never been one to have close friends. She was always on her own after Mum died, so she's grown up thinking and acting
~~~~~

for herself. No, it's nice to see her enjoying someone's company. Please, just let her enjoy it."

James looked reluctant but nodded his head.

"I trust your gut, Max," he said. "If you think he's okay, I'll keep out of it. But if he hurts her in any way…"

"Yeah, yeah, you'll become a fist-fighting ogre," Max retorted. "I get it."

James laughed but backed off from saying anything more.

"So when are they letting you out of this place?" asked James. "You should be at home."

"The doctors are doing tests tomorrow. Then I'll know. Why? Are you getting sick of being here? Because you don't have to sit with me, you…"

"Calm down. It was just a question. Don't go thinking I don't like hanging out with you, 'cause I do," James said before smiling and speaking further in a whisper. "Besides the female nurses and doctors here are hot!"

After another eye roll from Max, James heard the question he'd pondered earlier but then forgotten.

"Did you find my car?"

Max saw the look of remembering come to the mind of his brother.

"No," James said. "A few times, we've headed out and asked around, but it's like it just vanished. Sorry, Max, but I can't give you any good news on that front."

"That's cool. I'll hunt it down when I get out of here," Max replied. "How far could it have gone?"

"Yeah, but you need to talk to Dad about it. He handles all the vehicle insurance. I don't know what he's doing about that, or what the police are doing to find your wheels, if they're doing anything."

"I'm not worried," Max said, smiling sadly. "My baby will come home. I know it."

~~~~~

Mitchell wandered slowly through the
~~~~~

supermarket. Now and then, he'd stopped and discretely watched his daughter chatting to Ash at checkout. He wasn't ready to give his little girl up, but he remembered falling in love. He wouldn't deny her the opportunity if it was on offer. Looking at the two of them and the way they looked at each other made him think back to when he'd met her mother. She had captured him completely - initially because she was so beautiful, but mostly because of her intelligence. The two of them could talk for hours on end and never feel like anything was stilted or uncomfortable. It had all been so natural.

Thinking about his wife, he felt emotional, so concentrated even more heavily on the task at hand. Still, on occasion, he cried when he thought about her. It had been nine years since she'd passed and left him with their six children, but thinking about her did make him cry when he gave into his thoughts and memories. It was wrong that she was taken so young. He'd had to step up and try to be not only a father to their children but also a mother to them - particularly Charlie, but she'd turned out fine. Hell, if he was honest with himself, she'd turned out amazing. She wasn't a social kid and never had been, but she knew who she was, and she stood tall in that.

"Dad," he heard her voice call out to him from behind. He turned to see her approaching him. "What else do we need to get?"

Mitchell was glad of the interruption into his thoughts. He thought Max might be discharged from the hospital. When that happened, he wanted the house to be well-stocked. As long as it would take, he would stay at home and monitor his son once he was home again. Everything was on hold, especially the family business. The jobs were important, but not as important as his kids' lives.

"Milk," he said, trying to give Charlie a mission that would occupy her and keep her mind stress free also. "Six liters."

Charlie looked at her father as if he were crazy.

"Are we expecting company? That's a lot of milk for us."

"I am hoping Max will be coming home any day now," Mitchell said. "You know how much he loves downing bowls of that sugary stuff he calls cereal."

Charlie laughed. There was no doubting that. Max had always veered toward sugary cereals. They were his chosen snack food. Not chips, cookies, or ice cream. With Max, it was always go to the kitchen, grab a bowl, and fill it with cereal and milk. She nodded at her father and then turned to walk to the milk chiller.

After a few more missions, their shopping trolley was full.

"Right. Are we going through your friend's lane, or are we avoiding it?" Mitchell asked her, amusement in his voice even though he was seriously asking the question.

"*Dad*. Ash is the only one on right now, so we have to go through there."

"Alright," Mitchell replied. "Let's go then."

Once at checkout, he slyly watched out the corner of his eye, studying the interaction between Ash and Charlie. There was no doubting that it was equal, whatever it was. He was glad. He would have hated to see his baby girl want something from someone who wasn't as into her as she was into him. Mitchell didn't think there were any worries there. The look on Ash's face as he looked at her was clear as day, even if he didn't realize it.

When all items had been scanned, Ash told Mitchell the total sum and quietly and professionally processed the payment.

"Thanks, Ash," Charlie heard her father say before he slowly veered away with the trolley laden with foodstuffs.

Charlie approached Ash, leaning over his counter

once more. He laughed softly, wondering if she *did,* in fact, know what she was doing, leaning in such a way.

"What time do you finish?" she asked.

"Not till six tonight, although if it stays as quiet as this, I might get away earlier. What are you up to?"

"I don't know, but I'd love to kiss you," Charlie said, seeming to temporarily stun him into silence before she saw him deliver the widest grin.

"I suffer from that feeling right now, too, but I can see my supervisor coming…"

Charlie immediately pulled herself away, smiled at him, and started to follow her father out the outer supermarket doors. Ash looked after her, his heart heavy. No plans had been made to see each other when he finished work. Perhaps that was a good thing. They had been spending a lot of time together, and that wasn't reality. *Now* reality was beginning again, with him working the different shifts he needed to. He wouldn't see her as much. He sincerely hoped that they didn't drift apart. There was still far too much getting-to-know-one-another to be done.

~~~~~~

"After we put all this away, I'm going to head off to the hospital to see Max. Do you want to come with me?" her father asked as they placed all their purchases on the large kitchen table.

Charlie wondered why her father still didn't bring up the subject of the ranch. Was he angry at her for going there? Did he prefer that it didn't exist? She wouldn't ask him. It wasn't the way in their family to question their father too often about too many things. If he wasn't talking about it, he had a reason he believed he shouldn't.

"Yeah, I'll come in," Charlie replied. "I hope he comes home soon."

Mitchell looked at her. Charlie and Max certainly didn't squabble like other siblings did. For that, he'd
~~~~~~

always been thankful, but he also knew that out of his six children, the two of them shared the closest bond.

"He'll be released when the doctors are sure he's okay. We don't want him home any sooner than that."

~~~~~

James looked up to see his father and sister enter the room where he'd been sitting with Max for what seemed like hours. He loved his brother but sitting in one place was enough to make him feel like he'd go nuts if he didn't move sometime soon.

"Hey, Charles!" Max threw out as a quip as the two newcomers entered the room. Ever since the day Charlotte had insisted everyone call her Charlie, Max had started to periodically remind her that Charlie was short for Charles. He didn't do it very often anymore, but when he did, he always made her smile at his silly humor.

"Hey, Maxine!" Charlie threw back and heard him chuckle slightly. They were always growing and changing. Regardless, now and then, it felt good to revert to behaviors of childhood.

"Has the doctor been through?" Mitchell asked.

Max nodded.

"Yeah. They're doing a few more tests later," he said. "I'm staying here tonight but should be able to go home tomorrow if everything looks okay."

James watched the interactions in the room for only a few minutes before he felt the calling to leave and be free.

"I'm outta here. I'll see you guys later," he said. His father turned to him and pulled him into a hug. It was a little out of character for Mitchell but James went with it and returned the masculine hug and slap on the back.

"Don't disappear," Mitchell said and saw James nod before smiling at his brother and sister and leaving the room.
~~~~~

As he walked out, he felt a sense of freedom fall over him. Recently he'd been splitting his time between the family business, sitting with Max, and trying to hold down a regular job too. Not that he minded sitting with his brother, of course. Max was the most likable brother he had. But as tough as he was on the outside, there were times when James wished he could be recognized for more.

People liked him, for sure. And the women - yep, no doubt about that. He'd learned early on how to charm the pants off them - literally. He wasn't cut out for love. He knew that, but he knew how to enjoy himself, and he knew how to make sure a woman enjoyed herself when she was with him. Who needed love? It was a big waste of time. People kept saying they were in love with someone, and later hated that person. So what was the point? No, he'd never fall into that trap.

With all that he'd been doing in recent times, however, he did feel long overdue in the *loving* department. Yes, that was a good idea, he thought as he walked out of the hospital doors for hopefully the last time. He needed to find a woman to escape the harshness of reality with - just for a few hours.

Pulling his phone from his pocket, he flicked through the contact list. If anyone ever saw it, they might shake their head in wonder at how many women's names and numbers were stored in it, but he was who he was. Sometimes he liked chocolate milkshakes. Sometimes he liked banana milkshakes. Sometimes he liked lasses such as Jessica. Sometimes he liked lasses such as … *Katy*! Ahh, sweet Katy. Yes, she had some tricks that he could enjoy. Immediately he called and was greeted by the sweet voice.

"James Stonewarden. It's been a while. What can I do for you?"

"Well, I was hoping you might like to … swing by my apartment for a couple of hours?" he asked, and heard her laugh at the end of the phone.

"You horny or what?" she asked, straight to the point as always.

"I'm horny for *you*," he replied, the anticipation of the possibility pushing him into an aroused state that was revealed in his voice.

"I can already tell," she replied. "Tell you what. I'm at work and have to be here for another hour. I can stop by after that if you want."

"I want," James replied, making her laugh again.

"Alright horny boy. I'll see you then. Answer the door naked."

James smiled and heard her hang up. Looking at his watch, he took note of the time. An hour she'd said. The smile on his face was broad. It had indeed been far too long.

When he entered his apartment, he was reminded of how little time he'd been spending there. The state of the living room, as soon as he walked in the door, overwhelmed him. Not that Katy would see anything. He knew what she was like. Straight to the bedroom was her style. She was a kindred spirit. She knew that sex was sex, and it was sometimes needed just like a scratch was to an itch. They'd never dated. They'd never even suggested such an idea. They scratched each other's itch. Nothing more. Perfect.

The first stop for him was the bedroom. They were play friends, but he still believed she deserved respect. Respect in that instance meant clean sheets and a perfectly made bed. It would get mussed up in an hour, but who cared? It was still nice to make the effort for her. Clean sheets, covers all in place, pillows fluffed up and perfectly placed - oh, and a handful of condoms on the side table. When he'd done all that, he stood back and looked at the room. The result made him smile, and aroused. He could almost see what they'd be doing on that bed soon.

Switching his mind away from his anticipation of pleasure, he jumped in the shower and got to work on his second job. It was always good to be looking and smelling fine for Katy. She deserved nothing less. After shampoo, soap, toothpaste, and a long, slow shave, he knew he was looking good. He wrapped a bath towel around his hips and walked out to the living room.

After the sweet smells of the bathroom, the lack of fresh air in there was even more evident. He opened the large sliding door to the balcony and felt the warm, fresh air flow through. The rest of the job didn't look so good, but he got to it. Pizza boxes flattened for recycling. Dirty clothes into the washing machine. Magazines, DVDs, and his comic collection tidied and put away on the bookshelf. One last tidy fluff-up of cushions. The only thing he wouldn't do was vacuuming. The floor could use it, but there was no way he was turning that thing on and risk missing hearing her knock on his door.

He sat down on the couch and closed his eyes, enjoying the silence and the solitude. He'd had to move out of the Stonewarden family home to find it, and he loved it. Everyone had said when he left that he'd get lonely. Lonely? No, never. Horny, yes. Lonely, no. It felt good to be able to just have time to himself without constantly having to consider other people in close vicinity.

Leaning back as he was, his body should have been waking up to what was about to happen. Instead, he fell asleep.

Woken by the knocking on his door, he vaguely stood and went to open it. He was greeted by Katy, looking amused at the state of him.

"So this is how excited you get when I'm coming over? You fall asleep?" she teased him as she walked into the apartment. When she turned back to look at him, she saw him look sheepish as he ran his fingers through his thoroughly imperfect hair.

"I was dreaming about you. Does that score me any points?" he asked, making her laugh.

"Points scored. Although points lost, too, since you don't appear to be naked," she continued, pointing at his towel.

James could see her teasing in her eyes, but he could also feel himself becoming aroused the more he looked at her lips. The outline under the towel revealed precisely how he was starting to feel.

"Hmm," Katy said as she moved closer. "Yes, I think this needs to go."

James enjoyed the feeling that came from her moving right up to him and making the neatly secured towel fall to the floor. He was awake - *very* awake. His lips crushed down on hers as he felt her reach out and take him in her hand, stroking him. No more words were needed.

He pulled away long enough to secure direction as he walked her backward toward his bedroom. Kissing her deeply, he was even more aware of just how hungry he'd been in recent weeks. When they reached the edge of the bed, she pushed him back and watched him move up the bed. There he lay back and started to stroke himself as she slowly but artfully did a striptease for him. Always she loved doing that for him, and he had no objection whatsoever. She was good at what she did.

When naked, she climbed onto the bed and moved over him to kiss him. He moved both of his hands into her hair and pulled her roughly to him. When they'd kissed so much that he heard her moaning, he flipped her over onto her back and looked down the length of her body. She was in good shape. He loved it her beautiful flat belly, her toned legs, and the way she was always impeccably groomed.

Enclosing one of her breasts with his hand, he flicked his tongue over her nipple, immediately feeling her squirm under his touch. Always she was so receptive to his touch. As his other hand snaked down, he felt her open her thighs to grant access. He knew how to touch her. He knew how to *please* her. And whenever he felt her completely hairless there, his arousal grew stronger.

He kissed her lips once more, deeply, before moving down to taste her. It had been far too long since he'd done that. There was nothing like the taste of a woman. He indulged in her creaminess while enjoying listening to her sounds of acknowledgment that he was touching her exactly how she loved it. He was enraptured. When he was between a woman's thighs like that, he never wanted to be anywhere else. When Katy clenched her thighs around him, and he felt her shudder, he was ready. They never spent any time between her orgasm and him moving into her, doing anything loving like kissing and caressing. Whenever she was climaxing, James was already beside her, putting on a condom, and then plunging into her.

Katy gasped as she felt him fill her. He wasn't gentle, but he never hurt her either. It was like he knew the exact force she liked. She, too, was happy with their when-both-in-the-mood arrangement. Her life was her own, and she wanted it like that. She equally wouldn't trade time with James Stonewarden for anything.

She felt him push into her fully before pulling almost right out again, over and over. She felt him move into that place where he was in his own zone, and she enjoyed it. She liked feeling and hearing him grow more and more excited when he was thrusting into her like he was. He was a beautiful, strong, and well-toned man, and he moved in her beautifully.

James felt his orgasm coming and let it wash over him. It had been a long while since he'd last climaxed, so he had the mixed feeling of pain and pleasure as the huge amount of semen ejaculated out of him. When it had been too long, it felt like too much was trying to escape all at once. It was a different kind of feeling, but it didn't prevent him from experiencing the feeling of relief as his body finally released, and he was left with tingling throughout all of his muscles.

Katy lay still as she felt him slump down onto her. While his chin rested on her shoulder, she could sense him relaxing and getting his breathing under control. She stroked his back, from his shoulders to his buttocks, gently but firmly.

"You aren't going to sleep there, are you?" she asked with a teasing tone in her voice.

After a long while, she saw James lift his head and look at her. She thought he'd be smiling. Instead, he looked intense.

James pulled away and out of her. After ridding himself of the latex engulfing him, he lay on his back beside her, coaxing her to move against him in a simple cuddle.

"I can't stay long. My mother wants me to go to her place tonight for a family dinner," Katy said quietly.

James turned his head so that he could look into her eyes.

"Best we not waste a minute then," he said, finding the thought of having to enjoy her quickly quite enough for his body to wake up again.

He watched Katy as she smiled and kissed him deeply before straddling him. After he handed her another condom, he watched as she rolled it onto him and then slid down over him. He was happy to lie back and enjoy the view and the delicious sensations she invoked in him from her movements.

Riding him steadily, Katy felt in awe of how they felt together, but even the position she was in seemed suddenly not quite enough.

James watched as she lifted off him and turned completely around, straddling him again but with her back to him. As she slid down onto him, he thought he was in heaven. Her hands were on his knees. He held his head forward slightly as she started to move with increasing tempo and depth. Watching the back of her rising and lowering on him was almost more than he could bear, but he held back. He knew from their previous times together that she was magical in being able to orgasm in the position. He closed his eyes and tried to focus on anything else to hold back his climax until he felt and heard her reach her blissful place. As soon as he had that confirmation, he let go, his second orgasm intense as it flowed through him.

"Hmmm," he heard her say, as if in the distance. "I'm glad you called today. I think I needed that as much as you did."

He laughed softly at her as she withdrew and turned around to kiss him. He held her close to him, but soon she was pulling away.

"I need to get going, and you look like *you* need sleep!" Katy said as she started to dress.

James watched but didn't move. It was always the way with them. They served a purpose to each other, and they felt good together. But a little part of him was starting to wish that she - or *someone* - would want to spend more time with him outside of the bedroom.

"Hey, I'll see you next time, huh?" she said before walking out the door.

James lay on his bed, wide awake for a long time, his mind working hard. He didn't want a relationship - did he?

The thought was forgotten as his body took control, and he once again drifted off to sleep.

CHAPTER EIGHT

When Ash finished work, he contemplated messaging Charlie to see what she was up to. He contemplated it as he packed up and walked out the door. He contemplated it as he began his walk home. He even contemplated it when he entered his apartment. In the back of his mind was a nagging feeling that now that he was back at work and Max was on the mend, life might go back to how it had been before the shooting. He would see Charlie now and then when she bought groceries, and she would never really notice him.

He changed out of his uniform and had a quick shower before sitting down to watch a movie. Being pushy wasn't something he wanted to be. He worried that he might push Charlie too hard and make her bolt.

Just after he'd started the opening scenes of the movie, his phone awoke with the sound of a text message coming in.

'I'm leaving the hospital soon. Are you still working?' Charlie's message read.

Ash considered his options on how to respond and *whether* to respond. Ignoring her message wasn't something he'd do. He couldn't be dishonest with Charlie. She deserved better than that.

'I am at home now. Just put a DVD on.'

'Want some company?' her text asked, making Ash smile.

'I want YOUR company.'

'I'll be there in half an hour. Don't press play yet!'

He read the messages over and over. The desire to keep spending time together wasn't one way. It couldn't be when she was sending him messages like that.

Thinking of ways to fill in the time, he moved to

his kitchen and pulled out his popcorn maker. By the time Charlie arrived, the tiny apartment was full of the smell of fresh buttery popcorn.

"You cooked? For me?" she teased.

"Haha. Smartypants," Ash said, grinning. "Movie, popcorn, and you beside me. Sounds like a perfect evening to me."

Charlie kissed him and wrapped her arms around him. She was glad he didn't seem to want to push her for specific details about her visit to the ranch. It was too early for her to be able to talk about all that she'd learned. He still didn't know the kind of people her family actually were, even though he'd met just about all of them.

Ash kissed her softly, then with more pressure. Every time they kissed, the time from the first touch of lips till the moment when he felt himself grow inside his jeans was lessening. She was affecting him more often and more deeply each time they were together. Aware of the reaction of his body, he kissed her once more but then pulled away, leading her to the couch.

"Come on over and sit right here beside me," he said, sitting down himself and patting the seat beside him in invitation.

Charlie gladly moved to his side and cuddled into him. She was more than ready to turn her mind off to everything except the movie and the feel and smell of him next to her.

During the span of the movie time, they ate, laughed, and held each other. Ash's hand held hers, but now and then, during the quieter moments of the story, Charlie could feel his fingers slowly and lightly caressing the back of her hand. She closed her eyes during those times, focusing on the exquisite simplicity of delicious feeling that came from his touch. More and more, she found herself wishing for him to touch her more and explore her - to wake her up and let her know how good things could be between them if they both let down their guard and indulged in it.

By the time the movie finished, Ash was enflamed. It had been an exercise in just doing something uneventful together, but the closeness of her beside him was almost excruciating. After turning off the TV, he moved his body slightly so he was facing her. Looking into her eyes, he felt sure the feelings weren't one-sided. Definitely not. She looked like she was alight. He raised both of his hands and cupped her head in them, her mouth only inches from his own.

"Do you know what you do to me?" he asked her.

Charlie could hear his voice much lower than it usually was, and quieter. The tone of it added to her extreme alertness and the feelings rushing through every muscle in her body.

"I do," she said. "You do it to me too."

The contrast between what Ash's body was screaming out for them to do, and what his heart and mind were also calling to him to do, was unbearable. He couldn't think. It was too hard to. Instead, he crushed her lips with his own, letting his desire take over. They were beyond being happy with simple kissing. Their tongues needed to meld and be even closer, for even longer.

Their bodies moved together while remaining fully dressed. The layers between them stopped them from moving to where both had said they would not. The barrier of clothing encouraged the glorious feelings to flow from the friction created.

When she pushed him back and straddled him while kissing him, Ash could feel her hips grinding against his own, pelvis to pelvis. The level of excitement he felt was immense but bittersweet. He wanted more, but he also wanted it to stop. The excitement was growing to a dangerous level. Ash had a fleeting thought - if he couldn't hold back, at least it would be contained. Regardless, he was determined to do all he could to stop himself from going over the edge into a climax.

Charlie rubbed herself against him. The sensations she was feeling, she'd never felt before - not quite like that. She'd kissed boys. She'd even had a boyfriend who had put his hand up her t-shirt and groped her. Those situations hadn't prepared her for how she felt when with Ash. She felt like she was in free fall, and it was glorious!

As their tongues danced together and Charlie continued to rub against him, she felt a wave flow over her. Without any idea how verbal she was about it, she rode it out and enjoyed the experience of the new feelings.

The deep groan that emanated from her as she climaxed pushed Ash over the brink. There was no more holding back as he felt orgasm engulf him, followed by the realization that he was now wet inside his jeans.

For a long while, they looked at each other while remaining silent.

"I've never felt anything like that," Charlie said.

Ash believed her. Orgasms weren't new to him. He was a 20-year-old male and had learned about them years earlier. They were a frequent part of his life. That didn't stop him thinking he'd never before felt like he had when he'd climaxed with her on top of him. Looking into her eyes, he was inspired to keep kissing herm showering her with soft, short kisses, over and over again.

"I need to go to the bathroom," he said, feeling slightly uncomfortable with the wetness in his pants. "Wait. I'll be right back."

Charlie moved off him and watched him walk away from her. She felt a little surprised at what had happened but liked it.

Ash stood in the bathroom, cleaning himself up. Looking in the mirror, he could see that there were no visible signs of what had happened. The outer layer of his jeans at least was still dry. He looked in the mirror and cursed himself slightly. He was the older one of the two of them by two years. It was up to him to be responsible and not let them go where neither of them wanted to go. It wasn't easy. Not only did he feel a strong emotional bond with her, but she was just so desirable and *hot*.

Charlie waited on the sofa for him to return. The time alone gave her a moment to think. She knew her thoughts on waiting to have sex were rapidly changing. Her body was on fire. She wanted it all, and she wanted it with him.

When Ash returned to the small living area, he sat beside her once again. They looked at each other before he kissed her. Those lips just couldn't be looked at and ignored.

"I should get home soon," Charlie said.

Ash nodded, suddenly overwhelmed with emotion at being in her presence   .

"I'll walk you," he replied. He felt like he should say something else - something more. If he was honest with himself, he was slightly stunned at the way his feelings had gotten away from him. He wanted to yell out to her and the rest of the world that he loved her. He knew that was crazy. They'd only just met.

When she stood up, Ash followed. Before they left the apartment, he pulled her into his arms and kissed her lovingly. He was desperate to make sure she understood his feelings through the kiss. He was glad when she responded by seeming to melt against him.

Finally, they pulled apart and began their journey to her home.

After kissing her sweetly goodnight on the front porch of the large homestead, Ash walked back to his apartment. His heart felt warm inside his chest. The feeling he tried to quash. Obviously, it was the sexual release that had triggered a false feeling of love. It needed to be ignored. It wasn't real. It was just his brain playing tricks on him, trying to make him equate sex with love.

It just wasn't real.

~~~~~

"When are we doing the next job?" Charlie heard as she entered the front door of her home. She was smiling when she came through the door. She stopped smiling as soon as she heard those words.

The talking immediately stopped. That told Charlie that whoever was in the room had heard her come in. Leaning around the doorway, she briefly smiled at Vic and her father before running up the staircase and going to her bedroom. She didn't want to hear about the family business. She didn't know what her father and brothers were going to do next. Her bedroom door was closed. That was her way of closing her mind to the subject at all.

Downstairs, Mitchell turned to his oldest son.

"We're not, at least not for the moment," he said. "Max comes home tomorrow. I want him to be able to focus on getting completely better. I don't want him hearing pockets of information and doing something rash when he isn't ready."

Vic nodded. He looked forward to the day when his father would hand the reins over to him to run the business, but he could wait. The idea of having a break from the intensity of research, planning, and preparation wasn't a bad one. They didn't have a schedule of jobs set out. For them, their business ran on opportunity and knowledge. When the perfect opportunity appeared before them, they spent as many months as they needed to, to plan for it. Then they took full advantage of it. Vic had been doing it long enough to understand how the business worked. He knew the individual strengths of his father and brothers and how they needed to work together to ensure everything went smoothly. He was
~~~~~

ready to take over, but he would wait. When the time was right, he had no doubt that his father would summon him and tell him to step up. When that day came, he would gladly do it.

"Alright. I'm going to head home," Vic said before he walked out.

Left alone, Mitchell sat on the couch and closed his eyes to relax. His son was awake from his coma and was coming home. That was a relief. If he wasn't well enough, the hospital wouldn't be releasing him, so it was great news. He knew he should be focusing on the business, but something had changed in his perspective since the shooting. He believed in family honor and commitment, but he'd also been reminded that life could be short. It was a lesson he'd learned when his wife had died nine years earlier. He knew to make the most of each day. Somewhere along the way, he kept forgetting it.

Taking a moment to think about his wife, he also let his mind wander to his daughter. She was on her own journey of discovery, learning about her heritage. He believed that she knew he was aware of her spending time at the family ranch, but he didn't approach the subject with her. He didn't want to influence her there. She could push as hard as she wanted to, and Tom would tell her all he knew. If she didn't want to know, that would be okay too. Mitchell knew it had to be her choice, just as it was her choice to act as she wanted in love.

Ash. Mitchell thought about him and sighed. His baby girl was growing up. Would Charlie want to marry, settle down, and become a mother? He silently scoffed at his thinking. Just because she was a female, he assumed she wanted love and children. He never made such an assumption with his sons. His wife would have been appalled at such blatant gender assumption, but maybe it wasn't so much the matter of their gender differences that made him wonder such a thing. Perhaps it was more just an accurate analysis of their personalities that made him wonder where Charlie would want to go in the next few years.

He already knew she didn't want to do what he and the boys did. She had made that perfectly clear to him when he'd sat her down for their conversation on her 18th birthday. He, in turn, had told her that she would be moving into the business when she turned nineteen. Even he wasn't sure if he would follow through with that one, but he was moving forward as if he would. Everyone was recruited on their 19th birthday. It would seem unfair to simply let her choose to not be a part of it.

But the boy - what was he to do about that? What would her mother do, knowing their daughter was getting involved with someone? Would the two of them sit down and have girl-talk about Charlie's feelings? Would they avoid the conversation entirely? Always, since he'd become her lone parent when she was young, he'd had to take time to think about how to handle the different things that came along that affected girls only. Periods. Bras. Tampons. Geez, he'd learned a lot since he had to step up and be a father *and* a mother.

Resigned to at least give her the chance to talk, Mitchell rose, walked upstairs, and knocked on his daughter's bedroom door. After hearing her call out, he entered and found her sitting on the bed, looking through photos.

"Dad. What's up?" Charlie asked.

Mitchell sat on the edge of the bed and grabbed a handful of photos. As he prepared himself for whatever chat they were going to have, he pretended to look at one photo after another.

"I wanted to ask how things are with you and Ash."

Charlie was surprised. She had expected the conversation about the ranch was coming. Once again, her father was silent on that subject.

"How things *are*?" she queried.

For the first time that she could ever remember, she thought she saw her father look uncomfortable. She considered he might even have been looking embarrassed.

"Are things serious?" Mitchell asked.

"Dad. I don't want to talk to you about that," Charlie replied. "And why are you asking anyway?"

Mitchell looked closely at his daughter. She was his baby girl. He knew he had to acknowledge that she wasn't a little girl any longer, but instead a rather lovely young lady.

"Ash has seemed nice when I've met him, but I want to be sure how *you* feel about *him*," he said.

"I like him. I like spending time with him."

"And have you ... do I need to talk to you about..."

Charlie saw her father's discomfort level rise. She was glad. She wanted the conversation to end as much as she suspected he did. The only way to make that happen was to be completely blunt.

"We aren't having sex if that's what you're wondering," she said and immediately saw a combination of shock and relief on his face. "Dad, I'm not giving my body away to any guy - not easily. I can't tell you I'm going to be like this forever, but for now, I'm not even close to having sex. I'm just not ready."

"But he..."

"He feels the same way, so don't worry. We aren't doing it, and if we ever do, it won't be anytime soon," she said. She saw him start to bring up another point or question, so hurried to cut him off. "And when it does happen, don't worry. I know how to be prepared, and I know how to say no. You can put your mind at rest and never talk to me about this again."

Mitchell breathed more easily. She was a funny

thing, the way she could talk so candidly about some things that others wouldn't be able to. In his heart, he knew that really, she'd made his job of being a sole parent to a little girl extremely easy.

Charlie watched him sit still on her bed for a long while. He had the look on his face that he sometimes got when he was thinking about her mother. Charlie couldn't remember him dating any other woman in the nine years since his wife had died. For a moment, she wondered if he ever got lonely. The consideration made her sad.

Mitchell was surprised when he saw and felt Charlie's arms wrap around him.

"You're a great father, Dad," she said. "I couldn't have had a better life than the one I've had with you."

Although surprised by her statement, Mitchell gently squeezed the arms that enveloped him.

"And you are a great daughter, Charlie," he said. "I am proud of you, and I do trust you to make good decisions. Ash is a good kid. Just don't rush into anything. You don't need to rush."

"I know. I won't," Charlie replied. "Promise."

That was enough for Mitchell. He knew she might be just saying what he wanted to hear, but he suspected she wasn't. He would give her the benefit of the doubt.

Charlie watched as he stood, smiled sadly at her, and then quietly left her room. It had been a strange interaction and one she wouldn't forget in a hurry, but it had been nice too. He could have ranted and raved, demanding she not see Ash. He could have threatened to lock her up day and night to keep her out of any guy's way - but he hadn't. Ash had won her father over, and that alone spoke volumes about what kind of guy Ash was.

Seeing it was getting late, Charlie prepared for bed and then climbed into it. Her mind thought back to her time with Ash earlier. Her body had reacted in a new way. She knew it had been an orgasm. She had read about them in her romance novels, and it had been just as they described. A wave of pleasure, like an eruption - yep, that was definitely it. She smiled at the thought. Then she pondered the knowledge that he'd had an orgasm shortly after she had. He hadn't said as much, but she was pretty sure he had. It was a lot to think about. She hadn't ventured that far with any guy before. It felt good, and yet there was no danger in what had happened. They hadn't even taken their clothes off.

She liked it, and she wanted more of it.

Sighing, Charlie picked up her pirate romance novel. She needed to learn what that sexy pirate captain was going to do with the voluptuous naked woman in his cabin.

CHAPTER NINE

The next day Ash found his familiar routine feeling more normal again. After showering, dressing, and having a quick breakfast, he took himself off to work. He'd lain awake late into the night thinking about Charlie. How could he not think about her? She was beautiful, and she turned his blood hot, but he didn't want to focus so much on that side of her. He knew they had more than that. They had a friendship. It was only in its beginning stages, but he had to maintain the belief that it would continue for a long time yet.

During his half-hour lunch break, he felt his mobile phone vibrate. Taking it out and switching the screen on, he saw a text from Charlie. He smiled even before he read it. Just knowing that she was thinking about him was enough to make him feel good.

'Regan told me I was moaning in my sleep last night. I think I was dreaming of you.'

Ash read the text twice before he believed it said what it said. He burst out laughing.

'Oh, really? I might have been doing the same,' he replied.

'You dreamed about you too?'

He laughed again at her humor and then heard another text alert sound.

'Can I see you today?' she asked.

As he read that text, Ash felt his pulse quicken.

'I finish at six again.'

'Would you like to come to my place?' Charlie asked.

Ash breathed out heavily. Going to her house meant going home to her brothers and her father.

'Isn't Max going home today?'

'Yep, he's here.'

Ash felt like he was interrupting special family time until he realized that he wasn't the one who'd started the conversation.

'I can come there, or wherever works for you,' he typed.

'Okay, I'll see you here after 6.'

It was decided. No doubt, the whole Stonewarden clan would be there. It wasn't the most relaxing thought, but Ash was glad to do it if she wanted him there.

'See you then.'

As the afternoon wore on, he felt himself become increasingly nervous. By the time he saw the clock show 6pm, he was concerned. All of the Stonewarden men in one place in their home? And Ash was going to walk in there, knowing how protective they were of their sister and daughter? He shook his head. He'd made a commitment, and he would see it through.

He approached the house apprehensively. When he reached the door, his instinct was to turn and run. Then the door opened, and Charlie was there. Still in her usual jeans and t-shirt, to him she looked like the most beautiful creature he had ever seen. As she smiled at him, Ash's nervousness melted away, and all thoughts of the men inside the house were forgotten.

"Come in, Ash," he heard a much deeper voice call from within.

Charlie opened the door wider to allow him to step past her. As he did so, she felt his hand brush across hers lightly. It was subtle but felt intense to her. His touch was magical.

Within the foyer, Ash could see that most of the family was there. He'd already met James, Vic, Regan, and Max. Also in the mix was her father, Mitchell.

"Sorry, it's a bit hectic down here. Come upstairs," Charlie said.

Ash was panicked for a moment, not sure if

walking to her bedroom might be tempting trouble with the testosterone in the room.

Charlie laughed at him and leaned in close to speak quietly to only him.

"They're absorbed in one another," she whispered. "They won't even know we've gone."

Looking at her and then at the men in the room, Ash thought that perhaps she was right. He started walking quickly up the staircase, letting her lead the way.

It wasn't the first time he'd been in her room, but something felt different. They'd crossed one line in their interaction. Even though they'd been fully clothed, they had both climaxed from their closeness. Somehow it did feel like a new level of intimacy had been reached, even without any intention.

Ash watched her sit on her bed, with her back against the headboard.

"How was your work today?" she asked in a normal conversational voice.

Ash sat down on the edge of the bed, nervous but happy to be with her again.

"It was busier today. I think everyone is starting to stock up again, so it was good. The days pass quickly when we are busier," he said.

Charlie looked at him as he spoke. It wasn't missed on her that he was sitting a noticeable distance from her. She moved over more so that she was on the far side of the bed from where he sat. Once there, she lay down on her side, facing him.

Ash watched her maneuver herself as she did. He didn't think she was trying to look alluring, but she certainly did. He let out a long deep breath at the sight.

"What was that sigh for?" she asked him, chuckling slightly.

"You look beautiful," he said quietly.

Charlie didn't respond to that. It felt raw and

intimate, the way he'd said it.

"Come and lie down beside me," she eventually said.

"Charlie, your whole family is downstairs…"

"Well, not my *whole* family. Fitz is absent, as usual."

Ash looked at her with mock seriousness but ended up laughing softly. He wasn't going to be able to argue against her. It was useless to try. Instead, he did as she asked and moved so that he was lying facing her, on his side. He left a noticeable gap between them - just in case.

"How is Max?" he asked, desperate to keep the conversation going so that he could stop thinking about kissing her.

"He's good," Charlie replied. "The tests that were done yesterday confirmed he's definitely returning to normal. He has to rest for another week, and Dad will stay with him to make sure he's okay."

"That's really good to hear. I know you've missed him."

Charlie nodded.

"I did miss him," she said. "I love all of my brothers, but Max is extra special. He was really there for me when our mother died."

"What about Fitz though? Isn't he between you and Max in age?"

"He is, but Fitz is different. Don't ask me how. He's just always seemed like the odd one out or something. I don't know. Sometimes I feel like I don't actually know him even though we're closest in age."

"I'm envious of you having so much family," said Ash. "I only have my mum and dad."

"They never wanted to have more kids?" she asked, curious how any family could be so small as his.

"I don't know. It isn't the kind of thing they would talk about with me," Ash said and paused a moment, thinking about them. "They have been great parents. I know I'm lucky to have them. I can only hope to be as good a father when the time comes."

His last statement surprised Charlie. For the moment before those last words escaped his lips, she had been silently wondering if he would ever want kids. She believed most guys didn't. She didn't know where she'd gotten that idea from - perhaps from having five older brothers who were all childless.

"You want to have kids?" she asked him and saw him grin.

"If I had my way, I'd have dozens of the things. I know I have a good life, Charlie, but I did grow up wishing I had a brother. Or even a sister. Yes, I do want to have kids. I want to be a dad. A *good* dad."

Charlie said nothing to him, instead leaning forward and kissing him softly. She felt him hold back slightly, as if with the determination to not give in.

"Scared my family will burst in here and catch you kissing me?" she asked, teasing him.

"Yes!" he responded in mock horror, making her laugh. "But I also know how much I love kissing you and I don't want us to get too carried away," he said as he raised his hand to lightly stroke her cheek. "I'd love to get away somewhere with you."

"I was thinking that I might go out and stay at the ranch," Charlie said. "Tom and his wife said I could anytime, and I think I'd like to. They did say you were welcome too - *in a separate bedroom.*"

Ash laughed in relief. It might work better than going to a hotel somewhere, where they might have to share a room.

"What do you think?" Charlie asked, her heart beginning to beat faster at the idea of being in another place with him.

"When are you going?"

"When do you have days off?"

"I'm working another four days, and then I'll have three off," Ash said. "So next Monday to Wednesday, I'm free."

Charlie nodded, her mind thinking and planning.

"Okay, well, I could go there tomorrow and spend a few days there alone, and you could come out Monday morning? Then I could get all the chat about my mother out of the way 'cause I don't think Tom wanted to talk about that in front of you."

Ash smiled. He loved her candor. She didn't express any regret, apology, or sympathy for the fact that Tom didn't want Ash party to some information. She spoke truthfully without any emotion or feeling to it. It was just one more thing he loved about her.

Hearing those words pass through his mind startled him. He quickly pushed them aside.

"It sounds like a plan," he said quietly, his focus returning to her lips again - her very plump, red, and kissable lips.

Charlie saw his eyes refocus on her mouth and felt a longing inside of her. She didn't want to be pushy, but she wanted him to kiss her. She spoke softly to him.

"Please kiss me."

As soon as he heard the request, Ash happily did as he was asked. They didn't move from their spot even though their lips moved and caressed. Charlie could feel Ash's hand lightly rest on her hip and then start to caress her outer thigh, hip, waist, and back again. He didn't move to lie on top of her or encourage her to lie on top of him. Lying like they were, facing one another, felt right.

They were startled apart at the sound of someone hitting the door and calling out, "Stop that kissing!"

Recognizing it was Regan's voice, Charlie shook her head and rolled her eyes. Regan was trying to be funny. On Ash's face, Charlie saw alarm.

"He's just winding me up," she reassured him.

"It's cool."

Ash nodded, but the moment was broken. He moved closer to her and pulled her body tightly against his.

"I'll have to leave soon as I have an early start," he said in almost a whisper before he kissed her softly. He felt her nod her head before she began kissing him back more forcefully. Ash felt like he could happily lie back and let her kiss him like that all night…

His own thought startled him, making him pull away, smiling but determined.

"Hmm, I think you're trying to tempt me to stay longer!" he said.

"Guilty," Charlie replied, laughing.

As the two of them got up from the soft comfort of the bed, Ash pulled her into a warm embrace.

"I'll walk you out past the pack of wolves," she said, making Ash laugh out loud.

As they walked down to the lower level, the volume of the male voices was still evident. Except for Regan, it was possible every guy in that room hadn't even noticed they'd gone upstairs.

Charlie walked him out to the front veranda, enjoying the warmth and stillness of the evening air. She wrapped her arms around him and held him tightly, encouraging him to do the same. They stood like that for a long while before he pulled away.

"I'll see you Monday, okay?" he said before kissing her warm lips again. It wasn't easy, walking away from her. Each time he saw her, it felt like it was that little bit more difficult than the day before.

After he withdrew, Charlie watched him walk away. Her heart felt heavy at the thought of not seeing him for three days. She knew her feelings were strong, but she also knew that passion could blind a woman to other aspects of a man. Her romance novels had told her that. Having a break from him might help her to more accurately identify how she truly felt.

As she went back inside, she heard words that put her on guard again.

"It's a sure thing. An easy job, Dad…"

The guys were all talking about another theft. Seeing building blueprints spread over the coffee table, Charlie knew it was a big one. It wasn't going to be just a theft. That job was going to be one of their large scale heists.

She spoke, pushing her voice over others'.

"Dad, can I talk to you for a minute?" she called out. She immediately saw her father turn and come toward her. When they moved through to the kitchen, she spoke again. "You haven't mentioned the ranch," she said simply. She wanted to see what he would say about it if she only just lightly broached the subject. Did he even know about the ranch?

"We don't talk about it," he said simply and saw her frown at him.

"I am going to go out there tomorrow and stay there for a few nights."

Mitchell opened his mouth to object but then considered. Vic had just provided temptation for a heist. Charlie in the house was something he always tried to avoid when they went into planning mode. If she were away for a few nights, they could indulge in full-on planning without him worrying about her hearing them or what she would think.

"Okay," he said.

"Okay? Just like that?"

"Charlie, you want to go, and I'm okay with that," Mitchell said. "Uncle Tom is a good man, and you can learn a great many things about our family there."

"Then why don't we all get told about it? Do the others know?" Charlie dared to ask.

Suddenly she felt her father's hands on her arms and saw the sternness of his face looking down at her.

"No! And I don't *want* them to know. Understand?"

Charlie knew not to ask another question with the way her father was looking at her. Instead, she nodded and lowered her eyes. Soon enough, he dropped his arms, turned, and walked back to the living area. Why it had to be some big secret, she couldn't fathom to guess, but her father wasn't someone she generally wanted to disobey. She would keep her knowledge to herself. If honest with herself, the ease at which he had just accepted her telling him that she was going was a surprise in itself, but she had his approval to go, so go she would.

~~~~~~

The following morning, Charlie felt excited in anticipation of going away for a few nights. She'd hardly ever been anywhere other than her family home, and certainly had never gone anywhere without at least one member of her family with her. On the bus journey there, she let herself be nervous. No matter what anyone else thought of just going to a ranch a short distance from home, to her, it was exciting. It was a new adventure - something to appreciate and enjoy.

Before she'd left the house, she had seen her father. He'd said nothing about her plan to go away for a few nights. It did surprise her, especially considering his chat with her about Ash. For all he knew, she could be going to stay with Ash and have sex with him. How could her father possibly be so calm about her going away on her own? It told her that they must have something big they were planning - something *really* big. Otherwise, there was no way her father would have simply said 'okay' to her idea. No, they were working on something of magnitude, and she was glad to be out of the house, and completely unable to overhear any of the details.

Once off the bus, she made the trek on foot as she
~~~~~~

had the previous two times. Even just walking up the long driveway felt like a holiday in itself. After a certain distance, the sound of the road could no longer be heard. All that Charlie heard after that point was the quiet of the occasional bird singing and a horse in the distance whinnying. More steady was the sound of the wind blowing through the trees that lined the driveway from the road right up to the house. The rustling of the leaves and branches moving as they swayed in the breeze made her think of water flowing.

When the house and stables came into view, she stopped walking and just looked at it from where she stood. She was on a ranch that belonged to her family. It had belonged to her family for generations. Until recently, she'd had no idea that it existed. That was the strangest thing about it - the family's commitment to keeping it a secret ... from themselves? How did that make any sense to anyone?

She closed her eyes and took a few minutes to breathe in deeply. The air was fresh and clear. It almost made her feel like she wasn't arriving as a visitor. To her, it felt more like she was coming home.

~~~~~

"Charlie!" she heard Molly call out to her as she neared the house. "Come with me, young lass, and I'll show you where you are going to stay."

Charlie was greeted with arms folding around her and a kiss placed on each of her cheeks.

"Thank you, Molly. I am so happy to be here," Charlie replied, excited. "Thank you for letting me come and stay."

"Oh! Think nothing of it, lass! We don't get near enough visitors here, and as much as I love Tom, it is nice now and then to be able to have some different conversation," Molly said as they walked into the front entrance of the house. "This is a part of your heritage. You *should* spend time here."
~~~~~

The foyer they stood in as they entered the front door, Charlie realized she hadn't seen before. She didn't consider herself any kind of house connoisseur, but the word that leaped into her head was *magnificent*.

When Molly realized Charlie wasn't following her, she stopped and turned around. Being in the house all the time, Molly had stopped thinking anything about it. When she looked at Charlie and could see the expression on her face, Molly was transported back in time to the first time she had entered that very foyer. She said nothing to interrupt Charlie's focus, instead just watching the younger woman's face.

When Charlie looked at Molly, she was almost speechless.

"I can't believe someplace so magical as this belongs to my family but we aren't all encouraged to enjoy it," she said. "Why is it kept from us when it is so wonderful?"

"That is something that has just always been," she heard Tom's voice add into the conversation. Charlie turned toward it and saw him walking through a side door to the foyer. "Everyone who comes here asks the same question, Charlie, but nothing ever changes. Always it is the same."

"But *why*?"

"That I cannot tell you, but it has proved important on occasion as a place for people to escape to," Tom explained. "The purpose it serves then is all the better for the fewer people who know about it."

Charlie looked at him, stupefied by what he was saying. It still made no sense to her. Even his words had made no sense to her. Despite her confusion, she wouldn't push for an answer. For all she knew, he possibly didn't have one. She tucked the question away in her mind, choosing instead to change the subject.

"Thank you for inviting me to stay, Tom. I'm so happy to be here," she said and immediately saw his face relax.

"Oh, lass! We are going to have such fun! Come this way so we can get you settled in your room," Tom replied as the three of them left the grandeur of the foyer. "What of your young man, Charlie? Shall he come to visit us again also?"

"He's working at the moment, but he has Monday, Tuesday, and Wednesday off. I thought that he could come and stay here then, if you felt comfortable with that?"

"Of course. Now, this is your room," Tom replied, smiling as he opened a large wooden door. "The next door here is a bathroom, and that one there across the hallway is where your young man will stay when he visits."

Charlie smiled and followed Tom and Molly into the room. Upon entering, she dropped her bag as she found herself stunned - completely and utterly stunned. Ahead of her was a large four-poster bed with rich velvet drapes tied back by golden ropes on each of the posts. Behind the bed was a tapestry. As Charlie moved closer to it, she felt like she could stand in front of it for days and still not see every detail of it. The people in it were exquisite in the detail that came from the thread that had been sewn into it. In addition to people, there were animals - horses and sheep - and birds flying against a vivid sky of blue with white clouds.

Tom came forward and stood behind her, looking up at it also.

"It is beautiful, isn't it," he said.

"It looks old."

"Aye, lass. That one is just over 300 years old. It isn't the oldest we have, but it is certainly one of the most beautiful."

Charlie stood looking a little longer and then remembered her manners. Turning around, she saw a large freestanding wardrobe that looked like it must have been made for a giant. She moved toward it and ran her hands over the woodwork. Down the front of it around the large mirror that graced its center were hand-carved flowers and leaves, joined as if depicting a vine.

"It's a beautiful piece, isn't it Charlie?" she heard Molly's voice ask.

Charlie turned to smile at her. As she did, she felt tearful, and then incredibly silly at feeling tearful over a piece of furniture. "I had the same reaction when I first came here. Don't feel embarrassed. There are a great many things of beauty in this home. I'll take you on a good tour of all the rooms if you like, once you are settled."

Charlie nodded and smiled, wiping her eyes. "Thank you. I'd like that."

"Now, lass, why don't you take some time to unpack your bag. This wardrobe works," Tom said, opening the giant doors and revealing shelves and hanging space inside. "Feel free to hang your clothes up in there. There's plenty of room."

Charlie almost laughed. She had a duffle bag with a few t-shirts and a couple of hoodies in it. That was all. The thought of hanging them in something so beautiful seemed ludicrous, but she nodded and thanked him all the same.

"I'll be in the kitchen, Charlie, if you want to come down there when you are settled," Molly said with happiness evident in her voice. "Otherwise, Tom will be heading out to the stables again, and you can find him there."

Charlie was overwhelmed. She ran up to Molly and hugged her before turning and doing the same to Tom.

"Now, then, lass, no need to get all soppy," Tom said, a tear appearing in his eye. All three smiled and then laughed softly. "Go on with you. Unpack and then come and find me or Molly."

Charlie watched them leave the room, and the large door close. She walked around the room, touching things. On the walls were wall hangings and paintings. She couldn't help but touch the frames, having always loved the feeling of wood. To think that she was standing among items that were hundreds of years old played on her emotions.

Aware that she was a guest and her hosts wished to see her, she set to work. Despite it seeming completely unnecessary, she took her time hanging up her t-shirts and hoodies on the hangers in the large wardrobe. As she closed the large doors, she caught sight of herself in the mirror on the front. For a moment, she wondered how the women presented themselves in the time when the wardrobe had been made. She imagined that perhaps there was no way they would have even worn any kind of trousers, let alone something like jeans with rips in them. She wasn't a girlie girl, but for a split moment, she found she didn't mind the idea of putting on a dress in a place like she was in. Somehow it seemed like it might be a more respectful way to dress in a home of such history.

She shook the thought away and walked to the bed, where she lay down for a few minutes. She was going to sleep in a large bed with curtains around it. Why did they need curtains around the bed? Then she laughed at herself. She was on an adventure of learning, and it felt great!

~~~~~

"Are you all settled, Charlie?" Molly asked her when she had finally found her way through what seemed like somewhat of a maze to get to the kitchen.

"Yes, thank you, Molly. What are you doing? Can I help?"

Molly smiled at her. "I'm making some bread dough that I'll bake later in the day as rolls for us to have with our dinner. Have you made bread before?"
~~~~~

Charlie laughed softly. "No! I have no idea how bread is made."

"Would you like to learn?"

"Yes, please."

"Come over here then, lass. Wash your hands properly. That's always the first step in food preparation, you know," Molly said. After Charlie had done so, she spoke further. "Good. Now come. The dough has just been mixed, but now it needs to be kneaded. It can take a while, but when you see it come together, *that* brings a great moment of achievement."

Charlie moved to the bench and worked under the guidance of Molly, taking her time and learning the technique. It was a workout for her arms, no doubt about it, but the more she did it, the more she could see the dough changing. Finally, Molly told her it was ready.

"That's it?" Charlie asked, making Molly laugh.

"That's the *first* kneading," she replied. "Now we leave it for a couple of hours so that it can rise, and then we will do it again."

Molly moved to the sink, and Charlie followed. Washing their hands, Charlie found herself full of questions.

"Where would you learn to do that?"

"Oh! When I first came here, Charlie, I knew nothing. Even in my day, making bread from scratch wasn't all that common. People were already buying bread by the loaf then. When I came, your Uncle Tom's father was running this place, and it was his wife who taught me skills in the kitchen. I was curious, wondering why anyone would make any food from scratch when they could just go to the supermarket," she said, laughing softly. "I came and stayed here for a week when Tom and I were married. Over that time, I was converted. This isn't my family home, but since that moment, I have felt like it *is* my home."

Charlie nodded. "I feel close to this place, too."

Molly looked pleased. "Yes, I think you do. Now, tell me more about this young man of yours. I haven't seen him yet. Is he handsome?"

Charlie laughed but nodded. "Well, *I* think he's handsome."

"But I think it would take more than just a good looking face to capture your heart, Charlie. Am I right?"

"He is … I *believe* he is a good guy. He has been thoughtful and kind toward me," Charlie said. "With him, I don't feel like he just wants something from me. I'm not sure how to explain it…"

"I think you explain it very well. I know what you mean. There's a difference between being with someone that you just like, and being with someone who makes you truly believe that they really want to be with *you* and no-one else." There was silence as she paused, looking thoughtful. "I look forward to meeting this young man, Charlie!"

"I hope it *is* alright that he's coming here."

"Of course it is," Molly reassured her. "Let me tell you something about my Tom. He never says anything he doesn't mean. If he didn't want your young man here, he wouldn't have invited him. Rest easy in that. The invitation was made because Tom wanted to make it. No other reason."

"Thank you."

"Now, how about you head out and see what Tom is up to? I think he is eager to get you close to the horses again," Molly said and saw Charlie laugh. "Don't worry. You will get used to them. They are a harmless lot."

Charlie cast Molly one more grin before leaving the kitchen and finding her way outside.

"Oh, there she is," she heard Tom call out as she tentatively entered the stable. "Come in, lass. Here's your brush. Yes, come forward and give Missy one of these nice ripe apples. Do that, and she'll love you forever."

Tom guided her in holding the apple before the

two of them began grooming the horses.

"Do you have questions about your family, Charlie? If you do, make sure you ask them. I am happy to share anything with you, and your father has given me full advance permission to tell you whatever you want to know about. But let's talk about such things before your young Ash arrives on Monday."

Charlie looked at him and understood the need for that. There was nothing to dispute there. She still worried about what would happen if Ash ever found out that her family had been responsible for the burglary at his parents' apartment. Even though they hadn't known it belonged to his parents, would he believe that? Or was there a greater chance that if he found out, he would think that the very reason she was spending time with him, was somehow related to her family wanting information for that burglary? She shuddered at the thought of how many ways that horrible situation could play out if Ash knew her family's role in what had happened to his mother at that time.

"When I came here, all I hoped to find out was anything more about my mother…"

"Ahh, young Caroline. Oh, she was such a beauty, but with that, she was so kind and generous. She had a very loving soul. I don't think I ever saw or heard of her being unkind to anyone, and she loved to help people," Tom said and stopped the grooming he was doing to look at her. "I think you might have the same nature, Charlie."

"Do you think so? I don't remember her, so I don't know what she was like."

"You remind me of her, and I suspect you might sometimes remind your father of her, too," Tom said.

Charlie took a moment to think about that. Did she remind her father of her mother? She tried to remember any instance where he had acted in a way that such an explanation would make sense. She couldn't think of any.

"Maybe. Sometimes I am envious of my brothers, especially Vic. He was 21 when she left us. He had already spent 21 years with her. She'd been there for him through high school, through his first crush, through him starting in the business."

"It is a natural way to feel, I think. Your mother left too soon, no doubt about it. Before she got sick, she was so lively, was our Caroline. She had an inquisitive nature and wanted to try everything. A bit like you, I think," he said as he winked at her, making her smile.

"Do you know how she met my father?" she asked. It was a question that began a conversation that lasted right through until dinner time.

While she listened to tales of adventures her mother and father had shared, Tom introduced her to different jobs that had to be done in the stables, around the horses, and further over in a field where donkeys were kept. Right from the moment she saw them, she was enraptured with them, but the stories being told were too interesting for her to stop and ask any questions about anything. She had always loved romance novels but the way Tom told the story of her father and mother meeting, and their long period of 'courting', left Charlie thinking she'd never read words of romantic fiction the same way again.

After standing for a while, enjoying caressing the head of one of the donkeys, Charlie realized that Tom had already stopped speaking. She turned and looked at him and saw him smiling at her.

"That's Jerry. He particularly loves to be scratched here," Tom said, showing a specific spot to scratch. When Charlie rubbed hard there, she heard almost a sigh escape Jerry's mouth. It made her giggle. The sound took Tom back to the day he'd met Caroline.

Because Charlie had almost exactly the same giggle as her mother had.

~~~~~~

Later that evening, the three of them sat in the dining room at the large wooden table, indulging in the homemade meal.

"This really is the best bread I've ever tasted," Charlie said as she indulged in a bread roll with a sound lashing of butter spread over it. "Tomorrow, can I help you with all stages of making it?" she asked, having overlooked returning to the kitchen to help with the second kneading.

Molly laughed. "Of course you can. Anything you wish to learn, I am happy to teach you, Charlie."

Charlie saw a look of knowing pass between Molly and Tom, accompanied by discrete smiles. She looked away in politeness but not before she felt a pang of hope that one day she might experience a depth of love like the two people before her obviously felt.

~~~~~~

Later that night, Charlie climbed into the large bed, conflicted in feelings. She was exhausted. She was also so excited about being where she was that she felt like she might never be able to get to sleep. She picked up her phone and saw a text message waiting. Opening it up, she saw it had come from Ash an hour earlier when she'd been in a living room still talking to Tom and Molly.

'How has your day been?' his text message asked, making Charlie smile.

'Really good. I love it here. Will you still come on Monday?'

Ash received and read the text with relief.

'I want to. Is it okay with Tom? Definitely?'

'Yes. They already have a room set up for you :) '

'Oh, a smiley face. That must be good then.'

Charlie sighed. Throughout the day, she hadn't had time to think about Ash too much. Now that she did have the time, she did feel like she was missing him.

'I am looking forward to seeing you on Monday,' she wrote.

There was silence as Ash lay in his bed, having read her last message. He'd missed her all day as well, but he knew it wasn't a bad thing for the two of them to have a break either. He wasn't sure either of them could be sure of their feelings when they were so wrapped up in each other as they had been since the day of the shooting. He wanted to be sure not only of his feelings toward her but also her feelings toward him. Finally he pulled himself out of his thoughts and typed his reply.

'I can't wait to see you, too, Charlie.'

'Goodnight, Ash,' she typed, not wanting to say goodnight but feeling like they couldn't keep sending messages back and forth all night.

'Sweet dreams,' Ash replied.

Ash put his phone back on his bedside table and moved down under his blankets. All those months he had watched her wandering into the supermarket, he would never have thought she could come into his life and affect him as she had.

He felt like he had been literally bowled over.

~~~~~

"Good morning, Charlie," Molly and Tom both said to her the next morning when she entered the kitchen. They were sitting at the kitchen table with what seemed like a buffet of goodness in front of them. "Come sit down and have a good breakfast as I have a lot for you to do today," Tom said with a distinctive gleam in his eyes.

Charlie sat down and looked in awe at all the foods before her. Toast, bacon, poached eggs, bagels, cream cheese, salmon, hash browns … the choice went on and on. Tentatively she took two pieces of toast and covered them with a couple of eggs.

"What would you like to drink, Charlie? Coffee? Tea? Hot chocolate? Or perhaps some juice?"
~~~~~

"Juice would be fine, thank you, Molly."

Tom and Molly both watched her as all three of them enjoyed a slow, relaxed breakfast. Each time he saw her, Tom was reminded of her mother, but more and more, he was slowly thinking less of Caroline and more of Charlie just as the individual she was.

"So, what are we doing today?" Charlie asked him, breaking into his thoughts.

"We have a great many animals here, so I thought I'd take you around and introduce you to all of them today. They all need a little bit of attention each day, in one way or another. How would you feel about that?"

Charlie eagerly nodded. "I'd like that very much."

~~~~~

For the rest of that day, and through the next, Charlie was pulled into the routines of the ranch. The animals all made her feel like they were grounding her. After a hectic time of feeling like she'd been in a whirlwind since the moment of the shooting, over her second and third days at the ranch she finally started to feel relaxed and human again. In some ways, she felt like she'd been doing and thinking far too much and was finally returning to a safe and even level again.

Every evening she exchanged text messages with Ash. At that time of day, she felt like she missed him even more than she had the previous evening. She was glad they were having the time apart. Although she had feared it might sever their friendship, she knew that her feelings weren't changing at all. Even working all day and not thinking about him so much as she was busy, still when she went to bed each night, she couldn't wait to hear from him, even if it was only a few words on a tiny screen.

'Only one more day and then I get to see you,' she wrote to him on their third night apart.

'I know. I can't wait to see you,' his reply said.

The words were so simple, but they affected her.
~~~~~

They were words that anyone could say to anyone else at any time, and they wouldn't necessarily mean anything. From Ash, she knew they did. She trusted he was always honest with her. She believed in his words.

They exchanged a few more not so personal messages before saying goodnight. Charlie then lay back and closed her eyes, eager to go to sleep so that she would then wake up, get through one more day, and then receive a message from him again.

Ash also found himself eager to get through the two nights and one day before he would be able to venture out to the ranch and see her. He loved his job, but all of a sudden, the days seemed to be much longer than they ever had before.

~~~~~

Back in the Stonewarden home, Mitchell was planning with his sons. All of them were on board for their upcoming heist. Even Max was sure he was up to it. The job wouldn't happen for a few weeks yet, but those few days and nights were the primary planning stage. Everyone was there, and everyone was focused - especially Fitz.

He was the enigma of the family. Even Mitchell was confounded by him sometimes with the ways that he was so different from all of his siblings, but Mitchell equally had full faith in Fitz when it came to the business. Then he was dedicated and professional, no matter what he did in his own personal time. That was always a secret. Fitz never offered information about what he did when he wasn't working with the family, and everyone had given up asking him. He was there when he needed to be. That always had to simply be enough, as far as his family was concerned.

During the planning stage, Charlie crossed the minds of everyone at one time or another. Mitchell had told them that she had gone away with friends for a week. Each of them wondered about that story, but no-
~~~~~

one dared ask. They knew their father would know where she was. They also knew there was no way he would let any harm come to her. It wasn't much as far as information went, but it was enough.

~~~~~

On the fourth evening on the ranch, Charlie sat with Tom and Molly during dinner. Both hosts could see the nervousness on her face and looked at each other with the certainty that they knew why she was nervous.

"Are you enjoying your time here, Charlie?" Molly asked, trying to get her to relax.

"Oh, yes! I love it here."

"You aren't finding the work boring and unexciting?" Tom asked, teasing her.

"No," Charlie replied. "To be honest, this is the first time I've had an occupation, and I really am enjoying it. I feel like I'm meant to be here. I know that sounds crazy…"

"No, it doesn't," Molly said, smiling. "I felt the same way when I came here with Tom."

Charlie saw the way Molly looked at Tom and was envious. Was it on the cards for her to have a love like that?

"You only have to wait for one more sleep," Tom said.

Charlie turned to look at him. He had a smile on his face that wasn't teasing. It was sincere and caring.

"I know. I do miss him," she said. "He'll only be here for two nights, but that's better than nothing, right?"

When she lay in her bed later, she eagerly picked up her phone.

'How was your day today?' she asked and waited for a reply. It seemed like forever that she was waiting, growing slightly anxious as minutes passed.

'My day was good, but I kept thinking about seeing you tomorrow. Do you still want me to come out there?' his reply read.
~~~~~

Charlie smiled broadly, even though he couldn't see her.

'Of course I still want you to come. I want to see you. And hug you. And kiss you.'

As Ash read that message, his heart skipped a beat.

'I want that too. I'll be there after 10.30am.'

'Yay!'

Ash laughed at the simple word. It was so simple but it said so much to him.

'Sweet dreams, Charlie. I can't wait to put my arms around you.'

'Sweet dreams, Ash.'

In his small apartment, Ash forced himself to sleep despite his excitement for seeing her the next day.

In her large bedroom on a large ranch, Charlie forced herself to do the same.

CHAPTER TEN

"I think someone is excited," Molly said quietly at breakfast the next day.

Charlie looked up from her breakfast of eggs on toast and smiled bashfully. "I know it's only been a few days, but it feels much longer."

Molly reached out and placed her hand over Charlie's. "I've been there, Charlie. I know exactly what you mean."

Once again, Charlie caught Molly and Tom looking at each other with so much love that she couldn't help but feel wistful. They made it look so easy.

"But Tom, what do I share with him, and what don't I?" Charlie asked. "I'm in this magical place, and I want to tell him so many things, but I can't, can it?"

Tom looked serious and a little sad. "No, lass, you can't," he said. "Things about our family have to be kept quiet. I know it makes no sense, but please understand. This place is important. When certain things happen, it has to be here for people who need it," he said cryptically, but Charlie didn't ask him to expand on what he meant. "The two of you can explore the ranch, and I would love for you to keep helping out with the animals. I think you have a real gift there. They love it when they see *you* coming! But anything about the Stonewardens - I'm sorry, Charlie, but it just can't be talked about."

"But the portraits … they are so wonderful to look at. I can't show him that room, can I?" she asked and saw Tom shake his head in response. "So much beauty that no-one can enjoy."

"Aye, it is that," replied Tom. "At times, I've thought about removing the names from the portraits so that they *could* be shown to others without anyone seeing the Stonewarden name, but things have to continue as they have done. It is just the way of our family. Many things make no sense at all, but each serves its purpose at the right time. Perhaps for the duration that Ash is here, think of this more as a holiday ranch than a family one. Hmm?"

Charlie smiled sadly at him and nodded. He was right. She was going to have the opportunity to experience a small holiday with Ash. It wouldn't be nearly as much fun if she weighed him down in talking about people who'd lived hundreds of years ago anyway.

"It isn't forever, Charlie," Molly said quietly. "It's only for now, with you and Ash being so young and so new to one another. The longer you're together, the more you'll be able to open up to him, but you *have* to let time pass so that he can prove his trustworthiness."

Charlie knew that Ash was trustworthy. She didn't doubt that, but she would put faith in the couple sitting with her. They knew a great many things that she didn't know and didn't particularly want to know - especially about the business.

"Now, do you want to come with me to the stables and see our friends out there? They are probably quite hungry by now, and eager to see the young lass with the red apples," Tom said and instantly saw Charlie relax, smile and nod.

~~~~~

Ash woke early and jumped out of bed with a speed that wasn't quite so normal for him. After quickly consuming a large bowl of cereal and a large cup of coffee, he jumped in the shower. He was going to see Charlie. His heart was already beating faster in his excitement about seeing her again. It had only been four days that they'd been apart, but it had been a very long four days as far as he was concerned. When he realized he might have been more than excited and instead rather *overexcited*, he took a little bit longer in the shower to
~~~~~

indulge his thoughts of desire. The climactic release was delicious. He hoped it would serve him well, making his body a little more relaxed when he finally saw her. She could turn his blood from lukewarm to hot in an instant. He was taking no chances. He'd needed release before he left his apartment and began his journey to the ranch.

Stepping down from the bus, he took a moment to look at the ranch sign hanging over the beginning of the long driveway. The reality began to set in. Beyond what he'd been thinking about - seeing Charlie again - was the actuality that he was going to be staying on the ranch with her. He'd be in a separate bedroom, thankfully, but it still felt like an intimacy. It would be the first time he'd be close to her in the same house for two nights.

Feeling his body twitch as an early indicator that it was considering springing to life at the thought of being close to her again, he shook his head and began to walk.

Just as Ash began to walk around the small bend in the driveway that would place him in view of the house, he saw her running toward him. He stopped still. The sight was delicious, but also a little bit humorous. He hadn't expected her to be so eager to see him as she appeared to be, bounding down the driveway toward him. Seeing her slight look of klutziness as she ran, he couldn't help but be enraptured. She was one of a kind. She also appeared as eager to see him as he was to see her. After far too much thinking, he began to run as well.

Charlie ran until she was right in front of him. She then stopped and just looked. He looked hot - in so many ways. As she laughed, she took one final step to him, then wrapped her arms around him.

The closeness was nice enough to Ash, but as he looked at her face, he couldn't help but kiss her ravenously. They stood for a long while, holding one another and kissing deeply until they slowly eased back from each other. As they did, Ash saw a tear in her eye.

He gently lifted a finger and wiped it away as it made its way to her cheek.

"You look beautiful," he said, his voice low and husky as his hand continued its journey over her cheek and around into her hair.

"So do you," Charlie responded before they both laughed softly. "Come on. I have to show you to your room," she continued, turning away and taking his hand in hers. "Molly and I set it up for you early this morning. It is *amazing*!"

Ash happily followed her, not bothered by the lack of words as they entered the house and walked through to the bedroom wing.

"I'm in this room," Charlie said, pointing to one door. "That is the bathroom," she said, pointing to another. "And this is your room."

Ash watched as she opened the large door, entered, and then gave a sweeping bow to him to indicate to him to enter. As he did so, he was in awe of the sights before him. He, too, had a large four-poster bed. The furniture in the room wasn't identical to that in Charlie's bedroom, but it did comprise the same level of quality and age.

Charlie watched as he walked around, looking at different items. When he turned back to face her again, she welcomed him walking right up to her.

"This is incredible. *You* are incredible," Ash said before leaning down and kissed her softly but longingly. He wanted to make the kiss last and not rush to end.

As Charlie wrapped her arms around him, she enjoyed the softness of the kiss. There was no need to rush to anything more. The feeling of his lips on hers was fulfilling in itself.

"Will you come downstairs and say hello to Molly and Tom?" she asked him when they finally pulled apart.

Ash nodded, feeling like he was under a spell. "Of course. I'd like to thank them for letting me come."

The two of them made their way downstairs and found Molly in the kitchen. Ash found himself wrapped up in new arms he'd never met before.

"Ash, it is a fine thing to meet you at last," Molly said. "This lass has talked about you so much that I feel like I know you already. Welcome."

"Thank you for having me," Ash replied quietly. He felt timid and shy but also incredibly appreciative.

Grinning, Charlie led him away from the house and out to the fields to look for Tom. When they found him, he was handing out feed to the donkeys.

"Ash!" Tom called out as he moved toward them with his hand extended. "Welcome, lad. It is good to see you again."

Ash accepted the handshake, smiling at the older man. "Hello, Tom. It is good to see you too."

"This one's been jittery for days now," Tom said, inclining his head toward Charlie while speaking to Ash. "I think she's been having withdrawal symptoms," he continued, winking at both of them and making them laugh. "Now, she'll be alright, with you finally here."

"Tom," Charlie said quietly, as if highly embarrassed, but saw him laugh in response.

"Ash here knows I'm just teasing you, lass," Tom said. "I'm just finishing up feeding these young'uns, and then I'm heading back to the stable. Perhaps the two of you would like to try your skills riding the ponies again?"

As Charlie looked surprised, Ash burst out laughing at the idea. After consideration, they gave in and later followed Tom to learn the art of putting on and securing the saddles.

"I think you can ride a bit further today," Tom said. "I know I kept you both within that little pen last time, but there is a larger paddock over there. It's fully fenced so the horses won't run off. There's a great tree out there, a few meters before the fence line. On a hot day like this is, it's a welcome place to sit down and relax."

He said nothing more, but Ash and Charlie both heard the suggestion in his voice. They smiled and laughed as they endured getting up onto the ponies without any assistance, then slowly tried to get them to move.

Tom chuckled beside them, reminded them *how* to get to the horses moving, and then saw them on their way.

Neither Ash nor Charlie was interested in moving faster than a slow walk. It was a good time to concentrate on the horse riding only and nothing else.

"There's the tree Tom spoke of," Charlie called out after they'd been walking forward for what seemed like a very long time. "Come on. Let's park these guys up and sit down under the shade."

Slowly and with much giggling on Charlie's part, they reached the tree and then dropped to solid ground again. Looking around, Ash saw the tree had some kind of bar installed across one side of it as if designed for securing the reins of the horses to.

When he'd finished tying the reins to the bar, Ash saw that Charlie had already sat down on the ground with her back leaning against the large tree trunk. He joined her, sitting in front of her with her legs nestled in the gap between his hand that was leaning on the ground, and his body. He was perfectly positioned so that he could look right at her. She was a bit mussed up with her hair messy from the ride and her face slightly sweaty, but to him, she looked incredible.

"So what have you been doing out here? I want to hear everything," he said, grinning at her.

Charlie welcomed the question and told him about all that Tom had introduced her to with the animals, and all that Molly had introduced her to in the kitchen.

As she spoke, Ash listened intently. Her face was so full of animation and excitement as she shared her previous days at the ranch. Once again, he found himself intrigued at how different she was from how he'd seen her when he'd only noticed her at the supermarket. He'd always perceived her to be serious, but even that hadn't stopped him from wishing he could meet her. Now she was absolutely beaming.

For a long while after she'd finished telling him of her adventures, Charlie saw him looking intently at her. She did believe he had been listening, but he seemed to just be in some kind of daze, staring at her face. She liked the feelings it produced in her. In the past, she'd been stared at by guys who were obviously sleazy. When Ash looked at her, she liked the way that he did.

She watched as he seemed to wake up and realize that he was staring, even though she hadn't been speaking for a while.

Ash quietly laughed. "I've missed you. Now I'm doing some creepy staring thing. Sorry."

Charlie moved her body. She had been leaning back against the trunk with her legs stretched out in front of her under his arm. She pulled her legs back and moved her body forward so that they were both leaning on one hand but in opposite directions. Although their legs and feet were facing opposite directions, their faces lined up perfectly. She used the opportunity to look closely at him.

"I missed you, too," she said quietly before leaning in and kissing him.

For a long while, they remained still with only their lips touching and caressing. No other part of their bodies touched, and neither moved to change that.

Ash let his eyes rest closed. He concentrated on the feelings of her lips on his. Their softness and their subtle movement, combined with the sweet glimpses of her tongue sweeping into his mouth to tease, all played on his senses. He felt like he was sitting on the edge of a deep pool of warm water that he wanted to dive right into and immerse himself in.

Charlie pulled back from him and looked into his eyes before delivering him a series of short kisses, intermingled with pulling back and looking into his eyes again.

"Charlie, where are the horses?" Ash asked when he took a moment to try and focus on something other than the deliciousness of her.

When Charlie looked around, she saw that the bar he'd tied the reins to now held no reins at all - nor any horses. Both of them jumped up and walked around the other side of the tree. In the distance, they could see both ponies standing, eating what they assumed was much more delicious grass than where they had been.

Ash moved forward. As he did, the ponies moved further away, as if purposely moving away from him.

Charlie watched and started to giggle as the two of them tried to round the horses up but ended up just running around the paddock in circles. It felt to Charlie that they were playing a game of tag. Ash looked back at her now and then as her giggles seemed out of control. Her laughing was the most glorious thing he'd ever heard.

~~~~~~

Tom watched from a distance but did nothing except chuckle to himself. More than watching the humorous activity going on with the two young ones trying to catch the ponies again, what he was most interested in was the way Charlie and Ash interacted together. He was the oldest living Stonewarden as far as he knew. Although he wasn't considered the head of the family, he still would make sure that young Charlotte was alright. He would use the days that Ash was staying to watch and quietly assess to make sure the boy's heart was true. She was a beauty, just like her mother had
~~~~~~

been, but she was young.

As he watched them, he didn't feel any concern at all. From what he'd seen of Ash so far, Tom believed him to be respectful and good-hearted. He'd keep an eye on things all the same.

~~~~~

Over dinner that evening, Molly laughed softly at Charlie's version of events over the great horse escape. After much running around in attempts to secure the horses, Tom had simply whistled, coaxing both ponies had happily trot back to him. The ease of that after their stern efforts made the experience all the more memorable.

"Thank you again for letting me stay," Ash said to Molly and Tom as he and Charlie finished washing and drying the dishes from their evening meal.

"You are very welcome, Ash. You two run along now, and we shall see you in the morning. Nice and early, Charlie! Work to be done, as you know," Tom said with a wink to follow.

Charlie smiled at him and left the room with Ash by her side. As they reached the hallway where his room stood on one side and hers on the other, she felt nervous. She knew she didn't have to be. They had spent time alone a lot, but it did feel different. She didn't want him to walk into his room and just leave her alone. She also didn't want to push herself on him and make him feel uncomfortable. Neither option was anything that she needed to worry about.

Taking both of her hands in his, Ash kissed her softly just outside his door.

"I'd like to spend more time with you before we go to our separate rooms," he said quietly and saw her nod and smile shyly at him.

He opened his door and gently walked into the bedroom, walking backward while still holding her hands in his and kissing her every few steps. With the
~~~~~

door closed gently behind them, he edged her up against it then kissed her deeply. The groan that came from her pushed him on, telling him not to stop.

As Charlie wrapped her arms around him, she was eager to be a bit more aggressive. They weren't going to have sex. They both knew that, and neither would push for it. That made it easy for her to push back against him, walking him backward until she could gently push him down onto the large bed.

Ash happily moved up the bed until his body was entirely in the middle of it, and he felt and watched her move over him so that she was lying down over the length of him. No words were spoken before she began kissing him with the hunger that he suspected had been building in her for four long days.

He felt his logic dissolve as he was taken over by the taste of her lips and her tongue, and the sound of her breathing as it deepened. He wanted to restrain himself, but what she was doing to him made that impossible. Instead, he indulged in it. His hands naturally moved all over her, one stroking her back while the other held her head close to him.

Charlie heard his groan as she rubbed against him. They'd been there before, and she'd loved it. She wanted it again. She wanted to feel those new feelings flow through her body again. She would stop if he asked her to. Until then, she had no intention of that whatsoever.

Ash held on but could feel he was at breaking point. He didn't want to stop her as he could tell she was on her own mission. He forced himself to think about anything else that he could, just to hold on and not climax in the deliciousness surrounding him. When he knew she had reached there, he used all the force that he could to flip her onto her back. He wanted to slow things down. Although he was bursting, close to orgasm, he needed to take a step back for a moment.

Looking down at her, he could see the passion raging in her eyes. That, combined with how red her lips were from their kissing, broke his resolve. He couldn't help it. He dived in again, hungry to feel her lips on his once more.

They lay like that for an extended time with him holding his body back from hers just enough to have some room to relax a little. After the kissing slowly eased off, he pulled away from her completely. She looked at him as he gently stroked her cheek and then kissed it.

"Do you have any idea how much you affect me, Charlie?" he asked, his voice quiet and deep.

She could have smiled then and made light of his question. Instead, she looked at him with an intense look in her eyes.

"I do know, and I love this with you," Charlie replied. "I love how you make me feel when I'm with you. I even love how I feel when I'm away from you but thinking about you. I think you're amazing, Ash, and I love spending this time with you."

Ash wasn't often speechless. At that moment, he absolutely was. She hadn't said many words, but he felt the power behind the ones she had. In years he knew she was only eighteen, but something made her more mature than her years. Perhaps having lost her mother at such a young age, and having had to step up and work with the rest of her family to simply get on and get things done, had made her as she was. Perhaps it was just being one girl in a house full of men. Perhaps it was that she was the youngest of a large family and that somehow had made her who she was. In the quiet of his mind, he pondered each of those options and then dismissed them all. The *why* didn't matter. All that mattered was that she was who she was, and she was incredible.

"Marry me," he whispered. He hadn't intended the words to come out. It was just a natural thing to cross his mind and roll out of his mouth at the same time.

Charlie thought she must have misheard, and it showed on her face.

"What?" she asked.

Ash had an opportunity to pretend he hadn't said it, but then he realized that he *did* want to say it. "Charlotte Stonewarden, I love every minute I am with you. Will you marry me?"

With the words cemented and secured, Charlie couldn't pretend she hadn't heard him. She was overwhelmed in emotion. She was happy at the thought. She was also scared at the thought.

"Ash, if I was wanting to get married right now, in this instant, you know that you would be the only person I would consider getting married to," she said. "I've never felt like this before, and I don't want this to end. I love the thought of having you as my husband, but I'm too young - *we're* too young - and we haven't been together long enough."

Ash heard the words and felt heartbroken, but wasn't ready to give up.

"But Charlie, be honest with me," he said. "Do you not want to marry me, or do you not want to marry me *now*?"

She took a deep breath. In that question, there was room for compromise. "The latter."

Ash watched her lean toward him before he felt her lips on his.

"How do you feel about a long engagement?" she asked.

Ash smiled as a tear came to his eye.

"Really?"

Charlie laughed at him. That she could affect him as much as he affected her was an incredible realization. "Really," she said. "I don't want us to marry this soon or this young, but what about another year from now? One year from right now, we'll have this discussion again and see how we're both feeling. What do you think?"

Ash nodded and kissed her. "What I think is that you are amazing and beautiful, and sexy, and…"

His words were cut off by her laughing softly, pushing him onto his back, and then kissing him deeply. It wasn't a move designed to turn him on. It was just to let him know she was serious about how she felt.

"I should get to my own bed. My heart is very full right now, and my body is making me think naughty things," Charlie said, making Ash laugh out loud.

"Agreed. My body is making me think naughty things, too," he said and stood up with her to walk her to the door. There, he pulled her into his arms and kissed her softly. "Sweet dreams, Charlie."

"Sweet dreams, Ash."

CHAPTER ELEVEN

The next day, Charlie and Ash worked around the entire ranch, sometimes with Tom, other times with Molly. By the end of the day, both were ready to fall asleep nice and early. No more was said about their conversation of the night before. Neither made any move toward quite so much kissing.

Down in the kitchen, after they had gone to bed, a conversation sparked about them.

"I think they are very much in love," Tom said quietly, making Molly smile.

"I think you are right," she replied. "Those two aren't just passing time. They aren't just having a fling. They are really in love, even if they don't quite know it yet."

"It isn't easy being a Stonewarden and bringing someone into your life," Tom said as he reached out and took her hand in his. "The conflict between family honor and secrets, and trying to let someone in and get to know them, is tough. I still remember how much I had to keep from you…"

"Hush now, Tom," replied Molly. "That is in the past, and I wasn't scared off by your family, even though you thought I would be. The truth didn't change how I felt about *you*. I don't think it will change how Ash feels about Charlie either. He is a good man. I can see it in him. He will accept her place."

"She doesn't want to be part of their business, you know."

Molly nodded. "I know. But does she have to be? You and I aren't getting any younger. We could use the help around here."

"Aye, and she does seem to love it here," Tom

agreed, nodding. "It would work for everyone, wouldn't it - except maybe Mitchell. I think he really does want her to be part of their crew."

"Perhaps he can be persuaded otherwise," Molly said, grinning. "Perhaps by a caring uncle?"

Tom laughed softly and lifted her hand to his lips. "Maybe. I'll talk to her when her young man has left and see what she wants to do."

~~~~~

Ash woke up to an angel lying beside him, looking down at him. When his consciousness kicked in, he smiled.

"How long have you been sitting there, watching me?" he asked shyly as Charlie moved a little closer.

"I just got here. Sorry. I probably woke you."

Ash put his arm out and pulled her even closer so he could kiss her lips softly.

"I've never woken up with such a vision," he said. "I kind of like it."

Charlie chuckled and huddled as close as she could get.

"You're leaving today," she said in almost a whisper.

"Yeah, I don't particularly want to, but I do need to get back and get myself organized for work tomorrow morning," Ash said. "But Charlie, this has been amazing. I know we haven't talked about it again, but I haven't forgotten - I *won't forget* - the conversation we had. I really do want us to be husband and wife."

"I know. So do I," Charlie said. "I won't forget either. What time is your bus?"

"They go past every hour, I think. I'll have breakfast with you, and then I'll wander out to the bus stop. I know you have a lot to do today. You're becoming quite the sexy cowgirl," Ash said, making her laugh. "You laugh at my words? I'm very serious," he continued as he nudged her onto her back. "The way you
~~~~~

chased those horses the other day..."

The vision made Charlie giggle. No matter how long they would have together, she knew that would be a happy memory that she'd retain for a very long time.

Ash looked down at her and kissed her. "When am I going to get to see you again? Are you heading home sometime, or do you think you're going to live here forever?"

Charlie pondered that. She hadn't even thought about going back to her family home. She'd become so comfortable on the ranch that it had started feeling more like home than her actual home did.

"I don't know," she said. "I suppose I *should* think about going home. I can't just live here forever, can I? I'm surprised my father hasn't asked for me to go home yet, actually. I should call him and see what is happening there. I would like to see Max and make sure he's okay."

"Well, come back with me today if you want."

"I need to talk to Tom about a few things before I leave," she said. "I still have some questions for him, and I don't want to leave until I have answers to them."

"Alright."

~~~~~

At the end of the driveway later on that morning, the two of them clung to each other.

"I'll see you soon," he said.

Charlie nodded, feeling a pang in her heart that made her wonder if that would indeed be true.

~~~~~

"Charlie, I would like you to talk to me about how long you wish to stay here," Tom said to her after she had watched Ash leave on the bus.

"Oh, Tom, I'm sorry," Charlie began to say. "I didn't mean to invade you for so long..."

"No, no, young lass," Tom reassured her. "That is not what I was meaning. Molly and I were talking. We had an idea that I want to put to you, but I don't want you to think that you have to say yes. It is an idea only."

"Alright," Charlie replied tentatively.

"You have to promise me - no saying yes just because I'm asking. You have to think about the idea and work out what is right for you," Tom continued, waiting until she'd nodded before he spoke again. "When you first came here, you said you didn't particularly want to do what your father and your brothers do."

"No. I know it's some great thing I'm supposed to be excited about, but I just can't be. I just don't look at it the way that they do," Charlie said. "I know my father is disappointed, and he will still make me be part of it…"

"Well, that is what I wish to talk to you about. Molly and I have been talking, and, well, we won't be able to keep up this place by ourselves forever. The ranch will need someone to take it over eventually," he said and immediately saw Charlie's attention sharpen. "I thought that if you *do* feel strongly about not joining your brothers and father in their crew, you might like to work here full time, with a view to taking over full control of it further down the line. Molly and I won't be retiring for a while yet, but when we do, it would be good to have someone already trained up and able to take it over without any further training or fuss."

Charlie was temporarily stunned into silence. She took a few minutes to find words.

"You want me to live here? And learn everything? And then run the ranch later on?" When she saw Tom nod, she instantly felt tears begin to well in her eyes. "Do you think my father would let me?"

"I cannot say for sure, lass, but at some point, he has to think about who is going to run this place," Tom said. "I already see how you are in the kitchen and with the animals. I think you have what it takes to keep a place such as this in order. I won't lie. It isn't an easy job. In addition to all the practical work, I'd be training you in the admin side of things like bookwork and ordering of supplies. It can be hard work…"

Before he could say any more, he saw Charlie jump up. With a broad smile on her face, she moved toward him then wrapped her arms around him.

"Thank you."

"It's not a done thing, Charlie," Tom said. "I need you to think about it before I talk to your father. Is there anything you need to ask about it?"

Charlie was quiet for a moment. Should she mention that Ash had proposed to her? Would that affect anything?

"There is something I should tell you before we think about it at all," she said. "The other night, Ash asked me to marry him. I put him off because I know we aren't old enough yet, but I do think that if I still feel this way about him a year from now, I would like very much to marry him. How would that affect things here?"

It was Charlie's turn to feel arms enclose her.

"Oh, lass," Tom said as he hugged her. "That is a fine thing to hear. I think he's a good lad, that one."

"Yes, but how does it affect your idea, Tom? How could I have him as my husband and still have this life?"

"He seems to fit in well here, don't you think?" Tom asked. "What do you see as the problem?"

"I haven't told him about our family."

Tom nodded. "It is difficult, I know. I kept everything from Molly for so long before I asked her to marry me. Right before I proposed to her, I had to speak and share our history. It wouldn't have been right to keep it from her. What kind of life would that be, for her *or* for me?"

"So you think I should *tell* him about what my father and brothers do?" asked Charlie.

"Only you can know what is best for you, but my advice would be to tell him, yes - not necessarily *yet*, but certainly before you say yes to marrying him," Tom said. "He seems a nice lad. He is entitled to make a choice based on the truth - the *full* truth."

Tom watched her face in its thoughtfulness. He fully understood the place she was in. He'd been in that same place decades earlier. It wasn't easy. Always, the conflict between family honor and finding a balance with new people and love was hard.

"If the family is to continue, it might be up to you to provide the next generation. Lord knows your brothers don't seem in any hurry to get on with that!" he said, laughing all of a sudden. "Are children in your future, Charlie?" he then asked, his voice soft and caring.

She nodded. "They are," she replied. "I want to be a mother, and I know that Ash wants to be a father."

"Well, young lass, that fact might be a turning point in your favor if you want me to talk to your father about this idea of ours," Tom said. "For any family to thrive, new generations have to begin, and it will be better for you to start a family in this job than *that* one!"

"I'll take a few days to think about things, I think, Tom," Charlie said. "I think I should probably head home and see my father."

"Aye, he is missing you. I do know that."

"You've spoken to him?" she asked and saw him nod. "He didn't want to talk to me?"

Tom laughed softly. "No, it was all about business with him, but he did ask about you, and he did ask when I was going to let you go home," he replied. "He didn't say it with words, but I could hear it in his voice. He misses you, and he does want to see you. Trust me, a Stonewarden knows!"

Charlie smiled and hugged him. "I'll pack up my things and head home then. Thank you so much, Tom. You have given me something amazing to think about."

A short time later, she sat on a bus bound for her hometown, then walked to her home. As she stood on the path leading up to the front door, she took a moment to look at the house. It was something she rarely took time to. In her childhood and teenage years, she had been ashamed of the state of it, if she was honest with herself. The way Ash had reacted to it had opened her eyes a little. He had given her the idea to really stand back and just look at it from an outsider's point of view. As she did so, she agreed with him. It *was* an amazing home - and it was a Stonewarden home. Where in the great scheme of things did it sit as far as her ancestors went? She had seen their portraits. Which one of them had been the one who had the large home built?

"Charlie!" she heard from the front doorway. When she looked up, she saw Max. His smile was infectious. "About time you came back. You have no idea what it's been like being stuck here with these guys, day in and day out. They're like mother hens, fussing over me."

As he'd spoken, he had been walking down the steps and toward her. Finally, Charlie was able to hug him.

"Max! Oh, Max, I'm so glad you are okay."

They pulled apart and then started their walk up toward the house.

"Where have you been, Charlie?" Max asked.

"What did Dad tell you?"

"He only said you were with friends," he said. "I tried to get more out of him, but you know what he's like. I only asked once, and I wasn't going to ask again!"

"Whatever he told you is what was happening," Charlie replied. "Leave it at that."

"Are you alright, though?"

She nodded at him as they walked through the front door.

"I'm fine," she reassured him. "Better than fine. Don't worry about me."

As they entered the house, they were greeted by James and Regan making their way out the door.

"Oh, hey, Sis. Hi! Bye!"

That was all she was going to get from either of them, but she smiled at them. She hardly ever saw James during normal circumstances anyway, with him having his own place. As he walked away from her, she realized she had actually enjoyed spending what little time with him that she had while Max had been in hospital.

While she was pondering that thought and watching her two older brothers walking down the path, she felt the presence of her father appear. When she looked at him, she saw him smile, albeit rather sadly.

"Welcome home, Charlie," Mitchell said as he pulled her into his embrace. It wasn't a regular occurrence, but she accepted it and hugged him back. "It's just the three of us for dinner, so what would you like? Your choice."

Charlie was surprised but thought carefully and said her favorite fast food. The name tumbled out of her mouth more like a question than an answer, she was so unused to being asked such a thing.

"Alright," her father replied as he pulled away from her. "You two write down what you want. I'll go and pick it up at dinner time."

She watched as he walked away, their conversation seemingly terminated. Picking up her bag, she began walking up the stairs, making her way to her room. As she did, she found Max right behind her. She didn't try and stop him, even though it wasn't normal for him to go anywhere near her bedroom. Once inside, she dumped her bag on the chair and then closed the door behind him.

"Sit," she said, pointing at the bed. "What's going on?"

Max looked at her. She was young but much easier to talk to than anyone else in his family. "They're doing another job - a big one. I'm not supposed to tell you about it, but Charlie, I'm really worried. How can we go on as a family when people are shooting at us because of what we do?"

She sat down beside him on the bed. "Is that why we were shot at though? Have the police confirmed that?"

"No," replied Max. "They haven't said anything more except that they have suspects they're investigating. I don't think anything will come of their questioning. You know who it was, don't you. You saw the car when they started firing…"

Charlie felt a shiver flow through her at the visualization of that moment. She could clearly see in her mind the car and the gun rising, pointing straight toward her. "I told the police all that I saw and remembered. They know who it was. I *told* them who it was."

"I know, but they have to prove it, don't they," Max said. "And those guys are good - not as good as us in business, but *really* good at avoiding the law, I think."

He was, of course, talking about the Leadbetter family. Also thieves with eyes on jewels of the city, there was an unspoken clash between them and the Stonewardens. The latter didn't want trouble and didn't have anything to do with the former. The former wanted trouble. They thrived on it. Two completely different families with two completely different techniques, but one goal that both wanted - gems. Max didn't know how long there had been such an unspoken feud going on. He supposed it didn't matter. What did matter was that the Leadbetters might be stepping up their attempts to stop his family from being their rivals in the race for jewels.

"Well, what about your car? Surely that must have turned up somewhere…" Charlie started to say, but saw Max instantly shake his head.

"No. My baby's gone," he replied. "I've accepted that. I'll start again. I'm thinking I might buy a ute, paint it blue and red, and call it 'Optimus'."

Charlie burst out laughing. A 21-year-old man

who still wanted to play with Transformers. Who would have expected such a thing.

"But seriously, Sis, is all okay with you? Really?" Max asked.

"Yes, all is fine with me," Charlie replied. "You don't need to worry about me."

"I'm always going to worry about you. What about that guy you keep kissing? Is he still hanging around?"

"Max! His name is Ash, and yes, he's still around," Charlie said. "I like him a lot, so don't give him a hard time whenever you see him!"

Usually happy go lucky, Charlie was surprised to see Max's face grow serious.

"I won't give him a hard time. I'm happy to see you happy, and I do believe he's okay. Nothing I heard when I was lying in the hospital made me think he's a jerk. He can stay."

Charlie laughed at him again but affectionately. As far as brothers went, he was alright.

~~~~~

Mitchell took his time picking up dinner. His little girl was back from spending time at the family ranch - the ranch that was kept secret from the majority of the family. He'd told her that she was never to tell the boys about it, and he trusted that she would follow him in that. She didn't understand why it was important they not know what it was or where it was, but she had seemed to perfectly comprehend the importance he saw in keeping it a secret. Only a sliver of concern haunted him over her knowing about the large property.

Tom had already called him and talked to him about the idea of her moving out there and working toward taking over management of it. Mitchell sighed at that thought. He would never have thought of the idea himself, he had always been so consumed with making sure she knew her place in the business along with her
~~~~~

brothers. As he pondered it as an option, it made far more sense. She didn't want to go into the business and do what he and the boys did. That wasn't really a consideration. Others before her had objected but still had to step up and do what was expected of them according to family traditions and honor.

The two points that Tom had raised had hit Mitchell hard in his consideration. Charlie was a young woman, and she wanted to become a mother - not yet, but certainly sometime in the future. He wouldn't want her wrapped up in what they did if she had children. He wouldn't have let Caroline be part of it as they started their family, and he didn't want Charlie to be part of it then either. Tom had also said that she had been working hard, eagerly learning whatever she could. Tom wasn't getting any younger. As fit and reliable as he was, that wouldn't last forever. He was getting older. That point, Mitchell had mulled over too.

Yes, it made sense to let her go and take her place there. She would still be a part of the business, but she would be involved in the safe part. There, she could raise a family and still contribute to the family in that way.

Charlie as a mother. That was a thought that caused slight panic but also a little excitement in Mitchell. Not that it was going to happen anytime soon. Well, it had better not anyway! No, he didn't think she wanted it yet. She was only thinking out to the future. He suspected Ash was part of that plan too. If they stayed together and things got that serious, Ash would have to find out about the Stonewarden family. What then? At what point would it be revealed to him that they were, in fact, the people who broke into his parents' penthouse apartment and robbed them? Mitchell groaned at the thought. The timing of all of that was just so messy. If he'd known Ash longer before that night, there was a chance he might have known his last name, and then it could have been recognized as his family's home earlier.

The burglary could have been called off, and it never would have happened.

But it did happen, and somewhere, somehow, sometime, the news might be revealed.

What would that mean for Charlie then?

~~~~~

As she lay in her bed later that night, Charlie's thoughts moved to Ash. Although she'd only seen him that morning, she already missed him. It had been a great few days together at the ranch. Every minute she'd shared with him, she had enjoyed. There was never any conflict between them. She loved that. He wanted her, but he didn't pressure her. He listened to whatever she wanted to say - *really* listened, like hearing even the trivial stuff was exciting to him.

He'd asked her to marry him. That was the most amazing thing of all. It wasn't something she'd even pondered before, but she liked the idea. She wanted him as her husband, to have and to hold forevermore. She wanted him to be the first and only man she ever shared her body with. She wanted to see him every morning and every night, and she believed that he felt the same. He wasn't like other guys. He had values, and he was willing to wait for her.

She sighed at the thought as she moved further under the blankets. Her thoughts were interrupted by the sound of a text message arriving. She picked up her phone from the bedside table and looked at it. Of course the text was from Ash.

'Did you get home okay?' his message read.

'I did, thank you. I'm at home now, in my bed, thinking of you.'

Ash read her reply and smiled and groaned at the same time.

'Don't put such an image in my head.'

'And why not? Don't you like to think of me in my bed, thinking of you?' Charlie asked.
~~~~~

Ash laughed softly to himself. 'I do, but stop thinking naughty thoughts and tell me about your return home.'

Charlie couldn't help but grin but did as instructed.

'It was fine. It's only been me, Dad and Max here.'

There was a short time of no more messaging before Ash sent his next message.

'I miss you already.'

'I miss you too. Are you still working tomorrow?'

'I am. I'll be finishing at 4 though. Do you want to come to my place after that?'

'Yes!!!!!!!!' Charlie typed.

Ash laughed out loud. She was just so … *everything*.

'It's a date. I should be there about ¼ after.'

'Okay. Sweet dreams, Ash.'

'Of course, Charlie. They'll be of you. Goodnight.'

~~~~~

"Hey, you," Charlie heard Ash say as he approached where she was sitting on his doorstep the following afternoon.

She watched as he seemed to bound up the steps and guide her to stand up so he could wrap his arms around her and kiss her deeply.

"Hey yourself," she responded when they finally stepped apart so he could unlock the door. "How was work?"

"Long, but good," Ash said before closing the door behind them and dumping his keys onto the kitchen counter. "I was looking forward to seeing you."

He moved to the sofa while holding her hand, then pulled her into his arms. "How was your day?" he asked and listened as she talked.

When she had finished her small talk, Charlie turned more fully toward him.

"Ash, you know what you asked me…"
~~~~~

"To marry me?" he clarified with a slight teasing in his voice and saw her nod.

"Before I left the ranch, Tom put an idea to me that I want to put to you," Charlie said. "I don't know if it will affect us or not. Maybe it will. Oh, but maybe it won't…"

"Charlie!" Ash broke in, slightly laughing although he did feel a slight panic at what was to come. "Tell me."

"He asked me to start working there and living there, like full time," she said.

"That sounds amazing!" Ash exclaimed. "What about that is worrying you?"

"Well, for now, I won't be here in town so I won't be able to just come over here like this…"

"That's okay," he said. "I can come and see you on my days off if you want me to."

"Of course I do! But Ash, I was thinking ahead more, to…"

"To when you are my wife, and I am your husband?" he asked, again slightly teasing her but loving the sound of those words.

"Yes," Charlie replied, nodding. "How would we make that work if you want to be here, and I want to be there?"

Ash looked at her lovingly and softly stroked her cheek before kissing her lips gently.

"Perhaps you will need a hand to do the work…" he said.

"I … hmm … yes…" replied Charlie.

"So perhaps I can come and live there and work there too."

Charlie pulled back in surprise and relief. "Really? You would want to do that?"

Ash grinned. "Of course I would."

"But your supermarket job…"

"Doesn't have to be forever," he said. "Charlie,

you and I living and working together at the ranch sounds incredible. If it is what you want to do, and you want me there with you, I'll be there."

Charlie was speechless. Being that speechless, all she could do was kiss him - for a very long time.

~~~~~

The next day, Charlie made the journey back to the ranch and told Tom about her enthusiasm to move forward. Neither of them had received any feedback from her father, but they decided they were going to keep working as if he had said yes. If he pulled her away on her 19th birthday, Charlie would have to accept that. In the meantime, she had a few months before that was going to happen.

"But what about when I turn 19, Tom?" she asked. "Something is going to happen either way, isn't it. I am going to have my father sit me down and tell me what I have to do with my life. How is that going to affect Ash and me?"

"I know, lass. It is hard," Tom agreed. "But don't get yourself worked up about it now. Wait and see how things play out. You have a few months yet. Anything could happen in that time."

As Molly appeared, she gave Charlie a hug. "Oh, Charlie, it is good to have you back again so soon. Is Ash coming to visit too?"

Charlie smiled at the thought. "He would like to come here on his days off if that's okay with both of you."

"Oh, yes! I like having such a handsome young man around, you know, Charlie," Molly said, making them all laugh.

~~~~~

Mitchell lay down on the bed in his bedroom. It was the bed he'd shared with Caroline during their marriage, right up until she had passed away. Some days he didn't think about her so much. It wasn't one of those days. Charlie had been to the house for one night and had then left again. She was sure the ranch was her calling, and Mitchell was reluctantly tending to agree. The fact that she had even found the place without any input from him also hinted to him that she'd found it because she was meant to.

"Oh, Caroline, I wish you were here. You would know what to do now. You would know the right thing to do and the right thing to say," he said. As he verbally voiced those words, he let the tears come. Nine years on, he still had days when he just missed her so much. He knew he'd done a good enough job raising their kids, but she should have been able to be a part of that. She should have been able to watch them as he had been able to. They were as much a part of her as they were a part of him. Why did she have to be taken away so young and so early? They should have been together, watching their kids grow and head out in the world. They should have been thinking about retiring together and all the things they would do when the business passed over to Vic.

His baby girl was making plans for her future. Although Charlie was only eighteen, Mitchell couldn't use that as an argument because he knew she was much older in spirit than she was in years. She had grown up, and now she was ready to work. She *wanted* to work. She had discovered the ranch and was eager to contribute to it. It was a good plan. She could do that while being safe and, if it were meant to be, she could help with the next generation of Stonewardens. She shouldn't be the first to do that, but Mitchell had to concede that his sons all loved women so much that it was uncertain if any of them would ever settle down. Charlie was the youngest, but she was the first to find what Mitchell could see was love. It seemed a little backward, and yet it seemed *right*.

Tom had told him about the marriage proposal. At first, Mitchell had been shocked. When Tom had said that Charlie had taken it upon herself to put the proposal on hold for a year, he was impressed. He was impressed with her for considering that and speaking up about what she wanted. He was equally impressed with Ash. Not every man who asked a woman to marry him would take such a response easily. If Ash could happily accept Charlie's one-year plan to wait and reassess how they both felt then, he was even more of an impressive young man than Mitchell had already thought.

"She's going to be okay, Caroline," Mitchell muttered, wiping his eyes. "Our little girl's going to be okay."

CHAPTER TWELVE

On each of the following five nights, Ash went to sleep with a smile on his face after the back and forth text message banter he shared with Charlie. He wanted to be closer to Charlie, but even he thought that having space apart was good. It seemed a way for them to see if they truly did feel the same way about each other if the deliciousness of close proximity of their bodies wasn't such a primary force between them.

Out at the ranch, Tom watched Charlie grow more confident with all of the animals. He chuckled as he watched her talking to each one every day as if she were finally learning to make friends. He hadn't known her in your childhood, but even he could see that although she grew up in a house full of people, for the most part, she was a solitary lass. She was a good worker. He had no doubt about that. Whatever she put her mind and soul into, she would succeed in. She had the same inner strength as her mother.

While she was living and working on the ranch, Mitchell and his sons were planning. Intel had made them aware of an incredible score that was coming into town. The plans had been established and, even with the advanced technological skills of Fitz, everything was being checked again and again. As always, everything had to go seamlessly. Mitchell's job in that regard was to question them all, over and over, throwing in every possible thing that could happen so that they all knew how they were going to deal with it should that possibility become a reality.

The time was drawing closer. Plans were double-checked then triple checked. Equipment needed to get into a vault where the gems were to be stored was inventoried and checked it was all in good working order. It wasn't going to be a small job, but it was going to be worth it.

They just needed to wait a little longer.

~~~~~

Ash had to stop himself from running up the long driveway when his next days off from work finally came. His heart was beating loudly in anticipation of being close to Charlie again. The time apart was a good thing, but also excruciating.

When Charlie finally came into view, he stopped walking and absorbed the sight running toward him. She was breathtaking, and, he noted as she got closer, she was out of breath. He laughed at her as she reached him, bent over, and tried to catch her breath as if she'd run a mini-marathon.

Charlie stood up, grinning while she tried to breathe again. Perhaps running at that speed down that long driveway was more than she was currently in shape for. As she looked at Ash's face and the smile gracing it, she couldn't stop herself from throwing her arms around him and indulgently placing her lips on his.

The feeling of lips locking was followed by a desperation to get closer, making their kiss deepen until Ash moaned in pleasure.

"Wait, now *I* need to breathe," he said, making her giggle as he pulled away from her, took her hand, and the two of them began walking. "You look beautiful.".

Charlie lifted his hand and kissed the back of it before leaning closer to him and attempting to kiss him while they were still stepping.

"Ash! Welcome, lad," Tom called out from the stable as they neared. "Get yourself settled, and then both of you come in here. I have something special to show you that's going to happen in the next hour or two. You don't want to miss it!"
~~~~~

Up in his room, Ash dropped his bag before pulling Charlie her into his arms again.

"I'm glad you're here," she said quietly to him as she felt the familiar warmth and comfort from his embrace. "Five days seems too long."

Ash laughed softly. "I agree, but it is quite nice having the anticipation of seeing you too."

As her lips found his again, he held her tight and breathed her in before he pulled away, smiling sheepishly.

"I think Tom is waiting for us. Come on," he said, taking her hand in his and leading her to the bedroom doorway. "We have our whole lives for kissing."

Walking into the stable, they saw Tom and Molly in one of the stalls, crouched around a horse as if keeping a close eye on her.

"Is she hurt?" Charlie asked, feeling emotional at the thought, but saw Tom and Molly both smile broadly.

"Oh, no, lass," Molly said. "She's going to give birth." After she said the words, she looked at the faces of Charlie and Ash and laughed. "Don't look so scared. She's well on her way. It won't be long now. You are both going to witness a true miracle."

Charlie felt Ash's hand reach out and squeeze hers tightly. When she looked at him, he looked quite pale. They both stood where they were and kept watching with a mixture of excitement and uncertainty.

Another half-hour later, they saw the birth of a live foal. Both were speechless as they watched it gain its confidence to the point where it could stand by itself. While they watched the new life seeming to grow before their eyes, Tom watched the young couple. Animals giving birth wasn't something everyone enjoyed or could easily watch. Whoever ran the ranch in the future would have to be able to not only endure it but also embrace it. The looks on the faces of Charlie and Ash gave him relief. They were a little pale, but they were also engaged in it and not turning away. It was a good sign.

~~~~~

"How long are you staying with us this visit, Ash?" Molly asked when they were having dinner that night.

"I'd like to stay tonight and tomorrow night if that's alright with you. I only get three days off work at a time, so when … if … I can keep coming here to see Charlie, it will always be two nights at a time. But you will tell me if I outstay my welcome, won't you?"

Molly laughed. "We would, but that isn't likely for the moment anyway, Ash. You are very welcome."

They were enjoying a quiet meal and quiet conversation when they heard a loud bang on the side door. Tom immediately looked at Molly with alarm evident on his face. It seemed to both Charlie and Ash that whatever was going on, the two older residents were familiar with it. More than that - there was a routine to it.

Tom stood up and moved quickly. Charlie and Ash sat where they were as he left the room. Molly sat where she was, looking slightly pale.

"What's going on?" Charlie asked quietly.

In response, Molly looked at her, shook her head, and silently indicated that they should be quiet and stay where they all were.

It seemed a long time before the door to where they were, opened. Charlie was surprised to see her father walk in, followed by four of her brothers, who also had a look of confusion on their faces.

"Charlie? What are *you* doing here?" Vic asked before looking at their father for answers. "Dad, what's going on?"

"What are you all doing here?" Charlie asked, her question overlapping his. "And if you *are* all supposed to be here, where's James?"

Mitchell looked around as if he only just realized that one of his sons wasn't with him. He focused his eyes
~~~~~

on Regan. "He came out with you, didn't he?"

Regan shook his head. "No. I thought he was with Vic."

Vic faced them all. "No, he wasn't with me."

"Fuck!" Mitchell shouted as he ran out the door again with Tom following him.

Ash and Charlie just sat and watched. With the exception of one brother, Ash was now among all Stonewardens that he knew of. They were full of powerful presence - each and every one of them.

"What's going on?" Charlie ventured to ask, daring to speak one more time.

Max looked at her and sat beside her. "We've just…"

"Max!" Vic's voice boomed out over the top of whatever Max was about to say.

Charlie knew when she wasn't wanted. She knew those moments of her father and brothers. They were either doing something that involved theft, or they were planning it. Either way, she was driven to stand and indicate to Ash to do the same. They left the room by the opposite door to where she had seen her father go.

They'd only just closed the door behind them when she heard Vic's voice. He was obviously talking too loud. He never would've risked Charlie hearing what he said, and he certainly would never have ventured to say his words when he knew an outsider like Ash was close by.

"Are you mad? You were about to tell her about the heist, you fucking idiot! You know that she can't know about this. She can't know about the score we just got. So SHUT THE FUCK UP!"

Charlie closed her eyes and cringed, opening them a little at a time in the hope that Ash hadn't heard. It was bad enough that she'd heard, but he…

She could see by his face that he had indeed heard. His eyes were open and looked round in that instant. She knew his expression. It was the one he had when his mind was working hard. She watched as his face went hard too.

Ash held out his hand to her.

"Come with me," he said, no love in his voice.

Although tentative, Charlie followed him. They couldn't stand where they were for fear of hearing more that Ash shouldn't hear.

When he led her into his bedroom and closed the door, she remained silent. His face had changed. It wasn't like she'd ever seen it. For that, she was regretful, but she would wait. He had to think of his words and his questions. Whatever they were, she would answer them. It was too late to try and cover up what they'd just heard.

She saw him pace a little before he turned and faced her with a look of almost hatred on his face.

"Your family … are *thieves*?" Ash asked and saw Charlie nod.

She prayed that he would ask as many questions as he wanted to - except *one*. Her hopes were shattered when his questions continued, and he asked the very one that she'd hoped he wouldn't.

"Did they break into my family's apartment and steal from my parents?"

Charlie stood with her head down, and her eyes closed, willing the moment to be some kind of bad dream that she would wake up from.

Ash took a step closer and yelled, "Did your family steal from *my* family, Charlie?!!"

He watched as Charlie nodded and raised her eyes again. As she faced him, he saw tears appear on her cheek. For a moment, he wanted to pull her into his arms and make her feel better. Then the realization hit him again. After he had met her, her family had made their way into his parents' home and robbed it. That couldn't be a coincidence.

"You *used* me," he said, his words sounding like a

hiss. "All this time, I thought you didn't know how wealthy my family was, but you *did* know. You used me to get to them. All of this was some kind of what? Some big plan to get my parents' wealth? Is that why you've given me all of this attention? Just to get my family's money?"

Charlie heard all of his questions but said nothing. She sobbed, wanting to tell him that he had it wrong, but how could she? Of course, he saw it as he was saying it. She remained silent as he turned away from her, grabbed all that he had brought with him, and walked out. He said nothing more to her. There was no goodbye, no sentiment that he'd enjoyed being with her, and certainly no mention of any kind of future wedding.

After he walked out, Charlie sank to the floor in a heap, not even trying to stop the tears that were readily flowing at an alarming rate. She remained like that with no desire to move. Such a short time earlier, she'd felt so happy. How could everything change with one stupid appearance by her family?

~~~~~

Ash didn't look back. He was in shock, and he was mad. He was angry for having let himself believe that she would want to be with him. She was beautiful and amazing. Of course, she wouldn't want to be with him. Why had he let himself believe that she did? He was so stupid to have fallen for it - and he had. He'd believed all that she'd told him. He had lapped it up and stupidly believed every nice thing she had said. And it was all just so that she could marry him and get his parents' money. Stupid! Stupid! STUPID!!

His own mind continued to abuse him, putting him down all the way back to his apartment. It was like a recording replaying in his head, over and over. The same words repeated again and again.

Once inside his home, he went straight to his bedroom and threw himself on the bed. He'd abused
~~~~~

himself enough. He was ready to let out sadness. Even though she'd used him, he had loved being with her. He'd loved everything about her.

It had all been a lie. That didn't mean that he didn't already miss her. As much as he didn't want to, he knew that he would be pining for her for a very long time.

~~~~~

Mitchell was panicked. They had scattered after the job, but he'd directed them to the ranch so that no-one could have led the cops anywhere near any of their homes. After a long while, James had finally made contact with him. He was at a friend's house and was safe. After receiving the message, Mitchell took a breath to recalibrate his emotions. It was then that he thought of Charlie. She had left the room with Ash, he knew. Although he didn't want to interrupt their time together, he needed to talk to her.

He made his way up to the guest wing. After walking down the hallway, he found her on the floor of a guest room, sobbing heavily. He rushed to her, knelt beside her, then scooped her into his arms.

"Baby girl, what's happened? Why are you crying?" he asked. When he looked around and saw no sign of Ash, his questions continued. "Where's Ash? Is he here still?" he asked and felt her shake her head against his shoulder. "I don't understand. Did you have a fight?"

As Charlie pulled away from her father, he saw her give him a look that kind of said, 'you really can't be *that* stupid'. He tried to think what he'd done, or what anyone else had done, that could have resulted in whatever had happened, happening.

"Did he leave?" he asked and saw her nod as a new lot of sobs erupted. "Did he leave because we arrived? I thought he was okay with us…"

"No! He's not okay with you!" Charlie yelled. "He
~~~~~

now knows that you are thieves. He knows that you broke into his parents' place and stole from them. And now he hates *me* because you did that, and that means that *I* must have been in on it."

Mitchell took a minute to process what she had just said. Dread fell over him.

"Why are you even here?" she went on to ask. "You told me that the boys weren't to know about this place, and now you all turn up here in one swoop? What is going on??!!"

Mitchell stroked her hair in an attempt to soothe her as he spoke the truth.

"We did a job tonight, Charlie," he said. "We got what we went for, but it was close. Things almost didn't work out well. I told everyone to avoid our homes and to meet here, in case any cops followed us."

"Why would you let that happen to Tom and Molly?" she asked, but as he sat silent and she thought more, the realization finally flowed right over her. "*That* is what this place is for. This entire ranch is some kind of mirage that has been built to hide the family when there's a danger they'll be caught and arrested. It is just one … big … hiding place."

Mitchell was slow in responding, but eventually, Charlie saw him nod with a sad look on his face. They sat in silence a long while, both absorbed in their individual thoughts.

"But what about Ash, Charlie?" Mitchell asked. "You said he now knows about us. What did he say to that?"

"I told you. He knows you robbed his parents' place. Now he thinks I've been seeing him all this time to get at his parents' money. He thinks I've been using him…"

"But that isn't true. That isn't what has been happening…"

"I know!" Charlie exclaimed. "*I* know that, but he

doesn't. Dad, you have to admit the odds of him meeting me, and then you guys ripping off that apartment are slim. If I were in his shoes, I wouldn't think it could be a coincidence either."

"Well, I can put that right. I just need to talk to…"

"No! You have done enough. Please, just let it go. This is just my life now. I'm not going to fight anymore. What other way can I live, being who I am?"

Mitchell heard the words, but more than that, he heard the tone. It was the sound of someone who was utterly defeated and had no fight left in them. He'd seen that in war. He wasn't going to let his baby girl feel like that. He said nothing more as he held her tighter. Despite her request, he was resolved. He would say nothing to her about it, but he definitely *would* say something to Ash. That kid had loved his daughter. There was no way Mitchell was going to let him walk away that easily - not without hearing and believing the truth anyway.

~~~~~~

The evening was long. Mitchell and his sons eventually all headed off in different directions after Fitz did his thing in investigation and assured them they were safe. Before they'd left, Max had visited Charlie and teased her enough to make her at least smile. He didn't know what was happening, and he didn't push for information, but he could see she wasn't happy. He perceived her kissy friend was gone. He also knew her well enough to understand that it wasn't a time that she needed to talk. It was a time when she needed to be alone.

Eventually, Charlie left the room Ash had been going to stay in and returned to her own room. As she lay in bed, she thought about Ash, and she thought about her mother. Both had now left her. They were the only people in her life who had left her that she could remember, and it hurt. It had hurt nine years earlier, and it hurt at that present moment. She wondered if she could
~~~~~~

let herself get close to anyone ever again if it kept happening. If people kept leaving her, why get close to anyone at all?

~~~~~

Mitchell drove straight to Ash's apartment. He didn't care what time it was. As far as he was concerned, that kid was going to listen to him. He banged on the door several times before Ash opened it, his eyes revealing that he, too, must have had a lengthy sobbing session. When he focused on Mitchell, his face accurately conveyed the confusion he felt.

"We need to talk," Mitchell said.

Ash felt a sliver of fear but let the powerful man in. He didn't suppose it mattered if he did or he didn't. If Charlie's dad wanted to hurt him, he would - inside or outside the apartment. He stood as he watched Mitchell sit down on the sofa.

"You know what my family does," Mitchell said and watched as Ash nodded. "I know you don't understand, but the fact that my family does this shouldn't have any bearing on you and Charlie."

Ash was bursting to yell at the guy but maintained an outward calm. He was pretty sure that sitting before him was a man who'd been trained to kill swiftly and simply.

"Are you kidding me?" Ash started, slowly and quietly. "I've been a target all along…"

"No! That is complete and utter rubbish," Mitchell said. "Charlie met you at the supermarket. Come on, Ash. Think! Do you seriously believe that what? She got someone to shoot at you guys on that day just so that she could reel you in and make you fall in love with her? Come on. You aren't that stupid. She met you because of the shooting. She got to know you - *you* - not your family - and she fell in love with *you*."

"And I suppose I am supposed to believe that she didn't know you were ripping my mother and father off?
~~~~~

That was one big coincidence?"

"I know that it doesn't seem possible, but it is the truth," Mitchell continued. "If I'd known your last name, maybe I could have prevented it, but I didn't. And for your information, Charlie has nothing to do with what we do. She is kept away from it, with good reason."

"But she knows what you do," Ash said.

"Yes," Mitchell confirmed. "When she turned eighteen, I told her what we do. I also told her that I wanted her to join us when she turns nineteen. And do you think she wants to? Of course she doesn't. She told me that long before she met you. She wants nothing to do with it, and now she's been working at the ranch, she is happy that she has an alternative plan."

"The ranch that actually is some kind of criminal getaway spot for your family," Ash said. "How did you get Tom to agree to that?"

"Tom is my uncle, Ash," Mitchell replied. "He is part of my family. That ranch is my family ranch. *Charlie's* family ranch."

Ash was surprised into silence. He hadn't heard that news from Charlie, Tom, or Molly.

"Just another thing she lied to me about..."

"No! She didn't know at first. When the two of you first went there, she had no idea. I have never told any of my kids about it. She found it by accident, but she has since been told what it is to our family."

"If you have so much wealth that you can afford a place like that, why have you set your sights on my parents?" Ash asked, his thoughts feeling chaotic. "You hope I will marry your daughter so she can get the money, and then what? What is the bigger plan? Will you kill me to make sure she gets it all?"

As he heard that last question, Mitchell had to control anger building in him. Such an accusation was almost inexcusable. *Almost.* He reminded himself that Ash was just a 20-year-old kid who was in love and was in the grips of heartbreak. He could have a little leeway.

"Look, you can argue with me all you want, but that won't change the fact that my daughter loves you," Mitchell said. "She wants to marry you for *you*. If she didn't, don't you think she would have accepted your proposal straight away and tried to get you to the altar as fast as she could? Is there really any part of you, Ash, that believes that Charlie is some kind of user? Some kind of money seeker? Do you see that in her nature? Because if you do, then you don't deserve her. She is a good girl. She hurt for a long time when her mother died, and I know that she wouldn't give her heart to just anyone."

Ash was silent for a long while. Mitchell waited to see if anything else could be said to help prevent the two young people from going through a wasteful and pointless breakup.

"I don't want anything to do with what you do. I can't have anything to do with it," Ash said with a tone of almost pleading in his voice.

The sound made Mitchell relax a little.

"Charlie doesn't want anything to do with it either," he replied. "That is why I agreed to her living and working at the ranch with a view to taking it over in the future when Tom is ready to retire. I know that she loves the idea of having you there with her, Ash - as her work partner, as her husband, and as the father to her children. Please believe me. She doesn't want anything from your parents. None of us do. She just wants *you*."

"I don't have any access to my parents' wealth. None of it will come to me," Ash said, putting one more test out there. "I work in a supermarket. What I earn is what I live off. My parents' money isn't mine."

"I care nothing for your parents' money. I care nothing for *your* money," Mitchell assured him. "All I care about is my little girl's happiness. If you're worried about money, go to a lawyer and get everything secured so that no matter what happens, Charlie can't touch anything. That is a perfectly normal thing to do before two people get married. It is wise, and, in this instance, I think it would put your mind at rest - if you still want to marry my little girl, that is."

"She lied to me."

"No, she didn't. She kept from you some small bits of information about our family, and she did that because I asked her to, not because she wanted to. She hates what we do, but she is loyal to the Stonewarden family."

"And what lengths will she go to for that, do you think?"

Mitchell stood up in frustration. It wasn't lost on him that across Ash's face slid a look of fear, just for a moment.

"Ash, I can't *make* you believe anything that I or anyone else says, but let me be very plain," he said. "My daughter met you, she got to know you, she fell in love with you, she wants to marry you and have your children, and she wants to spend the rest of her life with you. Just you. Now, you can either believe that, or you can pretend it isn't real. Your choice."

With that, Mitchell walked out, leaving Ash frustrated, sad, angry … and extremely relieved that the conversation was over.

~~~~~

The next morning Ash woke to more pounding on his door. Reluctantly, he went to open it but was a bit more relaxed when he saw Molly. After he welcomed her in, they sat together as Ash waited for her to speak.

"Ash, you are probably wondering why I am here. I hope you don't mind me turning up like this. Mitchell told me where to find you."

Molly saw Ash hang his head as if resigned for whatever was coming.

"He told you to come and see me," he said.
~~~~~

"No, not exactly," Molly replied. "It was seeing how upset Charlie is this morning that made me want to see you." She paused. "You know that I am not of their family, and I married into it when I met Tom. It wasn't easy for me either when he told me about what they did. Their ... *customs* ... are strange to me, too."

"But you still married him…"

"Yes, because I loved him," she continued. "It isn't his fault that he's part of the Stonewarden family, any more than it's Charlie's fault that *she* is. They are born into it, and when they reach a certain age, there are huge expectations placed on them. Charlie's father accepted his responsibilities in the family, and I believe that her brothers have as well. But from what I've heard, Charlie has put up quite a fight to avoid having anything to do with what they do."

"They break the law!" Ash exclaimed.

Molly nodded. "They do, although they do it for a good cause…"

"Good cause?! What could be so important that it could make them think it's okay to break into people's homes and violate their privacy??"

"There is heritage going back hundreds of years," Molly replied. "When ... if ... you come back to the ranch sometime, Tom will be able to share that with you. He knows the family history inside and out, and he is quite the storyteller, I can tell you!"

Ash looked at her for a long time. His head was confused. What was real?

"Look, I'm here because the little lass is beside herself. She loves you. You must know that…"

"I *thought* I knew that," Ash said. "Now, I think I've just been a pawn - probably one of many."

"Oh, no, I don't believe that you think that. You know in your heart, Ash. She is gaga over you," Molly continued and saw Ash smile a little bit at her terminology. "She wants you in her life, and she wants a life away from what her father and brothers do. That is why she's trying to secure a place on the ranch. She wants to work there as a way to still be a part of her family, but she wants *you* there too. Her heart is real. Her *love* is real. Don't let what other members of her family do taint what the two of you have."

"Molly, they burgled my parents' home," Ash said, feeling defeated. "Someone going in and doing that resulted in my mother being in the hospital. Even if all of this is true, and Charlie isn't in agreement with what they do, how could I look at any of them again in the future? Would I just shake their hands, knowing what they did to *my* family?"

Molly nodded, feeling intensely sad. "I do see your dilemma there. If I try and put myself in your position, with what happened to your family, I can't even imagine how I would've handled my relationship with Tom after that. But I hope you can at least believe that Charlie didn't know about it. There was no ... conspiracy. You weren't a pawn in a game. I know it seems ridiculously coincidental that of all the places they would visit, your parents' place would be next on the list after you met Charlie, but it *was* a coincidence. I believe that, truly."

The two of them sat together without speaking for a long time.

"Despite what his family does, I have never regretted marrying Tom," she continued. "He is a good man, and he has never faltered in his love for me. When you find someone who can turn your heart like that, don't turn away from it lightly. What someone's family is like, isn't who *they* are as a person. Charlie is young, and maybe things won't work out for the two of you anyway. I don't know that. None of us know that. But right now, Ash, that young lass loves you, and I believe that you love her. Life can be short. Seize it. If you care about her enough, consider looking past her family and doing something to not let her slip away. She is heartbroken. She really is. I know that in time she would get over that, but before you walk away completely, take a moment to consider if you really *want* her to."

Ash sat with his head down. He didn't know what the right thing to do was, but he needed time to consider his options. As he began thinking, Molly stood.

"I will leave you now, Ash. Thank you for listening. If we don't see each other again, I do want you to know it has been a pleasure meeting you. You are a fine young man."

She'd spoken as she had stood up and made her way to the door. Before she stepped out, Ash hugged her then closed the door behind her. Exhausted, he walked back to his bedroom and crawled under the covers. His emotions were a blended mess. He hated what that family had done to his, but he also missed Charlie desperately. He couldn't even get his head around not seeing or talking to her, his heart was so heavy. He would take time. He would tune out from it all and go back to work after a couple of days. That was all he could commit to at that moment. Sleep, eat, and repeat until time to go back to work.

~~~~~

Charlie woke late after a late night of weeping quietly in her bed. In real terms, it was only a short time earlier that her life had seemed normal and she'd had to sit with her father and hear how her life was going to change on her 19th birthday. On that day, she had felt like she must be in living in some alternate universe, or had woken up in the middle of a movie. But even on that day, she couldn't have imagined all that had happened since. The shooting, and seeing Max lying as he had been in hospital, had been a nightmare. Then there had been Ash. He'd so easily become such a big part of her life, and had made her feel new emotions she'd never felt before. He'd asked her to marry him. At only eighteen
~~~~~

years of age, she had now been proposed to. What a waste of a proposal that was now that he was gone.

He was gone. Ash was gone. She repeated those words in her head, over and over, as new tears formed and she fell into an abyss of sobbing again.

Finally, she forced herself to stop crying. Although she believed Tom and Molly would be understanding about her feeling the way she was, outside there were dozens of animals who relied on routine. They knew nothing of her heartbreak. She had no right to make them suffer for her unhappiness.

Slowly but surely, she got out of bed, ate a quick breakfast, and then got on with her day as best she could.

~~~~~

James lay in the large bed that belonged to another of his play friends. He and Jessie had used one another many times over the previous year. She was good fun, and he was glad she'd been home and open to him staying the night. When he'd arrived, he had been so fired up from the near-miss of the job that almost as soon as she'd opened her apartment door, he had her on her bed, naked, and wide open to him.

They'd had fun. They always had a good time, but he never fooled himself there. Behind the great sex, there was nothing else to him and Jessie. They had no common interest outside of the bedroom. If he was completely honest with himself, he regarded her as a little mindless with no depth to her whatsoever. For scratching that itch, she was a nice, stress-free solution.

He felt her arm reach out, and her fingers instantly enclose him, breaking his thoughts. The near-miss of the night before was still on his mind, but certainly less so as he focused on the hand moving up and down along the length of him. He was hard, he was ready, and he eagerly welcomed her moving closer. He said nothing as she pushed him flat on his back and then boldly straddled his face so they could mutually please
~~~~~

each other with their mouths. That was Jessie, through and through - straight to the point, not even bothering with kissing - well, not kissing each other's lips anyway.

There was nothing to complain about there. Jessie was one of his few play friends who was so comfortable with her body that she would straddle him like she was doing. James loved that. The feeling of her hovering over him, spread so widely, was one of the most amazing sexual things to him. Tasting her and being able to feel her arousal growing by the level of her creaminess, turned him on just as much as the glorious feeling of her having him in her mouth. It was morning, and he was happily having the best breakfast he could want. He lapped until he felt her pull her mouth off him. That, combined with the increase of volume in her moaning, told him she was close. The beautiful moment when she exploded right against his tongue was near. In those final minutes, he cared nothing for the fact that he wasn't receiving any attention himself. That was when she focused only on herself, and when he *wanted* her to focus only on herself.

As always, that was when he'd hear her speak, although he could hear her only quietly with his hearing restricted due to her thighs close over his ears.

"Ohh, fuck yes, James. I love your tongue on my pussy. Hmmm … I'm so close. Don't stop."

James happily did as instructed. He didn't stop. Soon he felt her convulsing. It was an intense release, he could tell. He kept his tongue on her until she called out again while lifting herself off him.

"Fuck, you're good at that, but now it's my turn to please," she said, her voice confident and sultry.

James lay still as he watched her move around and position herself in comfort to finish him off. The night before, they hadn't had any such pleasure. Always, on first getting together, they went straight for clothes off and him diving straight into her. It was part of their excitement and why they worked so well together. Some lovers needed foreplay first. Others, like Jessie, wanted to be fucked hard straight away. Hard thrusting, first. Softness, later.

The feeling of her tongue licking him all over like he was an ice cream cone was exquisite. It wasn't that all enclosing feeling that he would need to climax, but it was always a beautiful first course. He indulgently lay still with his eyes resting shut and focused on the feelings as her lips enclosed him. At the same time, she was caressing his scrotum with one hand. They had nothing else in common, but over the year that they'd spent time together as lovers, she had indeed perfected her method of pleasing him. In his mind, he replayed the vision of her the night before. On her knees in front of him, being highly vocal, she had looked and sounded exquisite from his position behind her. Replaying the image and sounds in his head, it was an extremely short time before he exploded in her mouth.

After she pulled away from him, Jessie moved up and kissed him.

"And *you* are very good at *that*," he murmured against her lips in between kisses.

She pulled away and looked intently at him. "Are you alright, James? Last night you were more intense than usual."

He looked at her, slightly surprised. That was a first. They never asked or said anything about *feelings* when they were together. He wasn't sure he liked her asking, even though it was nice that she was. He smiled at her and kissed her softly.

"Yeah, I'm all good," he reassured her.

Jessie pulled away from him and started to get out of bed.

"Okay, well, I have to get ready for work," she said as if her caring moment was exactly that - just one tiny moment that was over.

James was content to lie still and do nothing. That was until she turned toward him, gloriously naked with her nipples hard, wetness visible at the top of her thighs, and absolutely no shyness about it. "Wanna shower with me?"

Suddenly the thought of just lying in bed didn't seem quite so tempting to James Stonewarden at all.

CHAPTER THIRTEEN

Ash was finally back at work. He had spent far too much time lying in bed, feeling sorry for himself. It was time to return to reality. No resolution had come from spending all that time by himself. He'd wanted to contact Charlie, but at the same time, he'd found that he just couldn't. He felt like an idiot - a complete and utter idiot.

The morning was busy, so he had no time to think. For that, he was glad. After the lunchtime rush, it became quiet. He'd usually find himself looking around the supermarket at times like that, but for some reason, on that day, he found himself looking outside.

He didn't see her slowly and quietly approach. When he sensed someone at the counter, he turned back and was surprised by so many things. Firstly, that she was there at all when he hadn't expected to see her again. Secondly, that her eyes said that she, too, looked like she had been crying for days, just as he had. And finally, that, in his eyes - even in her ragged old t-shirt and ripped jeans *and* with red, puffy eyes - she was just so incredibly beautiful.

"Hi," Charlie mumbled quietly while looking uncertain if she should even say that much to him.

Ash had thought a few times about how he would act if he saw her again. No scene that had played out in his head seemed fitting for the reality of her standing before him.

"Hi," he said back.

He wanted to be angry with her. He had thought that if he saw her again, he *would* be angry with her. With her actually in front of him, anger wasn't even slightly present in his emotions. He could identify sadness and confusion but not anger.

His eyes automatically did a quick scan of the counter in front of him. In doing so, he could see that she wasn't purchasing anything.

"I miss you, and I'm not ready to just give up on us," Charlie said. The words were concise, but there could be no misunderstanding in their meaning. "We need..." she started to say and then seemed to take a moment to rethink her next words. "I would *like* for us to sit down and talk. Please."

Ash studied her face. It would be so easy to pretend that all that he had learned about her family, he hadn't learned at all. Maybe if they had just been thieves, it would have been a little easier, but they had been the thieves who had invaded his parents' home. If he looked past that, would that mean that he was being unfair and disloyal to his own parents?

Despite his mind working so actively, his mouth spoke much more simply. "Okay."

Charlie was visibly relieved. "When?"

"I finish at two today," he said as he glanced at the large clock on the wall beyond her. "I'll be here for another hour or so yet."

"Will you come to my place when you finish?" she asked and immediately saw him look at her in disbelief.

"Charlie, you can't seriously expect me to go to the house of the people who put my mother in hospital!"

Charlie cringed at his wording but then forced herself to stand taller and look straight at him. "I can, actually."

Ash was at a loss for words. He tried to imagine what she could possibly be thinking by suggesting such a thing to him. No sane reason came to his mind, but she was staunch. He could see that on her face. Even if he couldn't think of one, *she* must have known of a reason for it. Was that a reason for him to step into the lair of criminals?

"There are some seats near the fountain in the park over there. I'll meet you there just after two," he said and saw her eyes glistening. He then saw her facial expression change, like she wanted to argue with him and change his mind. Then she just looked defeated.

"Alright," she said quietly and walked away.

Ash didn't want to cry at that moment - not right there in his workplace. It took all his might to hold on and prevent any tears from escaping.

Charlie walked out and went directly to the seat in the park. It was a nice place to sit with the sound of the large water fountain in front of her. The water falling out of the mouths of gargoyle heads and crashing against the water in the main body of the fountain provided a soothing sound like a heartbeat in a womb. She had a long wait till Ash would finish work and come to talk to her, but she *would* wait because he was worth it.

~~~~~

As the clock passed 2pm, Ash slowly gathered his things and walked out of the supermarket. He wanted to run to Charlie and embrace her. He equally wanted to turn and walk away completely, leaving her hanging. The conflict inside of him was great. He didn't think he'd ever had to make any decision in his life of the caliber that he had to at that moment - if there *was* a decision to make. Perhaps there wasn't, and he was being overconfident. Maybe she was meeting him to tell him formally that they were over and she didn't want to see him again. Did he want to hear that, if that were the case?

He wandered over slowly. When he got closer, he saw her sitting on the seat. Her back was to him as she faced the fountain, unmoving. For a moment, two or three meters back from her, Ash halted his steps. Once again, he considered quietly turning and walking away. He didn't want to hear what she was going to tell him. If they were completely over, he'd rather it be a silent but
~~~~~

assumed thing - not something that was said out loud.

His hesitation was brief in real time but seemed like forever as he stood where he was, contemplating what to do. Looking at her, with her head hung low, he knew he couldn't walk away. She meant too much to him, no matter what her family was like.

Charlie saw his feet come into view when her eyes were downcast. Slowly, she moved her eyes up his body, wistful of having already missed spending days with him. When her sight reached his eyes, she saw his uncertainty so said nothing. If he needed to turn away from her, she understood. She sat silent, waiting for him to make that decision.

He didn't walk away. Instead, he moved closer and sat beside her. She watched him, unable to move her sight from his face. Generally, he'd always been happy when the two of them had spent time together. There was now a different Ash sitting beside her - a *very* different Ash. That was okay. It was more than okay - it was good. When she'd suggested to him that they wait a year before they seriously considered marriage, she had hoped that in that time, they would go through things that weren't always happy. She was young, but she wasn't so young that she believed life was continuously blissful and easy. It was realistic to expect that crap happened. She'd wanted them to have some tests before committing a lifetime to each other.

And this was definitely a test.

~~~~~~

When a long while has passed without him saying anything, Charlie turned her body so that she fully faced him. Watching, she saw him pivot his body the same way, giving her his full attention. Both waited for the other to speak.

"Charlie, whatever you need to say to me, please just say it," Ash said, feeling his emotions moving toward overload.
~~~~~~

Charlie heard the words. They sounded like a plea.

"Ash, I want us to get past this. What can I do to help you stop hating me?"

"Hating you?" he asked. "Why would you think that I *hate* you?"

"Because you ran away from me. Because you haven't tried to talk to me. Because you hate my family."

Ash let a deep breath flow out of him as he considered what to say. The most difficult thing was wondering to himself what he *did* want to say. Part of him wanted to yell and scream out in frustration. Instead, he took a moment to breathe deeply and make sure that he spoke with a soft, calm tone.

"I don't hate your family," he said. "Taking away and ignoring what your family does, I do actually respect your father. And I don't know your brothers so I can't *hate* them, can I. But what they do, Charlie … *that* causes me grief."

"Not just you," she replied. "*I* hate it too, but they are still my family…"

"Yes, and my family are still *my* family," Ash said. "You saw my mother in the hospital. She was there because of *your* family!"

Charlie felt her tears threaten. The hardest thing for her was that she, too, wished that her father didn't do what he did. She equally wished that her brothers didn't do what they did. Because of that, she couldn't even be annoyed at Ash for feeling like he was. His arguments and feelings were completely justified in her mind. The question was what to do about it.

"I didn't know they were doing that, honest…" she said, her voice pleading.

As she said those words, Ash felt his heart break for her. He knew she was in a difficult position with her family being something that even she wished they weren't. His resolve to be strong started to chip away.

"I know," he said quietly. "Charlie, I don't blame you, and I do believe that you weren't any part of it."

"You do?"

Her voice was so timid that he couldn't help but give her the slightest of smiles. "I do."

As he watched her face, he found it increasingly difficult to keep being angry about anything. With tears flowing over her cheeks, she looked endearing. He felt strongly about what had happened to his parents. He felt just as strongly about what was happening to her. Both of them needed to stand up for their own families, but Ash could see that at some point, in some way, they both needed to stand up for themselves as individuals *and* as a couple.

"My family won't change," Charlie said with passion in her voice. "They will always be who they are. If I could do anything about that, I would…"

"I know."

"Do you?"

Ash took her hand in his and kissed it. "I do."

"The only way I can be away from it is by doing something like working on the ranch. That is why I want to be there - so I don't get dragged into what they do."

"I know," he said, feeling his heart thaw just that little bit more.

"My feelings for you are real, Ash," Charlie said. "They aren't some kind of act. They aren't a lie, and they have nothing to do with my family *or yours*. I love who you are, and I love the way I am when I'm with you. I love the way I *feel* when I'm with you." She paused. She desperately wanted some feedback from him. When none came, she continued speaking. "I can't turn my back on my family. You can't expect me to, but I don't want to lose you."

"Then tell me - what *do* you want?" Ash asked her.

She looked at him closely. She could tell he had

been as upset by recent events as she had been. She lifted one hand and stroked his cheek as she looked so far into his eyes that she might see his soul.

"I want us to stay together," she said. "I want us to keep working toward a life together. I want us to find common ground while you accept that my family *are* my family. There has to be some way for us to find a place that works for both of us. I just can't believe that's impossible. Can you?"

It was a heartfelt speech, and the words, combined with the tone of her voice and the desperate look on her face, made Ash's anger melt further. Even his desire to *try* to be angry had begun to dissipate.

"I don't know," Charlie heard him say. She felt her heart heavy in her chest, expecting the final words were about to hit her. "Charlie, I don't know how I will feel over the long haul about your family and what they do. But I don't want to lose you either, and I do want us to stay together. Things might not be doable in the long run. I can't promise you how my feelings will change, or even if they *will* change."

"What are you saying?" she asked, confused.

"I'm saying that if you want to, I would like you and me to get back on track together. I will try and look past what has happened between your family and mine," he said. "I can't promise that I'll be able to do that, but I am willing to try. I don't expect you to keep away from your family. I'd never ask you to do that. But you can't expect that I will ever be enthusiastic about them either."

"I know," Charlie said quietly as her tears began to dry up.

"But Charlie, you need to know for certain that the only money I have, comes from my work," Ash said. "That's it. If I work, I have enough to pay rent and live. If I don't, then I don't." It was a bold statement, intended for a reaction.

"Ash, I don't care about money. Look at me," she

said, indicating her clothing with her hands. "Do I look like I have *ever* cared about money? When I met you, you were just a guy working on a checkout in a supermarket. I didn't know anything about your family, and I didn't care that you were just working on a supermarket checkout. I didn't care then, and I don't care now. My dad said that if we did move forward and get married, we can get papers drawn up so that we can't touch each other's family's assets or money if there is any."

As soon as she said that, Ash felt guilty. He had only said his last words to try and assess how she would react. The thought of a prenuptial agreement made his skin crawl, but the conversation was open. He conceded it was better to have it, so there'd be no issue if it came up later. He nodded as she continued speaking.

"I'm happy for us to do that if it means your mind will be at rest about this," she said. "My family isn't poor either. We'll get a good agreement drawn up that works for both of us, that our families both agree on. If we do that, neither of us will need to worry about that." Silence. "Please, of all the things that could come between us, money can't be one of them - not when neither of us particularly want it. Working at the ranch won't bring me an income, and it won't bring *you* an income. If we work there, it will be free living but hard work. Tom said that all things bought for the ranch, including food and whatever else is needed, comes out of a trust - a well-guarded trust that is administered by lawyers. I'll be able to live, but it won't be free money either."

"*I* don't care about money…"

She moved closer to him and slowly leaned in and kissed him. It was a tentative move in her uncertainty if it would be welcome.

"I know you don't," she said. "On that, we agree. Neither of us will have money, and we will live like paupers, but if you want to as much as I want to, Ash, we can live like paupers *together*. Please. I miss you so much. I want you in my life, and I want to be your wife. I want to bear your dozens of kids," she said, making him smile softly. "I want *you*."

Ash's mind turned off, and his body turned on. She was passionate in her speaking, and her passion was igniting his, although in a different way. Her arguments were sound. He couldn't object or say anything against what she'd said. Lifting his hands to her jaw, he looked intently into her eyes before kissing her with all the desire that was heavy in his body.

The feeling of her lips on his was one that he'd missed. He had said all that he needed to say. It wouldn't be an easy road to where they'd been, but he couldn't just walk away from her.

They kissed for a long time, their desperation evident to anyone who saw them. When they parted, Ash saw Charlie's eyes were full of tears trying to brim over. As one made its way down her cheek, he lightly wiped it away.

"What are you feeling?" he asked with great tenderness.

"A lot of things. Relief. Release. Although I look like I'm crying, I do feel happier than I did before you sat down beside me," she said, crying and laughing at the same time. "I know it's been only a few days, but it has felt like a lot longer since we were at the ranch together."

Ash nodded. "I know. I've felt the same way. Do you want us to keep trying, Charlie? Really? Is it really what you want?"

"Yes!" she cried emphatically. "I know that anything can happen. Even without all of this happening, we might not last as a couple, but I don't want to give up yet."

"Do you still want us to keep thinking about marriage?"

"I want us to keep moving forward for the entire year, and then talk about it again. Maybe by then, we'll know we aren't supposed to be together, but maybe we will both be sure that we *are*." She waited for a response. There was none. "What do *you* want?"

Ash kissed her again, softly.

"I want you. I don't want to give up yet either," he said as he lightly moved a rogue clump of hair that had fallen across her eye. "I want to focus on just you and me. Our families, we can deal with later."

As Charlie nodded, Ash saw her tears beginning again, even though she was smiling. He pulled her into his embrace, and she gladly moved against him as closely as she could.

To Charlie, one thing was very evident - it was good to be back in his arms again.

~~~~~

To everyone's relief, including Mitchell and his sons, Charlie and Ash appeared to get back on track. As Tom and Molly watched them on the ranch during Ash's days off work, it seemed like there was some tentativeness between them. It was as if the two young people had woken up from a blissful dream and were finally moving forward in reality. Their initial flush of young lustfulness seemed to be transitioning into a deeper level of appreciation, understanding, and more grown-up feelings.

Mitchell had pulled Charlie aside and told her he supported her in moving forward as trainee manager of the ranch. He agreed with her moving toward becoming manager there in the future, whenever Tom and Molly felt it was time, and he supported her in being with Ash as partner, spouse, and work colleague. That speech was given before he pulled Ash aside and the two of them had a serious man to man talk. That comprised largely Mitchell telling Ash he had better not hurt his daughter, before Ash found great courage to turn around and tell
~~~~~

Mitchell right back that he and his sons had better not hurt her either. Mitchell's respect for Ash only intensified after those words were spoken.

Day to day, Ash and Charlie helped and learned from Tom and Molly. The days when Ash worked at the supermarket, Charlie got on and still did her work, missing him only when she went to bed each night. The days when Ash was at the ranch always ended up with the two of them in his room each evening.

CHAPTER FOURTEEN

Six months through their self-proclaimed year of consideration, the days grew colder, and the weather became more erratic. After their work was done one day in the stable, Ash and Charlie climbed the ladder that led to the loft overlooking the horses. They lay down on the straw and listened to the heavy rain that fell loudly on the roof. They had discovered the loft months earlier, and on days with such a glorious sound outside, it had become a favorite getaway spot for them. Still having three days at a time to spend together around Ash's supermarket shifts, it always felt like they had to make the most of their limited time.

Ash put his arms around her as they cuddled and listened to the heartbeat of the raindrops with the wind gusting outside. They were bundled up with thick coats on, but they were warm enough.

"Things are different as winter approaches, aren't they," Ash said. "I suppose we need to learn about all of the seasons and how things change with each of them."

In response, Ash heard a quiet 'hmm' from the head nestled against his chest before he saw Charlie lift her head and kiss him. Pulling her closer with his hand firmly in her hair, he drove his tongue into her mouth, his hunger for her evident. They never moved too far from that, Charlie having climbed onto him and rubbed against him only a few more times in preceding months. It was an unspoken agreement that they would try to place less emphasis on the physical feelings and more on the emotional and day to day ones.

Lying together and listening to the storm outside, Charlie suddenly felt a need for release. She wanted to feel him touch her - *really* touch her.

Ash felt her take his hand and place it on her breast. The move surprised him, excited him, but then confused him. "Charlie, we can't..."

"And we won't - not yet. Just touch me, please. Here," she said as she held his hand over her breast still. Then she moved it down to her crotch. "Or here."

Ash gulped. They had rubbed against one another on occasion, but hands had so far only been used for holding each other in embraces. She was asking him to touch her - there. He gulped again as he looked into her eyes, but began moving his hand all over that area of her jeans. He had no idea where she was supposed to be touched but moving his hand as he was seemed to be doing something as she began to breathe deeper and moan slightly.

He watched her face as he continued to rub his whole hand against her. Watching her and listening to her had made him hard, but he tried to tune out from that. It was far too exciting concentrating on her. When she reached down and undid her jeans, he was too surprised to act in any way toward stopping her. Soon he found his hand guided inside her underwear. There he found an area he knew nothing about, but he understood enough to know that the level of wetness he found was demonstration enough of how turned on she was. Lightly touching and listening to her as she spoke, he guided his finger this way or that. Between them, they found a tempo and lightness of touch that was perfect. It wasn't long before Ash felt her shudder against his fingers. He pulled his fingers out with reluctance. It was a warm place that he liked his hand being very much.

Charlie shyly did her jeans up and kissed him before she began hand rubbing him through *his* jeans. His hand stopped her.

"Charlie, not here. Please. It is enough for me to know you are excited. I don't need..."

"I know, but Ash, please let me touch you. I *want*

to touch you."

Listening to the pleading in her voice, Ash nodded in silence and let her do what she said she wanted to do. As turned on as he was, it took no time at all before the feeling of her hand moving over him resulted in him reaching orgasm. Inside his jeans. Again.

After letting the deliciousness flow through his body, he focused on her again. Over and over, he planted tiny kisses on her lips until she smiled and nudged him away.

"It's your birthday tomorrow. You know you're getting kinda old once you turn nineteen," Ash teased her. He expected her to laugh or at least smile in response to that. She didn't. "Why do you look so serious?"

"I promised you I would share things with you about my family," she said.

Ash nodded, feeling dread coming on.

"But do you really want to know?" Charlie asked.

"If there is something you think I *need* to know, then yes," Ash replied, preparing himself for whatever was about to be said. "Although, I'd rather not know about … what they are *doing* at any time…"

"Oh, no! You don't need to know about any of that," said Charlie. "Even I don't get told about any of that. No, my father knows how I feel on that matter."

"What, then?"

"There are strong family … *processes*, none of which I knew anything about at all until this past year. By tradition, when we turn nineteen, we are instructed by the head of the family in what will be our role in serving the family. Usually, that's when members of the family are inducted into … that."

Ash processed her words before moving away from her slightly with a look of alarm on her face. "Your father isn't going to make you … become a thief?!"

"I don't *think* so," Charlie said. "He told me that

he's happy for me to live and work here with Tom and Molly - and you, when/if you want to. But tomorrow is the day that he would normally come and talk to me, and things are set in stone, so to speak."

"But Charlie, like you said, he already gave you his blessing to keep doing this, and not join him and your brothers…"

"I know. I just … I just want both of us to be prepared, just in case he turns up here and does tell me something different. It might not happen. I hope it *won't* happen. I just want to be prepared for the possibility that it *might*."

Ash looked into her face for a long while, seeing real panic and worry in her eyes. He resolved to keep his concerns to himself. She had enough to think about already.

"It'll be alright," he tried to reassure her. "If he comes, you just have to deal with whatever he decides, I suppose. I'll be here for you, whatever happens."

"And if he turns me into a thief?"

Ash sighed and closed his eyes to the thought before he kissed her. "Let's confront that issue if and when it happens. Asking 'what if' never does anything except make people worry needlessly. I don't want that. Today is your last day of being an eighteen year old. What would you like to do?"

Charlie forced herself to relax and laugh softly at him. "Don't people usually celebrate their birthday? Not the day *before* their birthday?"

"Well, no matter what your father has planned for tomorrow, you have a big family. I think we need to at least allow for them wanting to see you…"

"You don't want to see them…"

"That isn't an issue. I will treat your family as I always have, Charlie. I will still shake in my boots at the sight of them," he said, making her giggle. "But I will greet them with as best a smile as I can - for you. So! We have a fair few hours before we need to do our evening chores. I'd like to sweep you away and do whatever you want to do. Just the two of us. What do you think?"

Charlie felt slightly tearful with relief about how he was going to at least try to be okay around her father and brothers when he saw them. Neither of them should have been in the position for it to be that way, but she was at least grateful to him for being determined to try.

She nodded at him. "Yes, please."

Ash pulled her close and held her before kissing her and standing up. As always, they took their time using their hands to remove the straw from each other's bodies. It might have seemed an innocent thing to others, but to them, there was something blissfully intimate about being able to run their hands over each other from shoulder to ankle.

"Let's go."

~~~~~

After venturing into the township for a few hours to enjoy a good lunch and a movie, later that day they finished preparing the animals for the evening and then sat with Molly and Tom.

"I understand that tomorrow is your nineteenth birthday, Charlie," Molly said, surprising Charlie. "Don't look so surprised. All of your family details are kept here. We know when everyone has a special day."

Charlie looked at all three faces before her. She was relieved that since everything was out in the open about her family, she could sit like she was and freely talk about things. Nothing needed to be kept from Ash. That was as good a birthday gift as she could have hoped for.

"I don't know if turning nineteen is a happy day in my family," she said quietly and instantly felt Tom's rugged hand move over hers on the table.

"Yes, it is, lass," he said. "I don't think you have anything to worry about. Your father seems set on letting
~~~~~

you be here..."

"I know, but we don't know for sure," Charlie said. "He could think about it tonight - in fact, he probably *is* thinking about it tonight - and he could still change his mind. There's nothing to stop him coming here tomorrow and taking me away with him to force me to..."

"Charlie, please don't think that," Ash spoke up, quietly but forcefully. As the thought of her dressed all in black, moving through the city like some hooded ninja, appeared in his mind, he instantly dismissed it. Although she would probably look quite good in an outfit like that...

"It will be alright, Charlie," Molly added into the conversation. "What is meant to be, always is."

Unfortunately, those words did nothing to ease the concern in Charlie's mind.

A short time later, Charlie and Ash excused themselves, and he escorted her to her room. They lay down on the large four-poster bed. Neither moved toward anything physical, their minds too heavy with fears. It was comfortable lying together - so comfortable that lying there, fully clothed on top of the bed covers, they fell asleep.

~~~~~

"Charlie!" she heard a voice call out with a sternness that she knew could only be her father's.

She opened her eyes, confused. Then she felt someone move off her bed quickly. When she turned her head, she saw Ash hurriedly trying to stand while obviously still mostly asleep. The look on his face as he looked at her father was classic enough to make Mitchell want to smile, even though the moment called for him to be a bit more sterner than that. It wasn't lost on him that although they'd slept together, they were clothed and on top of the bed. Even if they hadn't been, he would have had to concede that she was an adult, albeit a young one,
~~~~~

and could sleep with - even have sex with - whoever she wanted to. Seeing them having just slept together fully clothed still kept Mitchell's opinion of Ash at a healthy height.

"Dad. What are you doing here?" Charlie asked as she tried to wake up properly.

She watched as her father sat on the edge of her bed and pulled her into an embrace.

"It's your birthday. Where else would I be?" he asked, seeing her head hang low. All she looked was deflated, and Mitchell suspected why. He turned to Ash, who was nervously hovering nearby, appearing uncertain of whether he should stay or go. "Ash, I would like some time to talk to my daughter alone, please."

Ash nodded and instantly left the room, relieved that he no longer had to try and guess what to do. He quietly walked back to his room and lay down on his bed. He knew things might be about to change, and not for the good. He might be presented with the knowledge that the woman he loved would be taken away and forced to live a life that he couldn't like. He might be left to decide if she was worth turning a blind eye to activities she would be forced to take part in.

He rolled onto his side and instructed his mind to shut up. He had only told Charlie the day before not to play the 'what if' game. Now he needed not to do it himself.

~~~~~

"Have you come to take me away?" Charlie timidly asked her father. Questioning wasn't something that was encouraged among her and her brothers, but she felt strong enough to ask. It was her life that was going to be affected, after all.

Mitchell hugged her. For a brief moment, he felt anger at his own family's traditions, but he had considered the situation with Charlie long into the night. His mind was made up.
~~~~~

~~~~~

When Ash heard the door to his bedroom open, he looked up and saw Charlie walk in with a smile on her face. She closed the door gently and then moved to lie down, facing him.

"Well?" Ash asked, even though his heart was hopeful, given her smile.

"This is it," Charlie said. "I'm staying here forever. He is letting me still work toward becoming ranch manager and living my life away from what they do."

For Ash, it took a moment for the news to sink in. When it did, Charlie laughed at the look on his face.

"No more worries about this?" he asked for clarification.

She kissed him while smiling broadly. "No worries about it at all."

Ash pulled her to him, kissing her back as she moved on top of him. "But what about today? What's happening today?"

"I am going to celebrate with my dad and my brothers, Ash," Charlie said. "He has invited you too, but he knows that you might not feel okay being around everyone. Do you want to come?"

Ash studied her face. Did she want him to go? Did she want him *not* to go? Sometimes, such as in that moment, she presented a poker face, and the only way to get a direct answer was to ask a direct question.

"Do you want me to come?"

"If it were all up to me, yes, I would like you to come, but I do understand if you don't want to," she replied. "It'll only be for a few hours, so you and I still have tonight and tomorrow morning before you have to head back to your apartment."

Ash breathed in deeply. He had to do it. If he was going to be with her for the rest of their lives, he would have to face them all and get on with getting on with
~~~~~

them sooner or later. It seemed as good a day as any to be the first that he looked at them all with the knowledge of what they had done to his parents, and try hard to ignore it.

"Alright," he said.

Charlie shrieked, indicating to Ash that he'd said the right thing, judging by the level of happiness on her face.

"I'll jump in the shower and then wait for you if you want to have one," she said, her voice full of excitement. "Dad is waiting downstairs."

Ash watched as she pulled off the bed and then left the room, her face alight with animation. It was the first time he'd seen her like that for many, many months.

~~~~~

"Hi Ash," Regan said as the three of them entered the family home.

He was the only brother, except for Fitz, who knew that it had been Ash's parents' apartment they had entered and stolen from. He felt bad for him. If someone had entered his family home and done that, and his mother had suffered... Instead of letting that thought flow through to completion, Regan held out his hand to the younger guy in front of him. He couldn't undo what had been done, but he could make sure that he never treated Ash any way that would make Charlie unhappy.

Ash shook Regan's hand and nudged away his initial apprehension at being amid the six Stonewarden men. Even Fitz was there.

Fitz kept himself back from Ash, partly because he was never a social guy anyway. Shaking hands with people wasn't something he'd ever felt comfortable with. Mostly he didn't want to face Ash because he was the one person who had known before they'd opened that safe that they were in Ash's parents' apartment. He was the one person who could have stopped that robbery right then and there. If he'd told his father what he'd
~~~~~

discovered when he'd seen that photo, he suspected his father would have told them to quietly leave and never think about that apartment again. But he hadn't. He hadn't said anything, and they'd gone on to rob Charlie's boyfriend's parents' place. No-one else knew it, but that was all on him. There was no way he would ever be able to be happy around Ash. Every time he would see him, that would be on his mind. Fortunately, Fitz was never friendly toward anyone. No-one would ever think anything about him not being friendly toward his sister's boyfriend.

Being around all of them in their family home was overwhelming, but Ash smiled as much as he could. As he watched Charlie, he knew she was happy as each of her brothers moved forward, hugged her, and presented her with some small gift that lit up her face when she opened it. Every few minutes, she seemed to turn and look right at him. He made sure he was smiling in those moments. No-one said anything serious to him. He wasn't even sure who knew about his parents' apartment and who didn't. He had to make himself not care - at least for that one day.

Such a family occasion of hugs, kisses, presents, and a large lunch spread out across the long kitchen table was something Ash had never experienced. For a moment, he thought about his future. If he and Charlie had kids, they would go to the Stonewarden house now and then. They'd sit down at the long table and talk to their uncles and grandfather about how their schooling was going and what their friends were like. It was an image that Ash liked, so long as he didn't also think that there was a chance that his kids would, at some point, be recruited into the Stonewarden business. That thought caused a chill to run down his spine. But he was getting well ahead of himself. When he turned to Charlie, he knew she'd seen his face grow serious for the few minutes his thoughts had been somewhere else. He smiled at her. That was all he could do at that moment.

~~~~~~

One by one, her brothers removed themselves. Fitz was first to go, as was expected by everyone. He hugged her briefly and said goodbye, and that was considered a lot for him.

Next to leave was James. He had been watching the way Ash and Charlie interacted with each other and looked at one another. He didn't want to admit it, but he found himself slightly envious. He could have any woman he wanted, and he didn't want a relationship, but sometimes when he saw two people have a connection like his sister did with her boyfriend, he wondered if room could be made in his life, for someone on a more permanent basis. When he couldn't watch them anymore without feeling his emotions spiking, he stood and went to her.

Charlie saw James coming closer and happily accepted his arms around her.

"Happy birthday, Sis," he said. "You look happy. I'm glad. You deserve happiness."

Charlie pulled back and looked at his face.

"James," she said quietly enough so that no-one else would hear. "Are you okay?"

For a split moment, he considered that she might be someone he could talk to about how his feelings about things had been changing, but then he pulled that thought in. It was her birthday, and she was with her boyfriend, who was looking at her like he knew that he was the luckiest guy on the planet. No, to James, it wasn't right that his nineteen-year-old sister should have to listen to his heart to heart complaints.

"Yeah, I'm fine, Charlie," James replied. "I'm tired, so I'm heading home to have an early night."

When James walked away from Charlie, Ash expected him to hold out his hand for a handshake when he approached. Ash was more than a little surprised
~~~~~~

when he was forcefully pulled into a manly hug.

"I know she's happy with you, so you get my vote," James said.

Ash pasted on as good a fake smile as he could when he was released. Silently, he wished could also leave sometime soon.

Shortly after, Vic left also, after giving Charlie a long, loving hug and shaking Ash's hand before he walked out.

"Are you okay?" Charlie asked Ash quietly when they found a quiet moment alone. She saw him nod but could tell he was doing it for her. "Do you wanna get out of here and go to your apartment?" she asked. She couldn't miss that he instantly looked visibly relieved.

"Don't you need to stay?" Ash asked. "You are the guest, after all."

Charlie laughed softly. "They won't miss me," she said. "Come on. I'll say goodbye to these guys, and then we'll go."

Ash stood aside and watched her say goodbye and then whisper something in her father's ear, prompting him to nod and hug her in return.

Soon they were walking to and entering his apartment. It had been a crazy couple of days, but it always felt good for him to get home. Once there, they sat on the sofa facing one another. For a few minutes, neither spoke.

"Ash," Charlie said when she had built up some courage. When she saw she had his attention, she took a deep breath and expressed her feelings. "Could I..." she started once. She felt herself grow flustered and nervous before she tried again. "Could I stay here with you tonight?"

Ash leaned in and kissed her softly. "Are we in agreement...?"

Charlie nodded. "We are. I just want to sleep beside you. I want to be close to you."

Ash couldn't object. It was her birthday. She was finally nineteen. Her father had assured her that her life was going to be her own, as much as it possibly could be. He also believed that she was sincere in her promise to him that she wanted nothing more.

After Charlie saw him stand and hold out his hand to her, she followed him into his bedroom. When she moved toward the bathroom for final pre-bed readying, he found her a t-shirt of his to put on and handed it to her.

While Charlie changed, Ash sat on the edge of his bed. He was nervous, but he would pretend to not be for her. When she came out, she looked vulnerable but also beautiful with only his t-shirt and no jeans on. He quickly stood and moved to the bathroom. He didn't think he could visibly watch her get into bed - not without losing at least a little bit of control.

Finally, he returned to the bedroom and moved under the covers to hold her. Charlie easily and comfortably moved into his arms. They didn't kiss. They didn't move toward anything more. It felt like they had moved one level deeper that day. She was older, and her family obviously accepted him. They also accepted that she was an independent woman. All of that made her want to be closer to him, but not physically - emotionally. Something had shifted in her emotionally, and she could feel it. All she needed on that night was to sleep in the same bed as him, enjoying the comfort and security that she thought would come from that.

Not having moved from that spot, both were soon asleep.

~~~~~

Ash was the first to wake in the morning. They'd previously slept on the same bed together one time. That had ended with the abruptness of her father waking them. This time, there was no such intrusion.

He turned his body slightly to face her. She was
~~~~~

still asleep but facing him. Her face looked at peace. Ash didn't dare move. The view was beautiful, and he didn't want to wake her.

When she did wake, Charlie saw him looking at her. She gave him a sleepy smile.

"I like waking up and seeing you next to me," she said and instantly heard him take a deep breath. "I hope that one day I will get to wake like this every morning."

Ash felt his heart pounding heavily in his chest. He wanted to move closer to her, but at the same time, he felt like he shouldn't. In the end, he gave in. She was in his bed, and she just looked far too kissable for him to stay as far away from her as he was.

Charlie accepted his kiss lovingly but made no aggressive move like she normally might when they were alone and kissing.

"I want to wake up next to you every morning, too," he said quietly.

"Whenever you feel like you are ready, Ash, I'm ready, too," she replied. "I don't need to wait any longer, but I *will* wait for as long as it takes for you to want it too."

Ash's heart pumped even harder as he swallowed heavily.

"Marry me. Please," he said. "Say yes to becoming my wife, Charlotte Charlie Stonewarden. Let me come and live with you and work with you on the ranch. Let me make babies with you and raise them with you. Let me *love* you for the rest of our lives."

He saw tears appear in her eyes as she nodded and attempted to smile.

"Yes. Please."

Then he kissed her. And kissed her. And kissed her.

CHAPTER FIFTEEN

"Are you sure about this, Charlie? It's not too late to back out. If you have any doubts..." Mitchell Stonewarden began to say on Charlie's wedding day. He'd had a rough night of sleep, mutually thinking about his daughter getting married, and his wife missing the day. It was bittersweet. In one way, it would be a happy day. In another, it would be incredibly sad.

"Dad!" Charlie exclaimed, grinning. "I want to marry Ash. Now. Today."

Mitchell looked at his daughter. His baby girl. Dressed all in white, she looked very much like her mother. He'd had to keep putting that thought out of his mind all morning. Waking up earlier with further memory that his Caroline was missing her daughter's wedding, had brought on another rage of tears as he'd laid in bed. She shouldn't have been missing it, but she was. On the other side of that, Charlie was missing having a mother to see her go through her special day.

"She's here, Dad. I know it. She's right here, with us," Charlie said, reaching out to take his hand in hers as if she could read his thoughts exactly.

Mitchell looked at her with pride and smiled. She was doing everything right. She had waited to get married. She had waited to have sex. She and Ash had both spent time with lawyers, getting their family's assets and everything else lined up and secured so that neither had to worry about anything to do with any of that. They'd also been working together on the ranch since Ash had resigned from his job a month earlier. Reports from Tom said that all was well. Charlie and Ash worked together well and they were both picking things up quickly and easily. Everything she did, she was doing well and she was doing right. Mitchell knew there was nothing more that a father could have wanted for his baby girl.

He pulled her close and hugged her tightly.

"I love you, Charlie, and I'm so proud of you," he said, holding back tears.

"I love you too, Dad, but come on! It's time!"

Mitchell chuckled at her but followed her out. They were on the ranch and the large portrait room had been fitted out as a banquet hall for the wedding ceremony and long reception afterward. All portraits had been covered with decorations that discretely hid the faces and the names of the people in them. Why Mitchell insisted that his sons still not know that the ranch was a part of their heritage, no-one but him understood. It didn't matter. As far as each of the boys assumed, it belonged to Tom and Molly; Charlie and Ash worked there; and it was the place they had run to on the night they'd almost been caught on a job. Mitchell saw no reason to tell them anything at all. Their assumptions would be fine, at least for the moment.

He walked into the large hall with Charlie holding his arm. For a moment, he wanted to scoop her up and carry her away. There was a moment of panic, like he wasn't ready to give his little girl up to another man - except that he knew he was. He had no concerns about Ash at all.

As she approached him, Ash turned and resisted the temptation to run to her. She was walking toward him, steadily moving closer as she looked like a beautiful angel. When she reached him, he took her hand in his and kissed it. Silently, he hoped the rest of the ceremony and celebration would hurry along. There were a lot of people attending once they added his family to hers. Even though he was an only child, there seemed to be a fair few cousins that his mother had invited on his behalf. He couldn't chastise her for bringing a few extra people. He had to work hard enough to not consider that his mother and father were unknowingly in the same room as the people who had stolen from them. It was such a horrible thing to think about that Ash had to turn his mind off to it. To broach that subject was something that could only bring pain to all concerned.

After vows were said and much had been eaten, he took his bride's hands and led her to the dance floor.

"I'm looking forward to getting you alone," she whispered in his ear.

Ash tried to restrain himself in his response, but couldn't stop a face-aching grin.

"I feel exactly the same."

~~~~~

Much later, the two newlyweds walked alone into the large bedroom Charlie had resided in since she'd first arrived at the ranch. Closing the door behind them, Ash pulled her into his arms and finally kissed her the way he'd wanted to for hours.

Charlie wrapped her arms around him and indulged in it. She had been holding back for so long, desperate to not make him feel pressured, but she would hold back no longer. For a very long time, she had been ready for their first night as husband and wife.

"Can you unzip my dress for me, please?" she said softly as she turned her back to him.

Ash leaned in to kiss her bare neck as he did as he was instructed. Taking care with the beautiful gown, he lowered the zip right down, then eased the dress carefully down and away from her as she stepped out of it. As she stood before him wearing only a strapless white bra and the whitest satin underwear, she looked glorious. For a moment Ash didn't move, he was so absorbed in the sight before him.

Charlie moved up to him and kissed him again before undoing his tie, slipping his jacket from his
~~~~~

shoulders, and then taking her time to undo the buttons of his shirt. She had seen him without a top on once and that was only as he'd quickly removed a t-shirt and replaced it instantly with a work shirt. Finally able to take her time to explore his chest, arms, and shoulders, she found him breathtaking. She was in no hurry to remove more of his clothing. They continued to stand as she kissed his neck and ran her hands all over him.

When Ash could bear it no more, he eased back away from her and undid his trousers. He'd had plenty of moments since he'd met her when he'd been embarrassed by how turned on his body had been. At that moment, he felt no embarrassment. He slid off all that he'd been wearing and returned to her completely naked. As her hand came down to enclose him and feel him, he forced his concentration to removing her last items until she was naked in front of him. The feeling of the two of them embracing skin to skin with no barriers was exquisite to both.

They lay down, moving together as if in perfect harmony about how things were going to go. Ash let her push him down on his back and didn't stop her when she straddled him. She had done it so many times when they'd been clothed, it seemed only natural that she would want their first time together to be like that too.

"I know there's loads we can do in foreplay, but Ash, I'd like to feel you … inside of me," Charlie said softly between their kisses.

Ash groaned heavily in response. He said nothing but nodded at her when he realized she seemed to be waiting for his confirmation. He lay perfectly still as she moved against him, firstly rubbing herself on him. Then he felt her find her way and he experienced for the first time in his life, too, what it felt like to move into someone.

At the same moment, they each breathed out each other's names. Ash knew it was going to be quick, but he hoped that would be okay and they would learn more each time they indulged like they were. He watched her face in-between kisses. He loved the way she was looking at him in return. As she started to move slightly faster, he kissed her to concentrate on her lips only in a desperate attempt to hold back for at least a while. He reached down with his hand and touched her as he had previously, just with his finger.

Charlie moved so that he could access her better. When she felt the orgasm coming, she welcomed it. She was full up with him inside her and she loved it. Other than a slight discomfort in the few seconds when she'd first lowered right down on him, it was a glorious feeling to be connected to him like she was.

Ash watched her face. Her expression, combined with her gripping him as tightly as she was when she climaxed, sent him over the edge.

They lay together, joined. He stroked her back with one hand and held her head close to his shoulder with the other. They had built up to that moment for so long, it was like a relief - in so many ways. When they had arrived in the room, they had needed to get to that point. Finally, they could relax.

Charlie moved off him and lay down on her back beside him. She had anticipated it would feel good when they finally connected like that, but what she had felt far surpassed what she'd expected. She watched him as he moved onto his side so that he was facing her. His eyes roamed over her, and he began to kiss her. His lips moved over her neck, and then, finally, over the breasts that had teased him with little cleavage views through the t-shirts she'd worn since the shooting. After all those cleavage hints, he was finally meeting them. He had to concede they looked like much fun to touch and kiss in all different ways. He was in no hurry whatsoever. He could stay right where he was all night.

"I am going to cherish you every single day and

night, Mrs Thomson," he said, happy.

"Hmm, that sounds nice. Mrs Thomson. God, it makes me sound so old!" Charlie replied and laughed softly before she felt his tongue flicking lightly over her nipple. "Hmm, keep doing that."

So he did. He flicked his tongue and moved his lips over every part of her body, wanting to get to know every part of her that he still didn't know. It was a night of exploration for both of them. After each round of learning new things, they came back together as he sunk deep inside of her, again and again, until both fell asleep, smiles etched on their faces.

For them, their life together was only just beginning.

The End

RUBY OF LAW
(FORBIDDEN CONFLICTS SERIES - BOOK #2)

For generations, the Leadbetters have lived off crime.
For as long as any of them know, fathers and mothers
have taught sons and daughters how to succeed in the
criminal world, primarily through theft.

Phillip Leadbetter is 29, and has devoted his whole life
so far to doing what his father and mother have told him
to do. The sacrifice for doing that is that he still lives at
home, and he hasn't yet met anyone who he believes
could accept the man that he is, because of his family.

One night, a potential tragedy brings him into the path of
Daisy, an up and coming professional in the legal sector.
Seeing him as her knight in shining armor, she can't stop
thinking about the rugged guy who saved her. She's also
very pleased when fate brings their paths to cross again.

Getting to know one another, both leave out major
details about who they are. She doesn't want him to
know she's a lawyer because some people just don't like
lawyers. He doesn't want to tell her about his family and
their long history of criminal activity.

How, then, will things turn when they meet up in a
courthouse, each learning at that moment who the
other really is? How will they deal with the fact that
she is on one side of the law, and he is very
definitely on the other?

DIAMOND OF WAR
(FORBIDDEN CONFLICTS SERIES - BOOK #3)

James Stonewarden is a playboy. He has been since the moment he first started to notice girls. He loves them all, and they all love him. Why would he want to get himself into a relationship?

Sasha Leadbetter's a hot-headed young woman, known to the law for her quick temper and harsh ways. She isn't one to mess with - especially with the way she keeps a blade in her pocket. To her, it's her security. It's something that makes her feel safe and comfortable. She's had it for so long that it's nothing for her to pull it out and hold it to someone's throat without any conscious thought.

Unaware of who each other are, or how their families are distantly interconnected through crime, the chance of James Stonewarden meeting Sasha Leadbetter is slim. But it happens.

A playboy and a young woman who has the mentality to kill. What kind of recipe could that result in? And what will happen when James identifies a car at Sasha's family home, that matches the description his sister Charlie gave after the supermarket shooting months earlier?

SAPPHIRE OF PREJUDICE
(FORBIDDEN CONFLICTS SERIES - BOOK #4)

Greg and Rhett. They've grown up together since they were teenagers. They've fought together. They've stolen together. They've even loved women together. But something deeper has existed in one of them for years. He's hidden it well. Being part of the great Leadbetter gang and family, the prejudice of certain situations has always been loudly expressed by many of its members - too many, and certainly enough to make anyone fearful of what would happen if feelings were revealed and brought out into the open.

A night has passed when finally, in a moment of wondering if he'd survive till morning, Rhett's taken the chance and kissed the person of his desire. Given their circumstances, what can they do, and where can they go?

Meanwhile, as Phillip Leadbetter continues on his path of happiness with his Daisy, someone from her past has grown obsessed with her and wants her back. To what degree will he put into effect a plan to get her back, and get Phillip out of her life forever?

~~ NOTE: This book does contain adult sexual content and LOTS of swear words.

EMERALD OF WISDOM
(FORBIDDEN CONFLICTS SERIES - BOOK #5)

When Mitchell Stonewarden lost his wife to cancer more than a decade ago, he vowed to never give his heart to anyone else. With all of his children now adults, and a new generation of Stonewardens having already begun, he's finally started to wonder - does he really want to be alone for the rest of his life? The handover of the family business to his oldest son, Vic, has seemed to be free of difficulty or issues - but has it? Mitchell knows little of his oldest son's private life away from the family. He is surprised by what is brought to his attention that he had no idea about.

While Mitchell finally starts to move on into a new chapter of his life, another of his sons - Max - is on his own path of discovery in life and in love. Previously well-known as 'Romeo' to his family and peers, he begins to wonder if Christy - a surprising addition to his life - has grown to become more important to him than any other young woman he's ever met. When her work at a homeless shelter tests the boundaries of her safety, Max's commitment to her is also tested, making him wonder if he will, indeed, end up hurting her.

Meanwhile, on the other side of town, the Leadbetter family is shattered by an unexpected turn of events that leaves Stacey wondering if she is going to lose the man she's loved for more than three decades...

www.ingramcontent.com/pod-product-compliance
Lightning Source LLC
Chambersburg PA
CBHW060436310726
48977CB00001B/216